IMAGINARY LINES

Douglas Grant

ISBN 978-1-938886-49-2

To Diane Grant,
Thanks for the extra pair of eyes on this one.

Acknowledgements

I'd like to thank the following individuals for their assistance with the research and creative development during the drafting of this novel: Leo Grant, Frank Grant, Bryan Burrows, Christian Asdal, Dan and Laurie Jovick, Janie Lane, Chris Thompson, Diana Grindea, Michael Price, Guillermo Sanchez, Dominik Huber, Karin Bilich, Denise Cassino, Chris O'Byrne, Debbie O'Byrne, Bob LaDue, Brian Donegan, Vic and Laura Tulsie, Michael Shields, Tristan Smith, and Tom Rau.

Preface

Their arrival had been planned, timed perfectly so that they were rolling up on the property just before dusk. This would give the three of them time to do an informal survey of the place just as the sun started to set over the Pacific during one of the most spectacular spring afternoons that Kyle Conway could call to memory. He'd seen the place; he knew a day like today was ideal for presenting it to his brother Kyp and his longtime associate Mauricio. They'd be sold, just as he himself had been sold within a minute of first laying eyes on the place. He was so confident that they would see the potential of this place that he actually had to refrain from showing too much enthusiasm until his companions could appraise the situation themselves. They would see the opportunity he saw, though. There was a reason the three of them worked so well together.

The first thing Kyp noticed upon arrival was how much dust his Ford F350 kicked up as they sped up to the front of the house. A gravel driveway. Unusual for the neighborhood. But then he noticed just how much property there was, concealed by the tall and unkempt shrubbery. This was a lot of land as well. Kyp was beginning to see why his brother seemed so optimistic, and they hadn't even set foot inside the place yet.

The trio got out of the big truck and individually took in the property. The lawn was overrun by weeds and crabgrass. The house was unimpressive considering the sheer size of the lawn and the particular location. Kyle had originally thought that perhaps this place had been haphazardly thrown together after a hastily conceived contract had been drawn up sometime in the 50s. He knew better now. The house had value simply because of where it stood geographically, and Kyle knew that a loophole regarding it offered an exceptional opportunity for profit.

His eyes ran over the two stories of cracked, slate-gray stucco that he, his brother, and Mauricio would make disappear, replacing it with the type of architecture that would complement a beautiful lot of land such as this. In fact, when Kyle took in the salty ocean air and felt the cool breeze on his face, he decided that such a picturesque setting practically demanded to be paired with a worthy man-made structure.

Kyp came up behind his brother. At twenty-eight he was two years Kyle's junior, but taller and stockier than Kyle, broad shouldered and well fed. He took his dirty Padres hat off and combed his fingers through his curly blond hair, looking at the house as if he was still deciding something. "Huh," he muttered. "I think I see what you mean."

Kyle suppressed a grin. His brother really had no idea why this particular house was going to be such a big score for them. Kyle had done his homework on this place, and now he saw dollar signs in the cracks in the cement where weeds were poking out. *This* was it. Their big break.

Mauricio joined them. His eyes were still scanning the property as well, although if Kyle knew Mauricio, his friend was summing up all the potential risks and estimating the inevitable overhead. But that was why Kyle needed level-headed Mauricio. It was true, Mauricio wasn't in a partnership with Kyle and Kyp Conway, but he was an invaluable asset to Conway Brothers Construction Company, and his pragmatism had helped Kyle to be more realistic. Kyp usually followed Kyle's lead when it came to business decision making. Mauricio's services as an advisor on top of being a valued worker had kept the brothers from making overly ambitious decisions in the past.

"This was Marc Cronenberg's referral?" Mauricio asked Kyle.

"Yes, indeed," Kyle said with unchecked pride. The Conway brothers had built a house for Marc Cronenberg, a successful local restaurant owner, in an up-and-coming neighborhood in Tierrasanta. Marc had been pleased, and Marc knew people. Visitors at his housewarming party had been awed by the Conways' subtle interpretation of the modern home that paid homage to both the Victorian and Spanish styles. Their talents had sold themselves, and now a whisper in the right ear could lead the Conways to a place in the big game, assuming they were up to the task. *Oh, we're up to it,* Kyle thought to himself. *There's no margin for error. Not anymore. We've got to play this right.* "Let's go look inside," he suggested.

The men walked up a short flight of stone steps and Kyle opened an unlocked front door. He held the door open as Kyp and Mauricio stepped to the foyer and took the place in. Kyp found the place offensively tacky in a 1970s porn house sort of way. Mauricio saw the folly in the construction, as if the place had been erected hastily in some kind of race to develop on oceanfront properties on the west coast. And yet this house wasn't oceanfront. It sat high on a hill almost at the top of the peninsula's ridge. The backyard wasn't on the sand and yet the altitude made the view more spectacular. And whatever shortcomings the building displayed were more than made up for by the view, the breathtaking view that even builders of such a novelty house such as this couldn't help but exploit. Almost the entire back side of the house was windowpanes, allowing sunlight to pour in when the sun moved toward the western horizon.

Kyp looked from the floor to the ceiling. "Demolition should be fun," he muttered.

"Let me show you something," Kyle said walking past his brother and into a medium sized kitchen on their right. Mauricio didn't know if he'd been addressed too. He stayed where he was.

Kyle led Kyp through a kitchen equipped with antiquated appliances and dated striped wallpaper. He opened a paneled door at the back of the room and pulled the chain of a light bulb overhead. Kyp peeked through the doorway and his eyes followed the steps of a rickety staircase down into darkness. It was more of a storage area than a basement. "Are we going down?" he asked Kyle.

"After you," Kyle gestured with his right hand. The brothers descended the creaky wooden stairs and entered a musty storage area with a dirt floor.

Kyp surveyed the area. "Mold?" he asked.

"I'm sure of it," Kyle responded.

"Asbestos?"

"Highly likely."

"Infestation?" Kyp continued since Kyle was being so frank.

"I believe a family of skunks at one time."

Kyp looked at his older brother incredulously. "So then what's with the shit-eating grin you've had on your face since we got here? You must know something I don't."

Kyle tilted his head slightly. "What, the property doesn't do it for you? Look where we are."

"There's something else. What aren't you telling me?"

Kyle walked over to the cinder blocks of the wall and ran his hand over the surface. He made a fist and punched the cement with the heel of his hand a few times. He then turned around and approached one of the pillars in the middle of the basement. He tapped it with his index and middle finger a few times. It was like he'd momentarily forgotten about his brother.

But the two had a shorthand when they worked together, and Kyp was catching on. "Nooooo," he said, starting to grin himself. "There's no way. Not this place."

"Oh yeah," Kyle said grinning, although his eyes remained fixed on the pillar. "We can salvage forty-percent," he continued, referring to the house's wall structure. Now he turned and looked at Kyp, wrapping his right arm around the pillar and leaning against it. "Now you know why I'm so chipper."

Kyp did indeed. If they could maintain forty-percent of the house's original structure intact, then technically it was considered a remodel. And a remodel meant lower labor costs as well as lower material costs. But perhaps most important was the fact that they wouldn't have to jump through all of the hoops of the California Coastal Commission. That, in and of itself, was reason for the brothers to be extremely optimistic about the potential for this place. But the real reason to be enthusiastic was the house's geographic location. If they could pull this off then this place would be a stepping stone to a more respected and lucrative position in San Diego's general contracting community. And that was too big an opportunity to pass up.

"Hot damn," Kyp said grinning. "You did alright, Kyle."

"I didn't do anything. It's our resume that got us this far."

"Oh, do I have plans for this place. The gears are turning."

Kyle chuckled. He was glad his brother was so happy. He glanced at the staircase. "What the hell is Mauricio doing? He should be in on this." Kyle turned and walked past Kyp and up the stairs. Kyp stayed behind; perhaps his imagination was working from the ground level up. Kyle left him to contemplate.

When he got back to the living room Mauricio wasn't there. Momentarily puzzled, Kyle surmised where he might have gone. He went upstairs and in the hallway that led to the master bedroom there was a narrow and treacherous looking black steel spiral staircase. Grabbing the railing with a steady hand Kyle ascended the stairs which led to a small vestibule with a sliding glass door. He slid the glass aside and found Mauricio on the rooftop deck, gazing out at the pastel pinks and oranges of the Pacific sunset. Kyle imagined that Mauricio was reflecting on the long and arduous journey that had gotten him here, in the states, with this job, with this family. Kyle also wondered if Mauricio was weighing just how much further he dared to dream. *Dream big, my friend. Things are happening for us.*

Kyle came up behind Mauricio, and who turned to face him. Mauricio was slight of build, with wavy black hair and a neatly trimmed fu Manchu. He had clear, stoic eyes that told a story: he was a gentle, practical man who'd seen his share of human grief in his youth. Another time. Another place. At least this is what Kyle had always assumed.

Kyle got right to it. "A remodel, Mauricio. Do you have any idea how much less of blow that will be to our change purse?"

Mauricio's grinned, and his grin grew into a wide closed mouthed smile that told Kyle that he did indeed know the importance of this news.

"And the CCC?" Mauricio asked expectantly.

Kyle laughed and looked out at the sunset. Mauricio was always one step ahead of him. He leaned over and rested his elbows on the railing. Mauricio posted up beside him and took in the sunset as well. "No red tape on this one, buddy. That's how it works with a remodel."

The sun started to dip behind the western horizon. Kyle didn't avert his gaze from the beauty when he said, "We never would have made it this far without you, Mauricio. You know that, right?"

Mauricio too held the sun in his gaze. It was a quarter of the way down. "It's the other way around, boss."

Kyle snorted. "Don't call me that, man. Not on today of all days. Not now. Not ever." Half of the sun had disappeared over the horizon. "Okay?"

"Okay," Mauricio said grinning.

The sun was three quarters of the way out of sight. Kyle stood up to his full height and laughed heartily. He slapped his companion on the back. "Point Loma, Mauricio! We're in! Can you believe it?"

"It never seems real to me, Kyle."

"It's real, buddy. It's definitely real. Today Point Loma. Tomorrow La Jolla. This is our reality." He shook his head as if he too didn't dare to believe it. He was a longtime cynic who was wary of opportunities that seemed too good to be true. "No, this is it," he said with conviction as he beheld the vast ocean view. "Our big break."

The sun disappeared over the horizon.

Part One

"The problem is that even now, margins on new homes are still pretty good, though well below the levels of a year ago. As a result, builders will just keep building until those big margins evaporate. High prices are sewing [sic] the seeds of their own demise. They always do."

—Shawn Tully
2006

Maria Solares came bursting out of the women's fitting room in a state of extreme excitement. Her mother, Lorena, bent down to receive her daughter and appraise her new look. Maria, however, stopped just short of her mother, and then turned around to gaze at herself in the mirror. She ran her fingers over the fabric of the patterned yellow sundress and then squealed with delight. She spun on her heals and turned in circles, rotating wildly and letting the dress flutter in the air. Dizzy now, she came to a halt and then shifted all of her weight onto her right leg. She put one hand up to the nape of her neck and then stuck her rump out, making a pouty and suggestive facial expression that was entirely inappropriate for a girl of eight years.

"Maria!" Lorena cried with her mouth agape, her own face a mixture of wry amusement and mortification. "Where in the world did you learn that?"

"Don't answer that, Maria," Cynthia Conway said with barely contained laughter. "It's better that your mom doesn't know."

"Excuse me?" Lorena said, turning to her friend with mild annoyance. "I believe I'll follow my own instincts when it comes to raising my daughter."

"Fine," Cynthia countered. "Have it your way." Turning back to Maria, she said, "Sweetheart, was it from one of your mom's magazines or one of her stories on TV?"

"Don't you dare suggest that I in any way influenced this," Lorena said indignantly. "I'm in no way relaxed when it comes to monitoring what my children are exposed to." She turned back to her daughter. "Maria, if you want that dress then you'd better stop trying to grow up too fast. That was very unladylike."

The exchange had become less about Maria and more about the way Lorena and Cynthia took playful jabs at each other when contrasting their parenting styles. Onlookers in the Marshall's fitting room area were involuntarily taking in this scene and wondering what kind of dynamic this portly golden skinned brunette shared with this dainty, freckly blonde. What a strange pair they were.

A young boy's voice called out from the men's fitting room to the left. "Mama? Necesito ayuda."

"Un momento," Lorena called back. She turned back to Cynthia. "Can you keep an eye on our little preteen here?"

Cynthia smiled. "I won't let her grow up any more while you're gone."

Lorena sighed and then looked questioningly at the fitting room attendant, and older woman who nodded approvingly at Lorena and said, "Go ahead." Lorena went down the hallway into the men's fitting room area. Cynthia heard a door creak as Lorena slipped inside and then heard it close.

Maria was once again focused on her image in the mirror. "I love it! I love it! I love it!" She spun again, this time to turn around and face Cynthia. "Aunt CC, don't you love it?"

Cynthia got down on one knee to face Maria at eye level. "I do, sweetheart. You look very pretty. But you know we need to find you something a little more appropriate for church. Something more formal."

Maria looked startled. "But I can still get this, right? I can wear this to the barbecue after church." Her worried expression deepened.

"Well that's not up to me, Maria. Your mom has to decide." Cynthia saw that Maria looked truly forlorn now, and she knew that although Lorena and Mauricio were great providers for their children, they in no way spoiled them. "Let's just say that I don't think your mom would have let you try it on if she hadn't entertained the idea of buying it for you." She winked at Maria, and it seemed to do the trick.

Maria smiled a little. "Thanks, Aunt CC."

"You got it, kiddo."

Just then Cynthia heard a door creak in the men's fitting room area and she turned to see her two sons, Cameron, 9, and Cal, 7, come racing down the hallway toward their mother.

"Stop pushing me!" Cal cried as his older brother practically trampled over him. "Mom, he's pushing me!"

"Boys," Cynthia hissed through clenched teeth. "Stop making a scene this instant!" She glanced nervously over her shoulder to see if any other shoppers were witnessing this spectacle. No one was taking notice except, once again, the fitting room attendant, who seemed to shoot Cynthia an *I've been there* look with a grin tugging at the corner of her mouth. The grin also seemed to say: *Where's your friend now to observe this?* And Cynthia knew that Lorena had probably heard the commotion. Trying to save face now, she said, "Cameron, act your age. You know better. You're going to hurt your brother when you should be setting an example."

Cameron ignored her. "Mom, we're not twins. Why are you trying to dress us up like twins?" Cynthia bit her lower lip in an attempt to mask her sudden amusement. The boys, both with stringy golden blond hair like their mother's, looked adorable in their matching blue blazers over white collared button down shirts and khakis. They might have been twins had Cameron not had a few inches on Cal. And Cameron's question was a valid one, but it hadn't been her intention to dress them up identically.

"How do they feel?" she asked them both. "Are they comfortable?"

"It iiiiitches!" Cal moaned.

"Cal, stop whining," she admonished. To Cameron she said. "How 'bout you? You don't both have to wear the same thing, but this outfit is on sale. At least one of you is leaving with it."

Cameron never had a chance to answer. Cal started jumping up and down and gesturing wildly to his older brother. "Him! Him! He gets to wear it."

Maria began to giggle at the spectacle Cal was making, but Cynthia was losing patience. She reached out and took hold of her son's wrist, bringing his bouncing to a halt. "Cal!" she snapped. "I will not buy you Baskin-Robbin on the way home if you don't turn your behavior around right now. Now get it together or I'm going to have a long talk with your father when we get back." That did the trick. Whether it was the threat of no ice cream or her husband's discipline she'd never know.

Lorena returned with her son Franco from one of the fitting rooms.

"Oh, my gosh," Cynthia said, momentarily forgetting about the issue at hand. She took in Lorena's son in his boys' size black blazer, slacks, and polished loafers. He was even wearing a clip-on tie. "Franco, you look so handsome. Maria, look at your brother."

Franco, shy by nature, uncomfortable with praise, and anxious around public displays of familial affection, was already self-conscious in this strange adult's suit. He'd never worn one like it before. But when Maria ran over to her brother and hugged him fiercely, his normally dark complexion turned scarlet. Cynthia felt for the boy. Maria had all the spunk and boldness of her mother. But Franco definitely took after his father.

"Hey, he looks sharper then we do," Cameron said as if he'd somehow been outmaneuvered in a game of grown-up dress-up.

Cynthia, amused with the fact that *sharp* was now part of her nine year old son's vocabulary, said, "That's because it's his day, Cameron. You'll have your First Communion next year."

"We should all have it the same year," Cal burst out. "Then the four of us could have one, big super-party."

Lorena laughed at this. "That's not how the church works. And anyway, the party doesn't get bigger for you just because there are more of you receiving the Sacrament."

"Okay," Cynthia interjected, short on patience and annoyed with the fact that the six of them had fallen way behind schedule. "Franco looks dashing. I say that if it fits then he should take it. Cameron, you're taking that outfit. Go get changed and then come out here and wait for Aunt Lorena. I'll take Maria and Cal and we'll go find them both something suitable to wear."

"Shouldn't they change out of that first?" Lorena asked.

"It's just one more step they'll drag out. And I *really* want to get out of here." She looked apologetically at Lorena, who now looked irked. "I'm sorry. I know how important this is and I don't want to rush it."

"No, you're right," Lorena said. "We've been here too long already. And Franco *does* look good in that. We'll take it."

"Wait! What about this?" Maria said in a panic, holding out the skirt of her sundress. She gave her Aunt CC a look that said: *Back me up here.*

Lorena looked back and forth between her daughter and Cynthia, wondering what the two girls had discussed in her absence. "What does Aunt CC say?" she asked Maria. Maria's pleading eyes went instantly to Cynthia as if she were now expecting a betrayal.

"I think she looks absolutely stunning," Cynthia said with a smile. Maria seemed hopeful. "But . . . "

Stricken again, Maria must have been wondering: *But what? She never mentioned a* but?

Lorena voiced Maria's concerns. "But?"

"But if she's going to own that dress, then she needs to learn how to wear it like a lady. No more adult poses. Okay, Maria?" Maria beamed. She could definitely handle that one small condition.

"Well that settles that," Lorena said. She shot Cynthia a soft-eyed look that expressed the utmost gratitude. *Thanks for coming to my aid after all.*

* * *

By no means had Cynthia and Lorena been considered close friends when they both attended Rancho Bernardo High School in the 90s. The two girls had a few classes together and they had gotten along well enough, but they had run with different crowds and rarely did they find themselves in the same social settings. Neither had they really crossed paths much in sports, where Cynthia had been a varsity field hockey player and Lorena a member of the dance team. And although it was seldom spoken of, the cultural differences at the time seemed a significant enough barrier to establishing the common ground that would normally characterize a substantial childhood friendship. About the only thing that the families of the two women shared back then was their faith. And years later that faith would bring the two families closer together. But in high school they were simply two girls from two different worlds. And that was alright. No one had ever said that they had to be friends. They graduated in '95 without any noteworthy incidences involving alcohol, drugs, or sex. They had earned good marks on their report cards and kept their noses clean and off of the public record. They were good girls from good families with good values.

Fate brought them together in their career paths. Both had decided, for different reasons, to pursue early childhood education, and both women ended up entering into a two-year associates' degree program at San Diego City College. One woman had parents who were somewhat dubious as to the motivation behind their daughter's chosen career path, the other woman with parents who thought it a logical next step.

Cynthia Conway, then Cynthia Heard, was career oriented, but her parents had been convinced at the time that their daughter could fly even higher than her aspirations. She had often countered, in gentle debates with her parents that never turned ugly, that she was passionate about working with children and wanted to truly make a difference in their young lives. She was also quick to point out that it had been a fairly smooth transition to a post-secondary educational setting, because while many of her peers would switch their majors two or three times during their bachelors' program, all while trying to decide what they wanted to be when they graduated, she already knew what her calling was. She considered herself lucky in this, and her parents felt that she was at peace with her decision, so they supported her in her endeavors.

Lorena Solares, then Lorena Cruz, was from an extensive Latino-American family. Not only was she the oldest of six siblings, but she was one of the oldest among a group of cousins that reached into the upper twenties. The family unit beyond her immediate one was one with very strong bonds and sense of community, and Lorena had spent a great deal of her childhood, and not reluctantly, helping to raise her brothers, sisters, and cousins. She had fallen somewhere in the middle, only slightly younger than some of her aunts and uncles and older than most of the children. She had taken great pride in her role in bringing up these kids, and she too knew that she'd found her calling by the time she graduated from high school. Her parents had supported her whole-heartedly. She had, after all, been running her own version of child care services since she was a little girl. She might as well excel at what she was already good at. At least this was their logic.

"Don't you want to have the full college experience just like your friends?" Cynthia's mother had asked her. "Most of them are going to State. I don't want you to look back on these years and regret your decision."

But Cynthia wouldn't regret it. She would skip the whole dorm life experience and share a two bedroom apartment in Little Italy with her friend Monica. She'd be done in two years and then she'd be ready to focus on her career. She envisioned for herself her own pre-school and day care center with a strong focus on cognitive, social/emotional, and physical development. She had no idea at the time that she'd one day be partnered up with her old classmate from Rancho Bernardo, Lorena Cruz.

Lorena hadn't allowed herself a similar vision. She'd always known she had the skills in ECE to be picked up by a reputable pre-school, but she'd never dared to dream that she would one day be running her own school with someone whom she'd hardly known back in her high school days.

As the two young women went through City College at the same time, finding themselves enrolled in the same classes and drawn to the same social functions, they realized how closely their visions of their futures were aligned. Both wanted to be on their career paths sooner than the standard four years. And both wanted to marry young and start families while they were in their early twenties.

For Cynthia this was fairly simple to imagine, for she was in love with a young man whom she'd met the summer after graduation, at the kind of party her parents had always persuaded her to steer clear of. And she knew from the very beginning that Kyle would one day put a ring on her finger.

Although Lorena had the same dream, she would have to wait a little longer than Cynthia to see it realized. And when love found her, it would not be in any way she ever could have predicted. Love would come in the form of an illegal immigrant named Mauricio Solares, a quiet and gentle man who barely spoke a lick of English.

* * *

"My friend Billy's got a mouth on him. So he downs his whole beer in one gulp and in the same motion proceeds to smash the bottle on the cement to show us all how pumped up for the game he is. And I'm just gaping at him, thinking *you goddamned idiot.*" Kyle swiveled on his barstool and manuevered himself so that he was now facing Mauricio more than the bar. Here was the turning point in the story. "So sure enough, out of nowhere materializes this gaggle of Raiders fans looking like a horde of Mongols. It was like they'd been patrolling Qualcomm's parking lot looking for a reason to draw first blood."

Mauricio was listening intently. He'd always enjoyed Kyle's particular style of storytelling. He took a swig of his beer and asked, "What, they were offended by the broken bottle?"

"Oh yeah," Kyle said with a sarcastic sneer. "Good Samaritans, these guys. So they start chattering at us in their drunken Spanglish, *puto* this and *pinche cabron* that, gesturing wildly and flexing." Kyle chuckled in a way that told Mauricio that although it hadn't been funny at the time, he could definitely look back on it now and laugh. "So Billy, wasted, comes to the forefront of our group and he starts mouthing off right back."

"Were you outnumbered?"

"Absolutely. But not only that; none of us were trying to get into it with these guys except Billy. We were pissed at him for smashing the bottle in the first place. So I reach out and grab Billy by the collar of his Merriman jersey and yank him back, trying to put out the flames. These guys would've killed us."

"Did they back off?"

"Noooohoooo," Kyle said while shaking his head. "These bastards were out for blood. So then this one gigantic hulk of a guy with his face painted half black, half silver comes to the front of their group, decked out in plastic medieval armor looking like Attila the Hun." Kyle downed the last sip of beer in his bottle of Pacifico and then exhaled heavily. "And he says to me, 'Hey, pussy, let your friend finish talking.' And he takes another step forward. I'm shitting my pants at this point. And now his whole crew is inching forward right behind him, closing in."

Mauricio smiled. "Are you going to tell me that you went up against them and won against impossible odds?"

"Hell no! We were saved by the bell. Lucky for us security guards at Qualcomm are no strangers to brawls between Charger and Raider fans. They saw what was going on and put a stop to it immediately. And we were cited for bringing glass in."

Mauricio looked at Kyle expectantly. He wasn't sure if Kyle could tell how much of a let-down that story was. He baited Kyle. "Great story, man. Action packed."

"Hold on, dick, and let me finish." Kyle motioned to the bartender, requesting another round. "You wouldn't understand the second part if I didn't set up the first part properly. So months later, Cynthia and I are eating at an Italian restaurant in the Gaslamp that I can't remember the name of and I don't think is even there anymore. And we're enjoying ourselves having drinks at the bar when the hostess comes to seat us. And who should our server's assistant be that night but none other than Attila. I'm still surprised I could spot him without all that shit on his face, but there was no doubt in my mind that this giant was the same guy from the game. And he doesn't recognize me. Yet."

"How did you get his attention?"

"Well the Chargers had won that day by a lot, and the Raider fans had worked themselves up to a state of frenzy by the time everyone was leaving. There were brawls that day, just not us, thankfully. So from the moment this freak starts filling our water glasses I start to do a play-by-play from that day that can only grab this guy's attention. And Cynthia, she's confused as hell because she has absolutely zero interest in the NFL, and suddenly I'm talking her head off about it. And then . . ."Kyle was grinning, savoring the recollection. "And then we lock eyes, and this guy remembers. 'Thanks, cabron,' I say as he fills my water glass. I down it right away. 'Hey, pendejo, some more water.' I actually start stuffing dinner rolls into my pocket so that I can keep him bringing bread. The guy can't come within fifteen feet of our table without me calling out to him with another demand. Cynthia has no idea what's going on except that I'm behaving very strangely. And even though she's finding it off-putting, I'm not about to tell her now because she'll put a stop to it, and I'm having too much fun."

"Weren't you worried he'd do something to the food?"

"He wouldn't dare. And that's why it was so thrilling to me. I could tell that I had brought him to his boiling point. Was he willing to throw it all away, the ridiculously low wage that paid for the room he probably shared with twelve other people? Anyone of interest takes a close look at him and it's, 'Back to Mexico you go.' He wasn't about to throw away his meager existence because of a bruised ego. He had to sit there and take it, and I was enjoying every minute of it."

"Did Cynthia figure it out eventually?"

"Yeah. I told her the whole story after taking my tenth piss for the night. Keeping that guy running around all night had been taxing on my bladder. And she wasn't pleased. You know CC. She's a moral high ground kind of girl. She doesn't approve of that kind of behavior."

Mauricio thanked his bartender for another beer. "Lorena might have slapped me if I had acted like that."

Kyle snorted. "Well lucky for you, my friend, you don't carry on like those animals. You know how to act in civilized society. C'mon, let's play darts."

As the two men got off their stools in this divey, dimly lit sports bar, Mauricio felt a pang of regret. Regret that Kyle had thought he'd meant Lorena would slap him if he'd mimicked the behavior of the belligerent Raiders fan, and not that of his long time friend Kyle who often seemed to purposefully erode the respect Mauricio had for him with his under-handed comments.

* * *

Cynthia wouldn't have been pleased about the conversation her husband was having with Mauricio. Even though at the time she'd been livid when she'd found out what all of Kyle's carrying on in the restaurant had been about, she could look back on the memory now and actually grin to herself. It was that kind of spunk that had first attracted her to Kyle. No, what would have upset Cynthia had she heard Kyle and Mauricio's discourse was Kyle's persistent insensitivity when speaking to a Latino who had struggled his way into the states and was trying to find his place in the world.

The problem was that since Mauricio had made it here—realized the American dream with the career, the wife, the kids, the dog, the house and the yard—Kyle, in her opinion, treated Mauricio as some kind of special case whose wise career choices had allowed him to rise through the ranks of his labor-minded countrymen and drink from the cup of those who knew what it really took to get ahead in Southern California. And an inexcusable by-product of this was that Kyle was forever making unfortunate remarks that put down the Mexican immigrants right in front of Mauricio. It was like, *Oh, you're not really one of them anymore, Mauricio. You're one of us now.*

Cynthia had called attention to this insensitivity on Kyle's part on more than one occasion. Kyle would deal with her assertions in different ways. One would be to point out to her that her opinions were preposterous, that he in fact worked side by side with Mexican immigrants on a daily basis and had nothing but admiration for both their work ethic and pride in what they did. Hadn't he employed dozens of men just like Mauricio, not only to oversee the daily fruits of their labors, but also to sweat with them in the sun? How could she possibly surmise that he treated them any differently than his own flesh and blood? Furthermore, Mauricio and Lorena were like family to them, sharing bonds that were tighter than the ones he shared with some of his own family members. Did they not spend major holidays together grilling up on the back patio while their kids played together in the yard? His own sons referred to Lorena and Mauricio as Aunt and Uncle, for God's sake.

When Cynthia didn't buy into this thinking, he had other cards to play. "I'm just kidding around," he would tell her. "You can't possibly take me seriously when I crack jokes like that." And they would go around in circles, not with heated arguments, but with strong differences of opinion regarding what was appropriate within the category of lighthearted banter.

Sometimes he would laugh off Cynthia's criticisms, saying that she was merely being silly and letting her imagination run away with her. But other times when she persisted, and Kyle began to grow irritable, he would point out the struggles of his own Irish ancestors, and the abuses they had suffered when they, too, had been trying to build better lives for themselves in a new country. "You think I give a damn when some one calls me a Mick boozehound or insinuates that I'm a half-retarded scrapper?" is how he might counter her accusations. "Shit, when someone on the beach asks me if they think my sunblock is really strong enough, I don't get all worked up and let it bother me. And it's not because I'm thick-skinned; it's because I know it's all in good fun. Some people take themselves too seriously, CC. I've seen the way you try not to cringe when Lorena is serving up the thousandth round of fatty carne asada tacos." His unfair reference was to how Cynthia would smile politely and serve herself up the tacos, topping the meat sparsely with cheese and foregoing sour cream altogether. Kyle, on the other hand, would take a generous helping of the meat, cheese, guacamole, and sour cream, and then say something like, "I see you've been broadening your horizons, Lorena. Flour tortillas instead of corn, and—wait—what do we have here? Cholula instead of Tapatio? You guys are really moving up in the world."

And Lorena knew how to respond to Kyle's baiting with a mixture of amusement and annoyance. "Oh, that's right, Kyle. I forgot. Tell you what, you go inside and help yourself to the Jameson in the liquor cabinet while I fix you a plate of unseasoned carne and some wet red cabbage. We'll throw some bland mustard on it and call it corned beef. How's that?" And Kyle would laugh and continue to play along, because as he'd told Cynthia: it was all in good fun.

But Cynthia wasn't so sure. First of all, playful humor in such a manner, especially when it relied solely on stereotypes and cultural differences, was low class in her book. Kyle fell into these kinds of transgressions more than anyone else she knew. One of these days he would go too far.

By way of contrast, Kyp hadn't turned out this way at all. He was sensible and ever aware of the line one did not cross when dealing with individuals different from him. How had it happened that while every other member of the extended Conway family could entertain themselves with good-natured and clean humor, Kyle only knew how to employ his own version of comedy that hailed from the Don Rickles era? His comments and insights were heavily laced with his own biases. Even if that wasn't obvious to everyone, it certainly was to her. And it bothered her.

At the heart of the problem was that she truly believed that the man she loved had a bigoted sense of entitlement, not one easily defined in black and white. And since it was such an elusive mindset her husband had, she often found herself confounded when she tried to address it. The bottom line was that Mauricio and Lorena Solares were like family, and were treated as such by both her and Kyle.

* * *

She awoke to the sound of Kyle's removing heavy boots, not at the foot of the bed but on the black leather armchair near the window by the bureau. Her first coherent thought in her drowsiness was that she wished he'd thought to do this in the foyer downstairs. The clopping of the boots hitting the soft carpet probably shouldn't have awakened her, but tonight Kyle's movements were heavier than normal. He hadn't meant to disturb his wife while she slept, and he cursed himself when he saw her stirring.

"What time is it?" she asked groggily, but he didn't bother to answer. He knew she'd be leaning over to read the alarm clock on the nightstand. "Quarter after one? Don't you have to work early?"

"I'll be there by seven," he told her. "It's fine. Go back to sleep."

"Have you been drinking?"

"Yeah, Mauricio and I grabbed some beers down the street from the site."

She watched him remove his sweat stained Padres hat and shake out his curly brown hair. "I hope you didn't drive today," she pressed. She sat up straighter in bed and adjusted her eyes to the light in the master bathroom.

"No, Kyp took me to work today and Mauricio brought me home."

"Well that's not much better," she stated with concern.

Having stripped out of the last of his clothes he went to brush his teeth. As he retreated to the bathroom he said over his shoulder, "Have you seen how slow he drinks? He had one beer for every three I had."

"And how many was that?" she said with her head hanging lopsided. He grinned at her without responding before he stepped into the bathroom, out of sight. She then heard the hum of an electric toothbrush.

The drinking and driving concerned her; it always had. But she knew Kyle was responsible and wouldn't have allowed Mauricio to drive him home if he thought Mauricio was close to .08. Moreover, she couldn't begrudge him the stress release of a few beers after a long day on the job, erecting a behemoth of a house. Kyle was working himself half to death on this project. The toll was both physical and mental fatigue. He'd lost weight, and he looked better, but there were baggy, lined sacs tugging at the bottoms of his eyes these days. And during the few times he'd made it home in time to have dinner with her and the boys he'd had trouble focusing on the conversation. She knew what finishing this Point Loma house meant to Kyle—meant for the whole family—and she decided that she was going to ride this one out to completion, and then she could have her husband back. He knew what he was doing, and he was good at what he did. Although she didn't consider herself materialistic or overly concerned with capital, she was excited about the prospect of this family coming into the kind of money that secured futures-IRAs, CDs, college funds, stock options, property taxes, car payments, vacation savings, HOA fees, 401Ks.

Furthermore she was proud of Kyle, of what he'd accomplished in his young life. This house he and Kyp were working on now could very easily be the stepping stone the two needed to enter into San Diego's elite within the housing industry. He had had his sights set on Point Loma for a long time, and he aspired to keep building north right up into La Jolla and Del Mar. These were big dreams, she knew, but it hadn't seemed so long ago when he and Kyp were contracting in Tierrasanta and Scripps Ranch, envisioning the kind of house they would one day build on the Point Loma Peninsula.

The odds had been stacked against them. Conway Brothers Construction was technically still in its infancy, but they'd quickly established a reputation for putting up modern dwellings of blended architectural design within the confines of very strict deadlines. Although the brothers were in a partnership, she knew that Kyle was the brains behind the calculated risk taking. At this critical economic juncture in the San Diego real estate business, a lot of energy and resources were being focused on the downtown high-rises that were being built to accommodate the increasing population, and that would result in building the Padres' ballpark, Petco Park, in downtown San Diego. Whereas previously San Diego's historic Gaslamp district was the epicenter of the city's commerce, it now had to contend with the booming businesses of the East Village, and, unlike Kyle, those individuals with an eye for such things thought they saw a business opportunity in the form of building up downtown San Diego's skyline. Their logic seemed sound at the time. *Build straight up into the sky. Build first. The tenants will come later. Up. Up. Up you go.*

Kyp had wanted in on this "build-up" movement. Kyle had advised his brother against it. It was risky, and it certainly wasn't their specialty. "Let's keep our eye on the ball, Bro," he would tell Kyp. "Let's keep doing what we do best." Six months later Kyle's caution and foresight had paid off. Early in 2007 it was still too early to tell whether or not the explosive growth in high-rises would lead to major successes or failures, but Kyle and Kyp Conway had truly carved out their niche.

Kyle came out the bathroom and crawled into bed with his wife. He leaned over and kissed her, some beer still lingering on his breath. "You want to fool around?" he asked her.

"You should get some sleep," she teased.

He didn't put up a fight. Too tipsy and exhausted to perform, he rolled over on to his side so his back was to her. She ran her immaculately manicured nails across his back. "My poor baby," she said half-jokingly with that same protective maternal instinct she used with their sons. "You work so hard."

"Not as hard as you," he reassured her. His eyes were closed and he was talking into a pillow. "You raise other people's kids all day long and then still find time to raise ours. *That's* hard work." He remembered then and there that she had been up to something that day that he probably should have been aware of, something he should probably ask her about now. "How did it go for you today?" he asked through a yawn, casting a net just wide enough so that she wouldn't suspect his ignorance to her day's affairs.

"Lorena and I took the kids shopping for formal wear. We're all set. Cameron and Cal each have outfits for church, and I really think that they've gotten all of the Sunday clothes protestations out of their systems. It seems like they're actually starting to take pride in dressing up. Maria looked really pretty in the dress Lorena picked out, and Franco looked like such a little gentleman in his suit. They all looked great." She realized she was prattling on at this late hour over topics that could wait. And she suspected Kyle had already begun to drift into sleep.

Kyle was asleep. He'd done the husbandly thing by asking Cynthia about her day, but his brain hadn't stuck around for her answer. Something about shopping with the kids. Some event that she would remind him about at the last minute, and he would either kick himself in the ass for forgetting and then go along with it with a polite smile on his face, or it would be something that conflicted with his work schedule and he'd have to excuse himself. It was as simple as that. The job was *everything* right now.

It was too bad that he'd tuned his wife out now, though. Had he stayed awake to hear what Cynthia was talking about, had he actually paid attention to whatever this event was that required all of them to attend some kind of special Mass, then he might have spared himself a whole slew of trouble in the days to come.

As it was, what she was talking about had nothing to do with Conway Brothers Construction Company or the career boosting house they were building. Therefore it was of little interest to him. He knew that his wife would allow him a certain margin of error, a little wiggle room, where it was actually acceptable that his mind sometimes wandered during conversations concerning the family and their plans. All that mattered right now was that he should keep his mind focused on work. After July 1 everything could go back to normal.

*   *   *

The remodel was coming along nicely, and yet Kyle found himself in a constant state of agitation. The pacing of the project was fine, but in his effort always to remain two steps ahead of any unforeseen setbacks, he was not afforded the luxury of letting his guard down and relaxing. When he arrived at the house today and ascertained that the men were merely *on* schedule and not *ahead* of schedule, he stomped around the property inspecting matters with a grim expression worn on his face.

Kyle and Kyp had agreed not to get too fancy with the experimentation they'd been praised for in their blending of styles. The decision had troubled Kyle because to pull back from the hybrid artistic identity they'd created for themselves might be to sell themselves short. But reason prevailed, with the subtle nudging of Kyp, which was so out of character for him. That latest decision making had almost involved a role-reversal. Kyp was right; they needed to play it safe.

Accordingly they went with the classic Monterey Spanish hacienda in the Adobe style. True to form, the house, when complete, would boast red clay tile roof over white stucco. There would be a matching, detached guest house in the back. The back yard would have a stone tile patio alongside a pool that was eight feet at its deepest end and adjoined a Jacuzzi at its shallowest. The patio would feature an outdoor stone hearth that held a propane gas grill on the left and a tapped kegerator on the right. Kyp had suggested that a nice touch for the stone patio would be to install twin trellises on opposite sides of the French patio door leading into the kitchen that could support Spanish ivy or even eucalyptus. Mauricio had trumped this idea by expanding upon it, conceiving of a stained oak arbor that enclosed the entire patio. The Conways had been sold on that idea.

The passive neutrality and hands-off approach of the New York couple who'd originally reached out to Marc Cronenberg for a good local contractor had allowed for the brothers' complete creative control. Mauricio had been brought into the fold. So the payoff for going with only one style that was anything but unique in Southern California was that the boys were enjoying themselves while kicking ideas around. It was as if the New York restaurant owners, the Molinellis, who had plans to open a sister restaurant here on the West Coast, wanted to be completely surprised with the final product without overseeing the hammering of even a single nail. They were, in fact, remaining back in Manhattan until the house was complete. Kyle wouldn't be surprised if Marc led the both of them to their house in blindfolds when they finally did arrive.

The freedom to expand their creative expression did nothing to assuage Kyle's ever-present fear of falling behind schedule. It was like a headache that wouldn't go away no matter how much aspirin he took. An arbor might look good on paper at the beginning of the construction, but it might not seem too practically appealing when it could mean even two days' extra work in the long run. Kyle was looking for Mauricio now for this very reason.

He walked around the house to the back yard and onto the patio. He glanced down at his feet. Fake grass had been another tough decision.

But they'd decided that the appeal of the plant life that coiled around the arbor and the lush beauty of the shrubbery and garden that ran along the length of fence in the back would outweigh the breaking with tradition. Besides, the three men had decided that the grass looked satisfactory and that it complemented the design of the slate-gray patio. It would never whither in the sunlight or yellow from animal urine; it would never have to be cut, and in a state where water conservation was becoming an increasing environmental movement, it never had to be quenched with inordinate amounts of water. It was easy. If the Molinellis ever uttered a word of dissatisfaction concerning the grass, then Kyle would see to it that it was pulled up and replaced with sod in less than two days' time.

He entered the kitchen area through the patio door and found Mauricio trying to pacify one of the newer guys—Emilio, if Kyle remembered correctly. Emilio was holding a wooden cabinet door in his outstretched hands and, with a look of concern, was showing it to Mauricio. He was speaking in rapid-fire Spanish that Kyle had trouble following even though he told other people that he was "fluent". *Probably some dialect from down south; that's why I don't catch all of it.*

Mauricio didn't appear overly concerned and this helped put Kyle at ease. More than likely Emilio didn't want to green light the kitchen cabinetry before some small matter could be cleared up, and Kyle was heartened both that the new guy would check in before moving forward and that Mauricio was in tune with the progression of this house. "What's the problem?" Kyle asked Mauricio.

Mauricio turned to his friend and his expression told Kyle that there was nothing to worry about. "It's fine. He says the kitchen cabinets are cherry wood and don't match the oak we used in the bathrooms."

Kyle blew out a small breath. Thank God that was all it was. "We know, Emilio; It was in the contract." His mind already began to drift on to the next thing. "Puede seguir adelante."

Putting his hand on Mauricio's shoulder he turned to lead him out of the house. As the two exited, he wondered how much of a setback it would've been had there been a mix-up and the wrong cabinets had been installed. How much time? How much of a headache? Probably not much of one in the grand scheme of things, but what Kyle was gradually becoming aware of was how compartmentalized his brain was becoming, how focused he had been these last few months on this very tricky balancing act that was called progress. These thought patterns of his were making him edgy.

"What's up?" Mauricio asked him when they were both outside.

"The arbor," Kyle replied. "It can't take more than a day and a half."

Mauricio had overshot his interpretation of Kyle's body language by quite a bit. "Is that all? No problem." He needed Kyle to know that he had things under control, even in Kyle's absence. And Mauricio would especially be expediting the construction of the arbor because it had been his idea to put it in in the first place. "We'll have it up in less than one." Mauricio had come to know how there was absolutely no detail, however minute, that Kyle did not oversee on one level or another. The arbor that Mauricio had thought up was so supplemental—window dressing in the literal sense—that Mauricio worried about Kyle at the same time as he admired his friend's aloofness. Kyp seemed relaxed with the pacing of the construction and seemed confident that they would meet their deadline promptly. Why did Kyle seem so stressed out? True, there were potential speed bumps along the way; there always were. But Kyle's inability to relax—all while trying to create the appearance of someone who was at ease with the progress of the house—had become a concern to Cynthia, Kyp, and now even Mauricio. And Mauricio suspected, as did Cynthia, that the stress that was eating away at Kyle, underneath the physical exertion and pressure from the deadline, had everything to do with how this one project would come to define Conway Brothers Construction and establish their place in society.

Kyle's eyes were scanning the property. Side to side. Up and down. To Mauricio he appeared feverish, and he wondered if maybe Kyle needed the drink he'd come to rely on every day to dull the fears that often tried to scare him into thinking that maybe this time he'd finally overextended himself. Mauricio reached out and lightly poked Kyle in the chest, as if to awaken him from a daydream. "Not to worry, *boss*. We'll get it done."

*　*　*

Cynthia and Lorena too had noticed an upswell in Kyle's deadline-driven temperament, but they were able to discuss it casually and light-heartedly over their lunch break one fine Tuesday afternoon. They were at one of their favorite local dining spots, an Italian bistro with a rustic patio area that was packed during the lunch rush. They passed on focaccia and olive oil, and began with Caesar and arugula salads accompanied by Tuna Carpaccio that they would share. There would be no imbibing of white wine as long as they had children to return to, so the light, low-calorie lunch would allow the women to be able to leave the restaurant with guilt-free consciences.

"Thank goodness Mauricio is so cool-headed," Cynthia told Lorena. "Kyp's usually been tuned in regarding his brother, but this time around he's seemed completely oblivious to what's going on with Kyle."

"Kyp's got a lot on his plate too," Lorena reminded her. "It *is* a partnership." The comment struck a chord with Cynthia. There had been no bitterness in the statement, but had it been anyone else besides Cynthia's friend who had uttered it, there might have been. And while although she knew that she was misreading Lorena's statement, there was an implication there that had always been at the back of Cynthia's mind: *Mauricio would never be a partner. Kyle and Kyp would always have a leg up on him.*

She and Kyle had had a discussion about the matter a couple of times. And each time it had been brief because Kyle had always promptly put an end to it. Cynthia had suggested bringing Mauricio into the fold. Kyle had flat out refused, and he had been borderline belligerent about it.

Kyle was one of those individuals with a conservative mentality that dictated that although he and Cynthia were partners in life and aware of each other's take-home, she had absolutely *no* business whatsoever sticking her nose into his professional affairs. And to say he was obstinate would be an understatement. He was unmovable on this topic. To him it wasn't even a topic. It was Cynthia wasting her breath, flapping her lips about things she knew absolutely nothing about. If one day he instructed her about a child throwing a tantrum, that would be the day she would be allowed to advise him on how to conduct himself in the field.

The furthest she'd ever gotten was pointing out to Kyle that statistically speaking, Mauricio did 33.33% of the work when it came to both the planning and the execution. Kyle hadn't even really addressed this point. He'd told her that that figure would jump up anywhere from

50% to 100% when Mauricio one day realized he had gone as far as he could go with the Conway brothers and left to go start up his own company. Cynthia had been galled on multiple fronts by this response. Mauricio would *never* walk away from Conways. He was too loyal, and what could he possibly hope to achieve on his own? He didn't even have his contracting license yet: his citizenship was still too new.

"Oh, he'll walk away," Kyle had assured her. There was a recent lesson in the Conway history that attested to this. "Everyone walks away when they're hungry for more."

Kyle had absolutely no regard for the percentage Cynthia had dropped on him, despite the fact that it was probably true. He'd meant what he'd said. Mauricio was an illegal immigrant who had made it in the states, had in fact surpassed thousands of border-crossers just like himself. He had a great job with an American-born wife and two delightful children. He ought to be happy with what he had, and what he was *not* entitled to was a partnership in the construction company that Kyle and his brother had built from the ground up. Kyle had insinuated that if there came a time when Mauricio was unsatisfied with his station and felt he could advance his position elsewhere, then Kyle would shake his friend's hand and wish him the best of luck. Until then Mauricio would remain Kyle's best employee.

Why did this bother Cynthia so? Because as Kyle would be quick to point out, Cynthia wanted their lives to be picturesque on very superficial levels. Cynthia and Lorena had the same profession, and so did Kyle and Mauricio, and yet there was an ever-present and very tangible divide between the annual incomes of the Conway and Solares families. This was not spoken of, because adults with class didn't speak of such things, but it was always apparent when the two families got together, whether it was the detailing on the finish on their respective SUVs or the way Cynthia noticed Lorena balk when Kyle ordered a $200 bottle of Monastrell while out celebrating. And it bothered Cynthia because if this Point Loma house the boys were constructing really meant as much to their futures as they claimed—in terms both lucrative and professionally developmental—then why not give Mauricio and Lorena a boost? Pretty soon they would have enough money to not have to worry about money, and she didn't see why Kyle failed to grasp that a little positive karma here and there went an extremely long way.

"He's such a good father," Lorena said with sad eyes, "and he truly loves what he does. I'm so lucky to have him."

Cynthia snapped out of it. She didn't recall when they'd starting discussing Mauricio. In her mind she deconstructed what Lorena had just said and she sensed a very subtle but peripheral *but* or *although.* The women locked eyes and Lorena could tell that Cynthia could sense how transparent she'd been in her declaration, with its lining that suggested not *all* was well. "What's going on?" Cynthia asked.

"It's nothing," Lorena replied dismissively.

"Lorena," Cynthia said more forcefully. "Tell me."

"No, I mean it. It's nothing." Lorena was searching for the right words. "It's like, I love this man; he's the man I married despite some harsh protestations." She leaned forward in her chair and squinted at Cynthia. "He gets so detached sometimes, CC. Sometimes I think it's like he left a part of himself down in Mexico. I know he had a tough childhood, but I often wonder if it was more than just tough. Like something really traumatic, y'know? Sometimes I feel like one of those wives whose husband's returned from the war with PTSD, and a small piece of him has died. Only I'll never know what he was like before I met him."

"Are we talking about mood swings or nightmares?"

"No. Just really, *really* long silences." Lorena tapped her finger on the linen tablecloth. "And not even like uncomfortable silences. He's just content to sit there and not speak if it suits him, sometimes for hours on end. And he'll answer questions minimally, with very little insight."

"Isn't that the man you fell in love with?" Cynthia offered.

"Yeah, but that was in the beginning. I thought he'd eventually come out of his shell. We have two kids now who need to be immersed in language, and one of them actually prefers to speak Spanish. And he's shy like his father."

"Mauricio's not shy; he's soft spoken. Could a shy guy ever have gotten you?"

"You know what I mean. I just worry about him. I'm his wife and I want to be there for him. He never opens up to me about his past."

"Well, have you talked to any of his cousins about those days?"

"On the off chance that I'm able to speak with one of them, they deflect. And it's not like I'm prying. It's casual conversation. And you know how strong the family unit is in Mexico. It's like as the leader of their pack he's given them instructions not to divulge any information."

Cynthia sat back in her chair and laughed. "Now you're letting your imagination run wild. That scenario's so implausible it's silly."

"You think so?" Lorena asked with a bit of challenge in her tone that suggested perhaps Cynthia was the one being silly.

"Yes, as a matter of fact, I do." Cynthia softened her expression. "Look, Lorena, I know you think that because you and Mauricio are soul mates that you're supposed to share this 'mind-meld'. That's not how it works. Mauricio is actually entitled to some semblance of privacy. You can't be part of every thought that goes on in his head. Just like he can't be part of yours. You're too focused on *his* past. You should be focused on *your* present. Both of yours. He's a great husband and a great father. That should be enough."

"Even if it means extended periods of monk-like silence?"

"That's who you married."

The busser cleared away the table and the server approached soon afterwards. He asked the ladies if they'd saved room for dessert and they politely declined. He soon returned with the bill, and both women made a grab for the black book. Lorena was a second faster than Cynthia.

"Absolutely not!" Cynthia said.

"I've got lunch today, sweetie," Lorena said with her body turned so the check was just out reach.

Cynthia began to argue the point, but then thought better of it. Better to let Lorena have this small victory and then pick up the next tab. Lorena handed the book to their server, and then the two women sat back in their seats, soaking up the sun on this glorious spring day.

"What time is Cameron's soccer game on Saturday?" Lorena asked.

"Eleven." Cynthia took a sip of water. "How 'bout Franco's Little League game?"

"Same time on Sunday. He's going to have to miss his game the week after, though. Mauricio and I feel like hypocrites because he tried to bail last week so that he could play video games. Never mind that that's a totally unacceptable reason, but we tried to instill upon him a sense of commitment to his team. And maybe his heart isn't one hundred percent into baseball right now, but he is getting better. We can see it in his batting and his fielding. Anyway, we give him this speech about how he has an obligation to his teammates, and now we're yanking him off of the field for his First Communion. Hypocrisy over irresponsibility. The lesser of two evils I guess."

"I'm sure his coach understands."

"Franco's less enthused about a formal church ceremony than a baseball game, let me tell you."

"Regardless," Cynthia reassured her," it is a big deal."

The server came back to the patio and approached the woman with an awkward smile on his face. His next task was always an uncomfortable one. "Excuse me ma'am, did you have another card you'd like to use.?This one didn't go through."

Lorena momentarily looked astonished, but then quickly collected herself to save face. With a quick change of composure, she asked, "It didn't go through? Is there something wrong with the magnetic strip?"

The server smiled cordially, but it was apparent from his discomfort that he hadn't wanted to pursue the topic any further. He came right out and said it. "No ma'am. It's been declined. I'd be happy to take another form of payment from you."

Lorena flushed a little bit with embarrassment. Cynthia made a move to dig into her hand bag, but Lorena reached across the table and took hold of her wrist. "It's fine, Lorena. Really."

"No," Lorena said more forcefully. "I've got this." She opened her purse and replaced the declined credit card. Trading it out with her bank card, she handed the new plastic to the young man and said, "Here, try this one."

"I'll be right back," the server said, sensing the mild tension and glad for the chance to remove himself from it.

It was a minor setback, and it happened to people all the time. But Cynthia could feel the humiliation in Lorena just underneath the surface, and it reinforced Cynthia's misgivings regarding the deficit between the two families' finances. A maxed out credit card could mean anything, sure. But it got Cynthia wondering if her friend was struggling financially in an effort to keep the charade of well off family indulging in a comfortable upper-middle class lifestyle. And it also had her wishing that life was fair, an utterly futile notion.

Yet she'd let Lorena pay the bill. For Cynthia to have picked up the tab would have been a bruise to Lorena's ego more damaging than the drain of a thirty dollar lunch, even if it did suggest hard times for the Solares family.

When the server returned the payment had gone through. He thanked the women and was on his way. In an attempt to make light of the discomfiting transaction, Lorena laughed and said," When it's Maria's turn for her First Communion, we'll see what gems we can uncover at the Goodwill."

* * *

Cynthia had found Kyle early on in her adult life, pretty much right out of high school. Their love was a true one, and the pair complemented each other well. What Lorena had always taken notice of was how good Kyle was to Cynthia. Even when he was stern, short on patience and single-minded about his ambition, he treated her like a queen. Without going so far as to call it envy, Lorena admired the couple and wanted something similar for herself. But in those first few years after of high school, when Lorena was trying to build her own career, she had been very unlucky in love. She had dated one loser after another, and always ended up hating herself for it.

She turned inward in an attempt to evaluate herself and perhaps come to realize what it was that she was doing wrong. Why did she attract men who treated her badly? The first conclusion she came to was that she was the classic case of a woman who liked to make projects out of men. Find a real jerk and see if she could change him—bend him to her will and make him respectable. This theory might have been a sound one had she ever successfully molded a man to her true ideal. But looking back on her string of failed relationships, she realized that not one man she'd dated had budged even an inch. It had been a battle of wits that she'd always lost, and the taste of defeat had left her bitter with resentment. Then she realized that changing a man wasn't what she wanted at all, so why even waste the energy? It only got her down on herself in the end.

She then convinced herself that she needed to change her way of thinking; that she was, in fact, putting out an energy into the air like a beacon that attracted the wrong kind of man to her. Whether it was a guy with a lack of drive, virtue, or regard for other people, she always seemed to find him and run to him. And it bothered her that she knew this about herself, and yet still remained un-cautious. These "boyfriends" always knew the standard things to say, and although they didn't know that she could see through all of their pretense, she still held out hope that there might be a positive outcome if she simply stayed the course. Then the relationship would crash and burn, and she'd go through an intense period of depression where she told herself that she had only herself to blame.

"Your problem," her mother had told her, "is that you're attracted to exciting men. Exciting doesn't work for you. Look at Cynthia and Kyle. Sure, he's a little rough around the edges, with his foul mouth and his propensity for the drink, but he's dependable and he knows what he wants out of life. He's also career oriented and a family man. He'll make a great father one day. I'm not saying go out and find yourself a man just like Kyle. Dios Mio, that man is gruff. But find yourself a man with the same set of values, Lorena. Small steps. It will take some time to figure out. But I think it would benefit you to reexamine what it is that you look for in a boyfriend."

Lorena had taken her mother's words to heart, but nothing could have prepared the Cruz family for the man she'd brought home to dinner one Thanksgiving. A chance encounter at one of Kyle's work sites had introduced Lorena to her future husband.

A parent of one of the preschool children had cooked dozens of chocolate cupcakes for her child's birthday celebration, and some leftovers had been given to Cynthia and Lorena. Cynthia had thought it would be cute to stop by the house Kyle and the boys were working on in Linda Vista and offer them the cupcakes. Lorena, Cynthia's ride, had driven her over there to an impressive two-story house in this neighborhood of one-story homes. Kyle, Kyp, and their team had graciously accepted the sweets. As Cynthia chatted with her husband about the coming weekend, Lorena had decided to give herself a tour of the house. Making her way through the remodel, she marveled at the home and could easily envision it in its final form. Imagining herself in a house such as this one day, she drifted up the staircase, running her fingers over the newly lacquered banister. Kyle and Kyp were talented indeed. She glanced in each bedroom as she made her way down the hallway.

Stepping into the master bedroom, she came upon a man on a ladder wiring a light fixture into the wall. She wasn't startled, but she'd believed she'd been alone up here. He too began to speak over his shoulder when he realized that his company was neither Kyle or Kyp. "Oh, hello," the man said, stepping down from the ladder and brushing his hands off on his jeans.

Lorena took him in. He was slight of build, with wispy black hair and a swarthy complexion. His navy blue T-shirt, jeans, and construction boots were dusty, and his skin was covered in sweat and grime. He reached his hand out to introduce himself, looked at his dirty palm, and reconsidered.

She reached out and took his hand before he could retract it. "Hello. I'm Lorena."

"My name is Mauricio," he said with a heavy accent.

She sensed that his acquisition of English had only just begun. "I haven't seen you before, Mauricio."

"I'm . . . the new guy."

"Well it's very nice to meet you."

What followed could hardly have been considered a courtship. She had been very taken with him upon their first meeting. He was charming, but quiet and reluctant to speak unless spoken to. She had started to pursue him by accompanying Cynthia on her frequent visits to the site, and always finding a reason to seek out Mauricio. Kyle and Cynthia weren't oblivious to what was going on, but they merely considered it a harmless flirtation that would boost Mauricio's confidence and perhaps help to facilitate his assimilation into American society. But Lorena's mother's words about the kind of man she should find for herself stuck with her, and the Conways had no idea what bold designs Lorena had for Kyle and Kyp's newest and most promising employee.

The situation was in no way forced. The attraction was reciprocated, even if reluctantly so, on Mauricio's part. He always complimented her on her new hairstyle or manicure, things that had always gone unnoticed by boyfriends of the past. She was drawn to him, now on sure footing on her new path in the pursuit of love.

But he was guarded. It never crossed his mind that the attention she gave him could be anything other than playful infatuation. He was a lowly illegal immigrant, and she was the daughter of a successful dental practitioner. It was the stuff of fictitious love stories, but not of real life. And he in no way desired to jeopardize the opportunity he'd been given by romantically entangling himself with the partner of his boss' wife. He had too much to lose, deportation being the greatest calamity of all. It hadn't been by chance that Mauricio had been working upstairs in the master bedroom when all of the other workers were keeping busy outside. Kyle strove to keep Mauricio out of sight as much as possible.

The situation came to a head one evening when the house was almost complete and Lorena and Cynthia were talking on the phone. While discussing a renewal in their licensing, the conversation had been momentarily interrupted when Lorena, through the line, had heard Kyle return home from work.

"You're home early," Lorena had heard Cynthia say to Kyle.

"Yeah, I'm dead tired. Mauricio's got it under control. He'll be there for a few more hours. I'm going to bed."

Lorena had ended the conversation as quickly as she could without arousing suspicion. Hanging up the phone, she'd hurried to her bedroom. She changed into her favorite skintight white pants and black halter top. She washed her face and reapplied her makeup. She brushed her hair and put earrings on. She dolled herself up with the resolve of someone who was about to make a big play for what she wanted.

It took her fifteen minutes to drive to the house in Linda Vista. It was dark when she arrived. That was good. She found the front door open and entered a dark house. Perhaps he'd already left. Creeping up the stairs the made her way to the master bedroom and found him on his knees tacking down the last of the plush white carpet that would adorn this luxurious home.

"Mauricio," she said with an effort to add a sexy rasp to her voice.

He straightened, startled. His clothes were much cleaner now that they were putting the finishing touches on the house. "Lorena," he said, taking a deep breath and putting his hand to his heart. "You scare me."

She slowly closed the distance between them and knelt down next to him on the soft carpet. She cupped his face in her hands and kissed him, softly at first but then more aggressively as she melted into him. When she sensed him clamming up—not because he didn't want her but because of what it would mean if they were somehow discovered—she took his hands and ran them over her breasts. She sensed his indecision, the dilemma going on behind his soft brown eyes, and she reached behind her neck and untied her halter. When it fell to the floor he was defeated by biology, her seduction a success. They undressed each other and made love right there on the brand new white carpeting. She would never breathe a word of her first night of passion with Mauricio to Lorena or Kyle. Kyle would have been livid. But she never once regretted it.

Not even after learning he'd impregnated her.

* * *

She'd hid it from her family for as long as she could. In the meantime she'd done everything in her power to endear Mauricio to her family. This had been a struggle when it came to her father, Eduardo.

Dr. Eduardo Cruz, or Eddie as his friends called him, was from a generation two steps removed from the one that had immigrated to the states in the early 1900s. And while his grandparents had had a fairly smooth transition of citizenship, Eddie saw himself as apart from those who made up the wave of immigrants pouring over the U.S. border on a daily basis. Yes, to him they had admirable work ethics and an uncompromising sense of family, but they came here looking for a quick fix and a meal ticket without paying their dues. His family had waited patiently and entered the U.S. legally, their backgrounds checked and their papers signed. The problem, in his opinion, was that immigrants today were too busy sending money back to their families in Mexico to bother ingratiating themselves to their American hosts. He had been appalled when he'd first learned that there was a day when Mexican-Americans didn't go to work in an effort to show Americans how much they depended on their cheap labor. And worse, they paraded down the streets of downtown San Diego honking their horns and wailing like banshees, Mexican flags flapping in the wind as if they were throwing some kind of coupe. No, Eddie had worked too hard in an effort to provide for his family to give away his eldest daughter to some swashbuckling Mexican refugee. But the pregnancy changed everything.

At that first Thanksgiving dinner, Lorena's mother, Luna, had been an outgoing model hostess, hoping to offset Eddie's standoffish passive aggression. Eddie, with a broad shouldered, solid build that he often inadvertently used for intimidation, stared stonily at his dinner guest as Lorena prattled on about what a great job Mauricio was doing for the Conway brothers and how they never would have been able to make it as far as they had without him. Eddie looked like a Latino version of Clark Gable with his pencil *thin mustache and the way in which he arched his eyebrow as he scowled at Mauricio.*

"So tell me about your family back home," *he commanded Lorena's love interest.*

"Not much to tell," *Mauricio replied meekly.* "I have many primos, a few tios and tias. They live in Oaxaca."

"And your parents?" *Eddie asked.*

"They died a long time ago."

Eddie didn't like this one bit. Who was this man? What kind of home did he come from? He could be anybody. True love be damned. How could this individual possibly hope to provide for his daughter when he could be deported at any moment? No, he had to put a stop to this. He would make Lorena end it. He cared little about her dating history. This was not the answer.

He tried to broach the subject tactfully a few weeks later. The last thing he wanted was to push his daughter away into this man's arms.

"He'll never truly be established here," *he persuaded her gently.* "I know you think you love him, but your expectations are unrealistic. He probably has a girlfriend back home."

"Daddy—"

"And regardless of what Kyle and Kyp have done for him, he can never hope to establish himself in a position to provide for you and a family."

"Daddy—"

"And let's face it, Lorena; he's uneducated. Sure, maybe he's good at laying down spackle, but the kind of man you—"

"Daddy, I'm pregnant."

That had changed everything.

* * *

Save for the help, Eddie had the house all to himself. Luna was out shopping and his kids were at school. He had no further dental appointments today. He sat at his mahogany desk in his home office, the index finger of his right hand pressed to his temple and his elbow resting on the desk surface. The fingers of his left hand drummed on the desk monotonously as he waited patiently for his guest to arrive. Through his office door he heard his housekeeper, Ana, respond to the doorbell and admit their guest. He con-tinued to wait as Ana directed the visitor down the hall and into the study. Eddie heard a soft rapping at the door.

"Come in."

Mauricio opened the door and stepped into the office, hat in hand. "Hello, sir."

"Sit down, Mauricio," Eddie said without preamble.

Mauricio came forward and eased himself in to a brown leather arm chair. Eddie noted how nervous Mauricio seemed. Good.

For a long time Eddie simply sat there and stared at Mauricio, with intense eyes and his mouth puckered as if he was about to spit. Finally he said, "How did you manage to defile my daughter, Mauricio?"

"Sir?"

"Oh, that's right. Your English is limited. Let me rephrase. ¿Como se-duciste a mi hija para entrar en sus pantolones?" How did you worm your way into my daughter's pants?

"Sir, I—"

"Careful now."

"Sir, I did not mean for this to happen. Tengo un gran respecto por usted. And I do love your daughter very much."

"Well you've certainly solidified a place in our family."

"Sir? Yo no comprendo."

Eddie shot up out of his seat, which went flying back behind him. "You had better learn English pretty goddamned fast, boy! This is my firstborn daughter we're talking about." He came around the desk and took two quick strides toward Mauricio. Mauricio, uncertain what to do, reflexively got up out of his own chair and faced Eddie while taking two careful steps back. Eddie kept coming at him until Mauricio's back was pressed against the bookshelf and they were nose to nose.

Eddie was fuming, breathing heavily and looking Mauricio up and down, sizing him up. Mauricio wondered if the older man would hit him. He decided he would let him if that was what he intended. Instead, Eddie reached into the breast pocket of his white collared shirt, retrieving a busi-ness card. He reached out and grabbed Mauricio's left wrist, plunging the card into his hand. "Take this," he barked.

Mauricio lifted the card to read it. "Eduardo Cruz, DDS."

"No. The other side, you simpleton. Flip it over. Read the back."

Mauricio did what he was told. Hand written in ink was the name of a man, a name Mauricio didn't recognize: Carlos Ruiz. Underneath the name was an address: Paseo de La Reforma 305, Cuauhtémoc, 06500, Ciudad de Mexico. "What—"

"Tomorrow you get on a plane for Mexico City. You'll go to this address."

Mauricio began to squirm with apprehension. Eddie grabbed him by the collar of his flannel shirt and pushed him more forcefully into the bookcase. "It's a chartered plane. No one will screen you." Mauricio's confusion was palpable, and Eddie took mild pleasure in having the upper hand in this situation at the very least. "When you land in Mexico City, you go to this address. You ask for this man, Carlos Ruiz. Do you understand? ¿Comprende?"

"Yes, but what—"

"This man will see to it that you're granted an immigrant visa. An official one. Then you get back on the plane and it will return you here. Then and only then do you have permission to marry my daughter."

Mauricio sensed a trick. He feared he wouldn't be coming back. To Eddie, that much was evident. He asked Mauricio, "Do you love Lorena?"

Mauricio collected himself. "Yes, sir. Very much."

"Then this is what you need to do. You'll be back in a couple of days. You need to be at the Palomar airport tomorrow at 8:00 AM. Make sure you're there on time. Do not fuck this up."

"I want to see Lorena before I go."

"The only way you're ever going to see her again is with a visa in your hand. Now I've called in a lot of favors to make this happen, and all because you've turned my life upside down. You do not want to cross me. ¿Comprende?"

"Yes, sir."

"Good. Now go."

When Mauricio had left, Eddie poured himself a scotch. Picking up his overturned swivel chair, he plopped back down into it. He took a sip of scotch and then massaged his forehead.

Abortion had never been an option. Not for Eddie's daughters. And although he suspected he'd rue the day he'd ever met Mauricio Solares, he *had to give the man the benefit of the doubt. A shotgun wedding for Lorena was something he never would have imagined. But Eddie was old fashioned, and sometimes when old fashioned guys learned that their first born had been knocked up by some shifty illegal alien, they made sure that the father manned up and took good care of their little girls.*

*   *   *

Eddie had summoned Kyle, too, a day later. Kyle had agreed to meet with Eddie in the mid-afternoon when he could steal away from work for an hour. Mauricio's inexplicable absence that day had left him worried, and he had considered rescheduling. Since he was in the dark about all of the events that had transpired so recently, it never occurred to him that Dr. Cruz would have the answer to where Mauricio was that day.

He waltzed into Eddie's office and checked in with his receptionist, noting the heavy smell of medicine and disinfectant. She showed him into Eddie's work office, and this time Eddie received his guest with his back turned, hands clasped behind him and staring out his window at the bustle of Scripps Ranch's daily commerce. He had removed his long white coat and hung it around the back of his desk chair.

"Hello, Dr. Cruz," Kyle said as the receptionist turned and left them in privacy.

"Kyle," Eddie said warmly. "I told you before. Call me Eddie. Please, come in. Have a seat."

Kyle took a seat opposite Eddie's chair. So preoccupied had he been with Mauricio's no-show that he was taken aback when Eddie said, "You must be wondering where Mauricio is today."

Kyle kept his apprehension measured. "Yes, sir. Do you know anything?"

Eddie turned from the window and pulled his chair back, easing into it. "Yes I do. He boarded a plane this morning bound for Mexico City. He'll be back the day after tomorrow." He watched as Kyle's mouth fell open just an inch and continued, "I put him on that plane. Do you know why?"

"No, sir. Would you care to enlighten me?" Kyle would remain patient and hear Eddie out, although he didn't take kindly to men who took it upon themselves to interrupt his business schedule. Mauricio's absence today had been a setback, and Eddie Cruz had better have a damn good explanation for Mauricio's having run off to Mexico.

"*I had to pull a few strings, but I wanted to make sure that Mauricio is documented here at the very least.*"

Kyle was puzzled. Eddie didn't strike him as a good Samaritan, and Kyle couldn't think of one good reason for him to have done this. "He went to obtain a work visa?"

"That's right. We won't have to worry about deportation."

"Sir—"

"Eddie."

"Eddie, if I may. Why would want to do that for one of my employees?" True, it was risky business having an illegal immigrant as one of his top guys, but that didn't strike Kyle as a reason for Lorena's father to step in, unless—

"Because he impregnated my daughter."

—unless Kyle and Cynthia's suspicions were valid, and something had been going on between Lorena and Mauricio. Kyle closed his mouth and slowly covered it with his hand. He looked away and stared out the window that Eddie had been gazing through only moments before. "Ho-ly shit."

"That's right, Kyle. Your golden boy got my precious Lorena pregnant. Lorena, who had finally gotten her career going and a bright future to look forward to."

"Eddie, if you think that either me or Cynthia had any idea—"

"No, no, Kyle. That's not it at all. Believe me, the look on your face right now is all the proof I need that you had no inkling that this had happened."

"Then what . . . ? I mean . . . what happens now?"

"Mauricio returns here and marries my daughter. Clean and simple."

The ramifications of what Eddie was telling Kyle were slow to sink in. Mauricio would be marrying his way into a U.S. citizenship. This made sense. And if Eddie could pull it off with all of his numerous contacts down in Mexico, then why shouldn't he? So what was nagging at Kyle?

Eddie. Why would he do this? His disdain for illegal workers here in San Diego was no big secret. Why would he be giving Mauricio the keys to his family? And why was he telling Kyle? This change in Mauricio's status would certainly help to protect himself and his company, but despite how close Lorena and Cynthia had grown since partnering up, he couldn't figure Eddie's angle here. "This is what you want?" Kyle asked.

"No, but this is the best way to save face in a potentially humiliating and disastrous situation. Have you thought about the danger a child out of wedlock could pose to the pre-school? Lorena's reputation would be damaged *beyond repair. Now you see how this affects you and Cynthia. It's scandalous. I won't have it."*

"So this is why you called me in? Or is there more?"

Eddie leaned forward and rested his elbows on the desk, his fingers intertwined. "What am I looking at in the days to come, Kyle? Is this man you found on the street worthy of my family?"

So that was it. Kyle was to play advocate for Mauricio. Kyle looked back and held Eddie's stony gaze. He began to understand the risk Lorena's father was taking in this bold move; he understood Eddie's need to take control of the situation before it spun out of control. And now Kyle had the chance to put Eddie a little more at ease, even if the situation was nightmarish in Eddie's mind. But right then and there he decided that he wouldn't lie to Eddie. Eddie had worked hard his whole life and had provided a fine home for his family. He deserved the truth. And as Kyle sat there and took a moment to gather his thoughts, it occurred to him that he didn't need to lie. The situation may have looked bleak on the surface, but the more Kyle thought about it, it was an opportunity to improve a friend's quality of life, and build a family in the process. "Eddie, I can't imagine what must be going through your head right now, but let me just say that this all isn't as bad as it looks. Especially if Mauricio comes back with that visa. I discovered Mauricio when he was just a kid; hell, he still is a kid in my mind." Damn it. Choose your words more carefully. *"But since then he has climbed the ladder in the company. He's our number one guy. He's one of the hardest workers I've ever seen, and I've never heard a single complaint out of him. And aside from that, he's gifted. He's given us ideas that have taken us in whole new directions. We wouldn't be where we are today if it weren't for him. There's no telling how far he'll go. What's more, he's a decent man. He's personable and ethical."* Kyle glanced down at the floor, trying to pick his words. *"I consider him to be family. Cynthia feels the same way. We have him over to our home for dinner regularly. The only difference between someone like him and someone like you or me is the hand life's dealt him. He just needs a chance. If you give him a chance, I think you'll come to see him as a very honorable and respectable person, someone who will always love and cherish Lorena."*

Eddie had listened to Kyle intently, without so much as a budge in his facial muscles. Rather than comment on what Kyle had just told him about Mauricio, he had one more question. "And what do you know of his background?"

Kyle sighed and frowned. "Not much. Only that he's from Oaxaca and didn't have an easy childhood. But I've met some of his cousins. I've even put a few of them to work. Hard workers, all of them. They're all very close."

Eddie sat there, unmoving in contemplative silence. Kyle wasn't at all confident that he'd convinced the man. "Sir," Kyle began carefully, returning to the honorific to be sure that Eddie knew that Kyle respected his elders. "I don't want to speak out of turn. But it seems to me that . . . it seems to me that you're in a unique position to understand what Mauricio's going through."

"Am I? I was born here in San Diego, Kyle."

"I understand. That's . . . that's not what I meant. But didn't your grandparents at one time come here, at tremendous risk, to create a better life for themselves?"

Eddie looked at Kyle with a lopsided half-grin, an expression that told Kyle that the man was amused by Kyle's naiveté. "Son, let me tell you something about what I have learned. I've done business with a lot of other dental practitioners down in Mexico. If someone comes to see me and needs a root canal but has no dental insurance, I will sometimes—and strictly off the record—refer that person to one of my associates down in Tijuana. There people can get the work they need done for a fraction of what it would cost to get the same work done here. It's not unethical, but it might be frowned upon if some of my colleagues were to learn of it. But what other options does this person have? Healthcare in this country is a broken thing.

"The point is that in my efforts to do right by these individuals I have brushed shoulders with a great many dentists south of the border and have even attended conventions there. We work together closely, sharing ideas and learning of new developments, and I'm proud to be partaking in my heritage. But in my travels there I've seen both the good and the bad. A policeman will join a drug cartel when he realizes he can increase his salary fiftyfold by running contraband instead of keeping the peace. Some men will sell their sisters into the sex-trade if there is monetary gain involved. And we Americans are often complicit in the Mexicans' woes. The gringos will sell a truckload of semi-automatic weapons to a Mafioso in the Sierra Madres without giving the slightest thought as to who they might be turned on."

Kyle's confusion was compounding. Not only had Eddie dodged his question, but he was now speaking in abstractions that had little to do with what they had just been talking about. He decided he would wait patiently and hear Eddie out, hoping that this was all leading somewhere.

"*The youth are the most vulnerable,*" Eddie continued. "*Find a boy and get sway over him, often with the promise of cash, and you can mold him into whatever you want him to be. Those with very little to lose who see opportunity are easy to manipulate. Men like you and me will never know what horrible acts we're truly capable of. But the boys poised to become men in Mexico are discovering these things about themselves every day.*"

Eddie paused, and Kyle wondered if he was finished. When the pause lingered, Kyle spoke up. "*But we're talking about Mauricio. He's not in Mexico. He's here in California trying to earn an honest day's pay.*"

Eddie smiled a little bit wider, as if Kyle had set him up for the point he'd been attempting to arrive at all along. And Kyle saw no mirth behind that smile. Eddie was not at all happy with his present circumstances. "*In my experience I've learned that there are two types of people who come here. Those who are running from poverty, and those who are running from something else. Which one is Mauricio?*"

This was something Kyle could comment on with conviction. "*I'd say he's the former.*"

"*Would you bet your family on that?*" Eddie had fire in his eyes. He was challenging Kyle, as if he'd hold Kyle personally responsible if something awful befell Lorena and her unborn child.

Kyle didn't answer right away. It was not an answer to be taken lightly. It was like swearing on the life of your children when you weren't entirely sure of the truth yourself. As it happened, Eddie spared Kyle from having to respond. "*This is what's eating away at me, Kyle. You can vouch for the boy's present, but not his past. And although my faith tells me that I should be willing to forgive a man for his sins, we're talking about a man who will be father to my grandchild, a man I know absolutely nothing about.*"

Kyle truly understood now the bind that Eddie found himself in. But working side-by-side with Mauricio had allowed Kyle to truly understand his hardest worker's better nature. So although he understood Eddie's apprehension, it was not something he shared with him. He knew Mauricio. Mauricio was one of the good ones. But to placate Eddie, he said instead, "*I'll be watching him very closely, sir. He is my employee after all. The second he screws up, you'll be the first person to know. Then we can both set him straight.*" Good. Now he knows we're on the same page. Now to lay his fears to rest. "*But I truly don't see that happening. I think as time goes by and you get to know him the way Cynthia and I have—the way Lorena has*—*then on your own you'll come to wholeheartedly accept him as a member of your family."*

Eddie looked away at nothing in particular. He didn't seem at all convinced, but he'd already set events in motion by sending Mauricio to Mexico City. He couldn't reverse his decision now. "I hope you're right, Kyle."

* * *

Kyle had put in a full fourteen-hour day, and although he was physically exhausted, he was in high spirits. If they kept up this rigorous pace, if he stayed focused on the task at hand, then the greatest house that Conway Brothers had ever constructed would be livable by their July 1 deadline. And though he knew that both he and the other men would be running on fumes by the time the remodel was completed, they would have nothing to do for the rest of the summer afterwards except relax, unwind, and spend quality time with their families.

He'd come home at 8:00 and reheated the dinner that Cynthia had cooked for her and the boys. Cameron and Cal had been put to bed, and Cynthia was currently luxuriating in a hot bubble bath, a book in one hand and a glass of zinfandel in the other. After finishing his plate of tri-tip, mashed potatoes, and green beans, he'd poured himself a glass of scotch and plopped down on the couch, feet up on the coffee table. He knew Cynthia would have wanted him to change out of his work clothes before risking dirtying their beige vinyl sofa, but he was simply too tired to care. He'd been flipping the channels hoping to find something uncomplicated and entertaining enough to dull his thoughts and help him to relax. Then he's stumbled across the perfect choice—one of his favorite movies: *A Fistful of Dollars*. He was on his second glass of Chivas Regal, enjoying his idleness immensely, when he heard a knock at the door. *Who the hell could that be at this hour?* Then he'd remembered he'd left several rolls of blueprints in Mauricio's truck that he'd wanted to go over before retiring for the evening. He was able to turn his body slightly and crane his neck so that he could see down the front hall to the door. "Hello?"

The door opened just a crack and Mauricio stuck his head just past the jamb. "It's me, Kyle," he said just softly enough as to not wake the boys.

"C'mon in, Mauricio," Kyle called with even less regard for his sons' slumber. He turned back to his movie and waited for Mauricio to approach.

Mauricio walked into the living room with three cardboard tubes under his left arm. "I'm going to put these on the kitchen table."

"Cool. Thanks again for bringing those by. Looks like I'm more distracted than I thought." He watched as Mauricio turned to his right and retreated into the kitchen. "Help yourself to a beer or make yourself a drink if you want."

Mauricio came back with a Dos Equis in his hand and sat down on the loveseat that joined the sofa to form an *L* shape in their living room. "So, I wanted to ask you—"

"Hold on a sec, man. This is my favorite scene."

On the television Clint Eastwood's famous character, The Man With No Name, walks down the main street of the Mexican border town of San Miguel. Kyle became more animated; he put his glass down on a coaster and leaned forward, resting his elbows on his knees. He already knew the lines by heart, but after all the times he'd watched this scene, he still grew eager with anticipation. As Clint passes an elderly, bearded man putting the finishing touches on a simple wooden casket, singing to himself and oblivious to Clint's presence, Clint turns to the man and casually commands him, "*Get three coffins ready.*"

Kyle's lips parted into a malicious grin. "Oh, they've done it now." Clint continues on his stroll after the man nods his assent, with anonymous onlookers taking notice of his careless swagger. The shot changes and now the audience can see that his destination is a stable where four tough looking pistoleros take notice of his approach. All the while Don Savio's score is picking up in tempo, the melancholy trumpet morphing into an even more despondent crescendo of wordless chorus. Two of the bandits climb up onto the top of the pen, perching there as the other two approach Clint with enough distance between them as to not give Clint a clear line of fire at the both of them.

"*Adios, Amigo,*" one of the men says to Clint. "*Listen, stranger. Didn't you get the idea? We don't like to see bad boys like you in town. Go get your mule. You let him get away from you?*" The man cackles as he goads Clint.

Kyle reached over and slapped Mauricio on the shoulder. "Not good to taunt him. No good can come of it."

Clint's arms are concealed under his long patterned brown-green poncho. Without any hint of animosity in his voice, he addresses the speaker of the taunt. *"See, that's what I want to talk to you about. He's feeling real bad."*

The man doesn't follow, and in confusion says, *"Huh?"*

"My mule," Clint clarifies. *"See, he went and got all riled up when you went and fired those shots at his feet."*

"It's on now," said Kyle, nodding his head.

The bandits glance away momentarily in contemplation, confused now. Then the man on Clint's right speaks for the first time. *"Hey, are you making some kind of joke?"*

Clint says, *"No"*, as if they were all on the same level and merely needed to clear up a simple misunderstanding. His right arm is exposed now, and he's taken the cigar out his mouth and is using it to gesture his intent to the men. *"No, see I understand that you men were just playing around, but the mule, he just doesn't get it. Of course, if you men were all to apologize . . . ."* He uses the cigar to point at the men, and then returns it to his mouth.

Three of the bandits burst into laughter at this absurd suggestion. However, the man on Clint's right grins briefly, but it's apparent by the perplexed look on his face that he's beginning to take Clint a little more seriously.

"Big mistake," Kyle said, shaking his head in disapproval this time. He turned to Mauricio and tried to put a mock expression of seriousness. "No one fucks with Clint's mule."

Mauricio did his best to conceal his impatience. It was getting late. He wanted to be back home with Lorena and the kids, putting his head on a pillow and getting some sleep before another long work day. He'd never seen this movie before, and he wouldn't have minded watching it at some other time. He thought it was rude of Kyle to make him sit and wait. Kyle, the man who'd become obsessive about keeping a tight schedule of progress.

Clint listens to the chorus of laughter and looks down at the ground, his face momentarily concealed by his brown cowboy hat. At the same time he uses his left arm to throw the rest of the poncho up over his left shoulder, and it falls behind him like a cape. Both his torso and his gun belt are exposed now. The shot changes to a close up of Clint's face, and he looks at the men with a menacing squint. With the cigar in his mouth, he gnarls at the four men, "*I don't think it's nice, you laughing. See, my mule don't like people laughing. He gets the crazy idea you're laughing at him. Now if you apologize, like I know you're going to, I might convince him that you really didn't mean it.*"

As Clint insinuates the deadly threat, the bandits' hands are slowly inching towards the holsters on their hips. A standoff ensues for the next few seconds of the film, while each bandit calculates whether they can beat Clint to the draw. The man to Clint's left tries first, but is sloppy and slow to bring his pistol to bear.

"Here it is," said Kyle.

Lightning fast and with deadly precision, Clint's revolver is out of its holster and blazing. His left hand flies over his gun, rapidly cocking back the hammer after each time his right hand squeezes the trigger. Five shots take out the four bandits in one second.

Kyle jumped off of the sofa and threw his fist up in the air, and with a total disregard for his sleeping children, yelled out, "Yeah! That's how it's done, Mauricio. That's how you deal out a comeuppance." And then he laughed, the drink in him causing him to sway just a little. The laughter died down after a moment, and then he turned to Mauricio once more and said, "Classic film. Never gets old." Mauricio played along with a smile on his face, hoping they could move on and then he could go home. "I will say, though, that Sergio Leone's dagos aren't convincing substitutes for your people. I guess you just gotta suspend disbelief."

Mauricio didn't really know what Kyle had meant by that, but he guessed that Kyle had inadvertently insulted him yet again. His impatience was beginning to get the best of him now, and he spoke what was on his mind. "Kyle, do you think I could get an advance on some cash on Friday? We still need some more food and decorations for the barbeque on Sunday, and I know we don't get paid until next week."

Kyle's grin dropped into a frown. "Yeah, sure, of course you can borrow some money, but . . . but what barbecue? What are you talking about?"

Now it was Mauricio's turn to frown. He couldn't believe that Kyle didn't know what he was talking about. "The party. For Franco. It's his First Communion party."

Kyle looked up at the ceiling, eyes darting back and forth, as if he was consulting a calendar in his head. "First Communion party? I thought that wasn't until next month."

It was tricky business when Mauricio got frustrated with his boss. It didn't matter that Kyle was also his friend. Mauricio had to be careful what words he chose—keeping his tone in check—to voice how flabbergasted he was that Kyle could forget such an important date. "Kyle, our wives have been planning this for weeks. You *knew* about it." And if Mauricio was bothered by the fact that Kyle had forgotten, then he was really going to be taken aback by what Kyle said next.

As if all this was just dawning on him, Kyle blurted out, "Wait a minute. *This* Sunday. No, no, Mauricio. This is no good. We have to work. Seven days a week from here on out."

Mauricio was speechless. He couldn't believe what he was hearing. How had Kyle let this slip his mind? "But Kyle, we talked about this. You knew this was happening. Cynthia and Lorena have been spending most of their free time lately planning it. You told me it was fine."

"How long ago was this? When did you ask me?"

Mauricio thought about it. "Back in April."

Kyle put his hands up. "I'm sorry, Mauricio. I must have miscalculated. I thought it was in July for sure. Which would have been fine. But we've got a deadline to meet. We can't afford to mess around."

Kyle was a father of two, and his eldest son would be having his own First Communion in a year. Mauricio very plainly tried to appeal to Kyle on this basis. "You're telling me I won't be able to celebrate my son's First Communion with my family?"

"Our families will be there. But you and me, we need to put in a full twelve-fourteen-hour day. I'm sorry, man, but this is the work we've chosen for ourselves. This is how it needs to be. We screw this one up, and there won't be any work for us in the future."

Mauricio's face fell and lost a shade or two of color. Had this been prearranged and not some astonishing turn of events, then he might have been able to prepare himself mentally. But Kyle's memory lapse and refusal to budge, when an apology followed by a one-time exception would have been in order, felt like a betrayal.

Kyle's expression softened. "Look, you can go to the Mass. Watch him receive the Eucharist and all of that. But right after that I need you to leave the church and come right over to the site. Believe me, I wish I could be there too. But we have got to see this through to the end." He took his wallet out of the back pocket of his jeans and opened it up. Taking out two hundred-dollar bills, he reached out to hand the money to Mauricio. "Here, will this be enough?"

Mauricio stared at the money in Kyle's hand for a long moment, and then looked up to meet eyes with his friend and boss. He reluctantly reached out and took the bills from Kyle's hand. "That should be plenty. Thank you."

Kyle didn't want to lose face by apologizing any more than he had. Excessive apology would have been a sign of weakness. Mauricio could have all the time off that he needed and go anywhere and do anything he liked, but *only after* July 1. "Okay. I'll see you tomorrow then. Thanks again for bringing those rolls by."

"Good night," said Mauricio, and he turned and left. Kyle heard the front door close and blew out a heavy breath. He downed his last sip of scotch. He bent down and reached over for the remote on the coffee table to turn off the television. It was time to retire for the evening. Another long day tomorrow.

"Are you out of your mind?" Cynthia said with unchecked hostility.

Kyle turned and saw her standing in the doorway to the dining room, which adjoined the back hallway and the stairs. She was in her satin bathrobe and her hair was still wet. He knew he was now about to catch an earful. Indeed, he always knew how these altercations would play themselves out. "Oh, God. Can we please not do this now? I'm exhausted."

"Well, I was ready for bed too when I heard all of your hooting and hollering. I came downstairs to shut you up and make sure you didn't wake up the boys. And what a very interesting conversation to stumble upon."

"I'll say it again. Let's not do this tonight."

She ignored the suggestion. She was irritated, and her voice dripped with condescension. "Y'know, I guess I really didn't see how one-tracked your mind has been lately. Has everything I've been saying to you over the last few weeks been going in one ear and out the other?"

Kyle rolled his eyes. "Yes, I've just been a little distracted," he muttered with boredom. He really didn't see why he needed to explain himself to her when she should have understood in the first place. "Look, I'm respectfully asking you not to try and get involved with my business."

"Oh, please. Family comes first."

"Really?" He switched tactics. "Do you like the hot water you just took a bath in?"

"Don't give me that. We're far above the poverty line. And I work too. You're telling me you can't spare Mauricio for even one day? That the whole project would fall apart without him?"

"That's exactly what I'm telling you. I can't spare him for even one day. We need him. Kyp would agree with me. And it doesn't really matter that I forgot, because it wouldn't have made a bit of difference. He still would've had to work."

"I can't believe this," she said shaking her head in disapproval. "Y'know, I saw how let down he looked when you told him. He was genuinely hurt."

"He'll get over it when he's holding a fat paycheck in his hand."

"Some things are more important than money. This is a sacred rite of passage for Franco."

Exasperation was getting the better of Kyle. "Oh, c'mon. How many Sacraments will there be for this kid? I can't believe we're arguing about a First Communion."

Cynthia knew that Kyle had never been a particularly religious man. He played along, sure, but that had been for her benefit. But what irked her was that he knew how important this was to Lorena and Mauricio. "Let me ask you something. If this were to happen next year for Cameron's First Communion, would you make the same choice?" She immediately regretted the question, because she already knew the answer.

"Of course I would. You're being silly."

"Oh, really!"

He was inclined to raise his voice, but knew that he couldn't. "Let me explain something to you, CC. If we don't meet this deadline, two things will happen. First off, we will lose hundreds and hundreds of dollars for every day we go over. Money just flying right out of the bank. Is that what you want?" He didn't give her the chance to answer. "Secondly, we will be seen as incompetent in the eyes of any potential customers in the future. Our reputation will be damaged beyond repair. And then we'll *all* have bigger things to worry about than whether or not Daddy can make it to his boy's First Communion party."

His patronizing tone pissed her off. His obstinacy got under her skin. So she took a deep breath and counted to five, all the while trying to see things from his perspective. It actually wasn't that difficult.

This house was a big deal. For what it could mean for his career. For the financial freedom it would give their family. They weren't talking about a friend's wedding and they weren't talking about a son's graduation. She understood that a First Communion would mean very little to Kyle when his whole career and everything he had worked so hard for hung in the balance. Some fathers were cops who worked on Christmas. Some were doctors who missed the birth of their own children. Some were stop-lossed soldiers who were on their third tour of duty in Iraq.

But at the same time she had trouble accepting that this was the only way. If Kyle hadn't been so inconsiderate, he would have remembered about this milestone of Franco's and planned accordingly ahead of time. Now, as it was, it was too late.

He walked over to her and took her shoulders in his hands. "C'mon, let's go to bed."

"This isn't right, Kyle."

He gritted his teeth. "Look, I'm very sorry your friend and partner seduced my architect and put us all in this situation." She shook herself out of his grip, but he put his hand up in front of her to calm her down. "I know what's best. You're just going to have to trust me."

"Lorena's going to have some choice words for you."

She just had to get the last word in. "Then let her come at me," he bellowed, wide-eyed. "I've got a few things I'd like to say to her about her behavior."

"Don't you dare bring up—"

"No, screw this. I'm tired and I don't need this crap. If you can't be on my team when these things happen, then I don't know what else to say." He reached over and flipped off the living room's light switch. He started upstairs, and then stopped halfway up. "You coming?" he asked, the challenge in his voice having left him.

He made her sad sometimes. After all these years she still loved the headstrong man she'd married. But that same quality often hurt her.

There were times when she felt as though their family was a throwback to the 1950s or 60s. He saw himself as the man of the house, the bread-winner and provider, and his decisions were always final. She missed the days when they would discuss issues like this and come to some mutually beneficial agreement. She missed when he would actually ask for and value her opinion. And she was tired of feeling underappreciated in her own career endeavors, as if all the hard work *she'd* put in was simply some hobby she'd taken up in order to kill time and keep from feeling unfulfilled.

But it *was* late, and these differences of opinion she had with Kyle that made her feel blue could wait another day. "I'll be up in a sec. I want to deadbolt the front door."

* * *

"Spectacular work, boys," Marc Cronenberg told Kyle and Kyp standing out in the street in front of an impressive house that only a few short months earlier looked like it had been ready to be condemned. "Really first rate."

It was dusk, and when Marc had pulled up in his gleaming black Audi on a surprise visit, the Conways had joined him on the sidewalk across the street to view the house from a distance. And the way the setting sun painted the house in a pink-orange luminescence made Kyle swell with pride. It was at this exact time of day when he, Kyp, and Mauricio had first laid eyes on what then was little more than a hovel.

"Thanks, man," Kyp said. "We couldn't have done it without you."

"Looks like everyone comes out a winner," Marc said. He was a tall, thin man in his late forties, with a hawk-like face and thinning gray hair. Marc was the proud owner of three successful seafood restaurants throughout San Diego, a shrewd business man with his sights set on unprecedented exponential growth, and with a work ethic to match. The Conway brothers could relate to this; it was one of the characteristics that had allowed them to get along with Marc so famously from the very beginning. "This is exactly what the Molinellis had in mind. They will be very pleased."

Frankie Molinelli too was a successful restaurant owner. When Marc had been a much younger man, he had been looking to break into the culinary world, and had moved to New York City to find his way. It was there that he'd first met Frankie, a slave-driving and abrupt executive chef at a high-volume Italian bistro. Frankie had taken Marc on as his sous chef, and Marc had built his career around the man. It was from Frankie that Marc had learned about the delicate balance of flavors involved when formulating port wine reductions, beurre blancs, crème fraiches, bologneses, and ragus. When Marc had gone off on his own, he'd taken his knowledge with him and made his way back to San Diego, opening up his own restaurant, Cádiz, which offered French and Italian cuisine. At its heart it was a seafood restaurant, with dining at its best, and he'd earned high scores in the ratings of the San Diego Zagat Survey before taking a huge risk and opening two sister restaurants of different names.

When Marc's one-time mentor had reached out to him and told him that he was thinking about coming to San Diego and trying his hand at an establishment nearby, Marc had been delighted. Frankie had seen a business opportunity on Shelter Island, and wanted to invest in one more source of revenue before an early retirement on the sunny Southern California coast. But he'd wanted a house somewhere close by, and Point Loma had been the logical answer.

However, before he'd started researching the real estate market, Marc had intercepted him and told him about how satisfied he'd been with the professionalism of the two "kids" who'd just remodeled his house. He'd urged his friend to hold off on any final decisions, and to fly out to San Diego and meet with the Conways. He took pictures of the inside and outside of the home that he and his wife had been so happy with, and conveyed to Frankie that these two brothers could remodel a home that would be well beyond the actual market value at a fraction of the cost.

Frankie had in turn surprised Marc with a gambit. He told the man he'd trusted with his kitchen in his absence that he was sending a check made out to the Conways in the amount of $300,000. If these boys were really as good as Marc claimed they were, then they should find a place suitable for a remodel close by and use the money he'd sent for building costs. If they needed any more than that, then he would send it. In the meantime he would busy himself with his latest business venture on Shelter Island. He didn't want to see the house until it was completed, and he would be ready to move to San Diego by July of 2007.

Anyone else might have suggested that this was a very foolish and reckless decision on Frankie's part. Why take a risk on something as important as a home in which to enjoy your retirement? But one would have to know the kind of relationship Marc and Frankie shared in order to understand why Frankie, seemingly impulsive, would lay something as important as this at Marc's feet. Marc knew Frankie would throw all of his time and energy into the new restaurant, and have very little left over for anything else. Marc also knew that Frankie was adventurous when it came to exploring new territory, and that he completely trusted Marc with the referral.

Kyle and Kyp wouldn't let his friend down. And although Frankie would never hold Marc personally responsible if the house wasn't everything he imagined, Marc knew the Conways would deliver. They had before.

"I wish I could toast you two right now," Marc said, glancing at both of the brothers. "I'd say a celebration is in order. How about a drink? On me."

Kyp was about to turn him down in light of all the work they still had to do when Kyle blurted out, "Sure. Why the hell not?" He looked past Marc to his brother. "Kyp?"

Kyp, following Kyle's cue, said dubiously, "Are you sure? I know it's already 7:30, but didn't you want to finish up today?"

Kyle waved his hand in dismissal. "Mauricio's got it. He and the boys can finish up tonight."

It didn't take much to convince Kyp, who had no kids, and a girl-friend who was out of town. "Alright. Let's do it."

"That's what I like to hear," said Marc smiling.

"Great," said Kyle. "I'll load up the truck." To Marc: "We'll follow you." To Kyp: "You want to tell them we're ducking out?"

"Yeah, sure. I'll be right back."

Kyp crossed the street, walked up the driveway and up the steps to the front door. He glanced up to the tastefully inconspicuous rooftop deck and smiled to himself. He, too, was full of pride. When he entered the house, he found Mauricio in the kitchen, downing a glass of water and studying the bubble of a level that was resting on the kitchen counter. The bubble rested evenly between the two black lines and told him that the counter was indeed level. When he saw Kyp he put the glass down and smiled. "Is he happy with what he sees?"

"Oh, yeah," Kyp said with a nod. "But he doesn't get to see the inside until it's done." He took his cap off and combed his fingers through his hair, a frequent habit that Mauricio had noticed that Kyp and Kyle shared. "Hey, we're going to bounce out for a drink. You got this?"

Mauricio looked dumbfounded. "You're leaving?"

The sudden change in expression unsettled Kyp. Mauricio had just looked like his parents were abandoning him. "Yeah. Is that cool? Marc just wants to buy us a drink to thank us for a job well done." Mauricio actually looked pained, and Kyp couldn't put his finger on why. "We don't have to. I can stay, at least."

"No, no," Mauricio countered, but his expression didn't change. "You two go. You've earned it."

Kyp wondered if perhaps Mauricio was hurt that he hadn't been invited, but Mauricio had to know that in both Kyp and Kyle's absence he was the foreman of the group who remained. He was able to communicate with those who spoke less than fluent English, and there were at least two of them still in the house. "Hey, man," he said lightheartedly, "of course we want you to come, but—"

"It's fine, Kyp. Go. Celebrate. Have fun."

"Alright, man. Thanks. We owe you one." As he walked out the back door and around the house to Kyle's Ford F350, he got the impression that there was something he was missing in that short dialogue he'd just had with Mauricio. He told himself he'd ask his friend later what was bothering him.

Kyle was revving up the engine, and he called out the passenger side window, "Get in. I'll bring you back tomorrow."

"You sure? One shot usually leads to another with you."

"Get in!" Kyle shouted with mock impatience.

Kyp climbed into shotgun and closed the heavy door. As Kyle backed out of the driveway and turned out onto the street, Kyp found himself grateful that they had someone like Mauricio who they could trust to finish up when they weren't there to supervise. It was trust that had led them to this point; it was trust that had made Marc declare that everyone had come out a winner. Frankie's trust in his one-time protégé. Marc's trust in the Conway brothers. And Kyp and Kyle's trust in their friend Mauricio.

* * *

Bells were ringing on a beautiful Sunday morning, and children were spilling out of the church through the heavy doors the ushers had propped open. Waves of bright white and black were breaking up as boys and girls turned to seek out their families. Most of the parents were still inside, but Mauricio had taken Lorena and Maria by the hand and led them out of the church a few minutes before the end of the Mass.

Lorena had been so happy to see her boy standing up there at the altar, so handsome in his Sunday suit, as the priest blessed Franco and placed the body of Christ on his tongue. Mauricio had destroyed that moment of bliss when he'd leaned over and whispered in her ear, "I have to go." She'd closed her eyes and stooped her shoulders an inch or two, and then excused herself and her family as the three of them squeezed past the other parishioners and out of the pew. She'd briefly locked eyes with Cynthia across the aisle; she and her boys had arrived a little bit later than planned, and hadn't been able to sit with the Solares. Never one to leave a Mass before the priest had walked out and the organ had proclaimed the final notes of the closing hymn, Cynthia had followed suit and tapped Cameron and Cal on the shoulders when she saw the Solares taking their leave.

When they were all outside, they scanned the crowd of children until Maria, in her father's arms, pointed out her big brother's passive face. "There he is! Franco!" She wiggled in Mauricio's grasp and said, "Daddy, please put me down." Mauricio acquiesced, and when Maria's feet hit the cement she bolted for Franco. Sweet and loyal little Maria— as proud of her brother as her parents were—reached Franco and threw her arms around him, the affectionate display making him uncomfortable in front of the other kids his age. "I'm so proud of you, Franco."

Lorena was so moved a lump rose in her throat, and she reached out to take Mauricio's arm. His arms were in motion, however, and she saw now that both of his hands were busy. He was already taking off his tie.

Why was he in such a hurry? Kyle and Kyp weren't even here; they'd never know if he left a few minutes early or a few minutes late. She *hated* that those two pushed him around like this. The mindset from those early days of their acquaintance had never been washed away completely. He was still their underling, and it made her sick.

Her husband was an American citizen now. He'd paid his dues. He was extremely gifted, and could break away from Kyle and Kyp Conway at any time and be picked up by any other contracting company in the city. Of this she had no doubt. Maybe if he got a job where his salary actually reflected his skills, he might one day be able to start his own company. But not as long as he was under the thumb of those two Irish hypocrites.

She looked over and saw Cameron and Cal congratulating Franco with very mature handshakes. She looked up and again Cynthia's gaze. CC had been reading her facial expression, and Lorena reflexively put a smile on her face. Lorena's displeasure at learning of Kyle's memory lapse had been no secret, but she'd resolved not to let it show on her son's big day. She smiled at Cynthia, and Cynthia returned the smile, although it was a weak one that did nothing to eliminate the mixture of sympathy and guilt that Lorena saw in her eyes. Lorena walked over to her friend and said, "Hey there. Thanks again for coming."

"Of course." Cynthia's expression softened, and she turned to Franco and put her hands on her knees. "Franco, you look so grown up."

Franco smiled. "Thank you, Aunt CC."

"Can we give him his present now?" Cal interjected.

"No, Cal. It's in the car. We'll give it to him at the party."

Mauricio came over and parted the crowd. He got down on one knee and lightly tapped his son on the sternum. "You're a little closer to God now, mi hijo. Estoy muy orgulloso."

Franco was filled with a feeling of honor. Maria, Cameron, Cal, Cynthia, and Lorena looked on silently. Everyone knew how much Franco idolized his father, and this was a ceremony unto itself. "Gracias, Papa."

The priest made his way over to greet the Solares and Conways, and before he could be interrupted, Mauricio hastily said to his son, "I have to go now. I'm sorry I can't be at your party today. Que te diviertas."

Franco glanced at the ground, but he put a smile on his face to show his father he understood. "Okay."

Mauricio stood up and kissed Lorena on the cheek while simultaneously giving Maria's shoulder a squeeze. "I'll see you soon," he told Lorena. "Don't clean up without me." A full day of work on a Sunday and he was still worried that Lorena would attempt to clean up after the party by herself.

"Hey, there's our little man!" Eddie Cruz called as he approached the group in a sharp ash gray suit, Luna trailing just behind him in her best powder blue Sunday dress. Eddie threw his arms out wide, and Franco rushed to greet him. Mauricio saw this as his cue to exit. Eddie slapped his grandson on the back, and then he ushered him into Luna's meaty open arms. As he did so, he turned to Lorena and Maria a few feet away, and over Lorena's shoulder he noticed Mauricio making his way across the parking lot. Lorena came forward and hugged her father, kissing him on the cheek. Maria hugged him around his right leg, and he scooped her up in the same fashion Mauricio had just minutes before. "Oh, look at you," he said affectionately to this kid that he was absolutely crazy about. "You look so pretty in that dress."

"I have another one for later," she beamed.

"Do you, now? Well I can't wait to see that one too." He turned to Lorena. He quickly made a mental note of her demeanor. Her body language told him that something was bothering her, despite the front she was trying to put up with the smile she wore on her face. He glanced at Mauricio's line of retreat. "Everything okay?" he asked her.

She crossed her arms and nodded with a grin that he didn't believe. "Yeah, fine. Everything's fine." She shot him a look that told him that this was neither the time nor the place.

He decided he would let this one slide. She'd pour her heart out to Luna if something was bothering her. Her mother would know what to say. "Alright," he said without conviction. Turning his attention back to his granddaughter, he declared, "Well, young lady, you've got a date with me at a barbecue."

* * *

Mauricio was putting the finishing touches on the bar that would adjoin the new house's luxurious living room. The top of the bar was gray granite, the same as the kitchen countertop, and he was just using a cloth rag to rub in the third application of sealer when Kyp walked in carrying a large cardboard box. Mauricio looked up and smiled to greet his friend. "What do you have there?" he asked.

"It's all about housewarming," Kyp replied. "I take it that won't be dry for at least another hour or so. I'd better set this on the floor."

"Yes. Good to be on the safe side."

Kyp knelt down and placed the load down on the carpet. Mauricio heard the clanging of glass bottles. He watched as Kyp reached into the carton, and one by one retrieved bottle after bottle of spirits. Walking behind the bar, he loaded the bottles onto the polished hardwood shelves: Belvedere vodka, Don Q rum, Woodford Reserve bourbon, Glenlivet single malt scotch, Patron Silver tequila, and Sambuca and Grand Marnier liqueurs. "Kyle and I decided this would be a nice touch." He tossed Mauricio a grin. "We can't brownnose this guy enough."

Mauricio returned the grin. "Where's Kyle now?"

"Oh, he's out and about running errands. You know how energized he gets, especially this close to the finish line."

Something was bothering Mauricio, but he couldn't quite place what it was. It wasn't Kyle's absence, although he certainly had a right to be bothered by that. No, it was the liquor bottles, and something else. Something about what Kyp had just said. "The finish line," he muttered more to himself than to Kyp. He realized what was nagging at the back of his mind, and he came right out and asked, "Kyp, what else is there to do?" He looked around the living room and through the doorways into the other rooms and halls. He glanced at the sparkling crystal chandelier hanging over the main foyer, and then behind him to the back door that led to the patio and the pool. The house was immaculate, as close to perfection before a move-in as could be.

Kyp looked puzzled. "You mean you don't know? I thought maybe Kyle told you. We're done, my friend. I mean . . . almost. Tomorrow we'll do a walk-through and test everything out, but come Friday we're handing over the keys to the Molinellis."

It was a strange wave of mixed feelings that washed over Mauricio. Surprise? Sure. Relief? Absolutely. Accomplishment? This had been his crowning achievement. But with this came a few feelings that he immediately recognized as characteristically negative, and he tried his best not to acknowledge them. "That's . . . that's great."

"I know, right?" said Kyp with a nod. "Makes you wonder why Kyle's been so uptight all this time. We all knew we'd get the job done." His tone turned slightly more serious. "I meant what I said before, Mauricio, about us not having been able to do this without you. This house has your name on it as much and mine or Kyle's. I hope you know that."

Those feelings again. Trying to outweigh each other as if they were on a balance. "I do, Kyp. I never dreamed I would make it this far. And I owe it all to the both of you."

Kyp snorted. "Nonsense. You've made your own way through life. It was our good fortune to have stumbled across your skills before anyone else could scoop you up and put you to work." Kyp momentarily second guessed the statement he'd just made. That had sounded like something Kyle would have said. He worried it might have come across as though Mauricio were merely raw talent simply waiting to be discovered and exploited by the architects of Southern California. Then again, wasn't that how this whole damn capitalistic society worked? He refocused. "Doors will open for us now, Mauricio. You'll see."

Mauricio nodded with a smile, but said nothing else. Kyp loaded up the last of the bottles and walked out through the patio door, perhaps to allow the sense of finality to really sink in for Mauricio. But when Kyp did exit, Mauricio didn't spend even one moment on reflection. What he did do, though, was take his cell phone out of his jeans pocket and flip it open. He double-checked the date just to make sure he hadn't been imagining things. No, he'd been right. It was June 10. For the last two and a half weeks they'd been working twelve to fourteen hour days, seven days a week. And tomorrow they would be done, more than two weeks short of the July 1 deadline.

* * *

"So you're Kyle?" Frankie Molinelli called across the restaurant dining room as he waltzed through the swinging kitchen doors. He glided across the carpeted floor at a leisurely pace as he went to receive his guest waiting patiently at the hostess stand. "Jesus, Marc wasn't kidding. You really are just a kid." He reached out to Kyle and took his hand, giving it a firm shake.

Kyle took in the man he'd worked so hard for in the last ten months but had never met in person. Frankie Molinelli was a stocky man in his late fifties, sharply dressed in a navy blue suit and shiny black wingtips. His dark hair, silver at the temples, was slicked straight back. Frankie regarded Kyle looking over the tops of his straight rimmed glasses. "Very pleased to finally meet you, sir," was all Kyle said. It felt good to be out of the T-shirts, jeans, and construction boots he'd been living in for so long now that he'd nearly forgotten how normal people were supposed to dress for special occasions. He'd arrived at the brand new restaurant, Emilia Romagna, dressed in a lightly starched, white button-down shirt over khaki slacks. Gone was the dirty Padres cap that usually hid his curly, light brown hair.

"Please, call me Frankie." He put his hand on Kyle's shoulder and led him toward the bar. "Come. Let's have a drink." They walked over to the bar area, and as they did Kyle made note of the elegant Italian décor of the restaurant's interior, and thought to himself that he and Kyp had done an excellent job of judging this man's tastes when they'd brought their vision of the Point Loma house to fruition. He stole a glance through the glass doors at the back of the restaurant that led to an outdoor patio area. From there he could see the ships docked in the Point Loma Harbor, and just past that, the San Diego Bay, which led to a lovely view of the downtown skyline.

Frankie pulled out two barstools and gestured for Kyle to have a seat. "Lucen," he said to the bartender, "let me have a dirty Grey Goose martini, up, with three blue-cheese stuffed olives. And for my friend here . . ." He looked to Kyle.

"Maker's on the rocks is fine, thank you." The two men sat down on their barstools. Kyle found this refreshing for some reason. He liked that Frankie was choosing to meet with him at the bar rather than some private table sequestered in some far corner of the dining area. He got the feeling that Frankie was the kind of restaurant owner who liked to get his hands dirty, working away in the trenches on a high-volume night. The man had gotten his start as an executive chef; he probably maintained a high level of quality control.

"So what do you think of my little West Coast experiment?" Frankie asked Kyle enthusiastically.

"I think it's stunning. I actually remember this building. I can't believe what you've done with it."

"Well, I'd have to agree with you there," Frankie conceded. "We really lucked out with this prime location. Speaking of which . . ." The drinks came and Frankie thanked Lucen. "Speaking of which, my wife and I walked into our new home yesterday, and we were absolutely floored by what we saw."

Kyle actually blushed. He'd been so nervous up until this point. "I'm glad you like it," he said with measured modesty. "We're all very proud of it."

"As you should be. Quite a feat for someone so young and ambitious."

"Well, lucky for us Marc knew exactly the kind of place you were looking for. We just had to make it a reality."

"And what a reality! If this really is the first phase of my retirement, then what an exciting new chapter in my life this will be." He switched gears. "And not to mention, from what I understand, a very promising stepping stone for Conway Brothers Construction."

Kyle shrugged, the modesty a little too forced now, as if anything could happen. "I certainly hope so. I guess we'll see."

Frankie saw right through the act. "Don't be afraid of a little bravado every now and then, son. It can do you some good. I wouldn't be where I am today without being guilty of the sin of pride."

Kyle felt very comfortable conversing with Frankie. Aside from his intuition telling him that Frankie was the type of guy who worked side by side with his line cooks when need be, he also suspected that Frankie was a fine maitre d', one who greeted every table of diners to make sure that they were enjoying themselves, perhaps beguiling them with amusing anecdotes from his days in The Big Apple, or maybe even the old country.

"Well I'm certainly happy with what we put together where you're concerned," Kyle said.

"Which reminds me," said Frankie as he reached into the inner breast pocket of his suit. "I have something for you." He retrieved a blank white business envelope and placed it on the bar in front of Kyle.

Kyle tried not to stare at the blank white paper for too long. Turning back to his host, he said, "Thank you, Frankie. Thank you for this opportunity."

"No, thank you, Kyle," Frankie said reaching over and clasping Kyle on the shoulder. "I have a feeling you have a very bright future." At this, Kyle smiled toothily. Frankie picked up his martini from the bar and raised the glass. Kyle did likewise with his drink. "To new beginnings," Frankie toasted.

"I'll drink to that," Kyle said, and lightly tapped glasses with Frankie.

* * *

Kyle tried not to appear overeager as he made his way across the parking lot toward his truck, the envelope next to his heart. What were a few more moments? He climbed into his truck and closed the door. Scanning the parking lot to see if there was anyone watching him might seem silly, but he wanted to relish this special moment unobserved. He regretted that Kyp was not there with him to share in this, but he slid his index finger up under the edge of the envelope's seal and carefully moved his fingers across it to break it. He looked inside and a saw single slip of paper. He removed it and lifted it up in front of the steering wheel so that the sunlight hit it. It was a cashier's check made out to the Conway Brothers Construction Company's business account in the amount of $1,100,000.

He simply stared at it. The ink. The bank logo. Frankie's signature. The dollar amount. $1,100,000 for ten months' work. He was more than just pleased. He was giddy.

He'd done it. He'd built his first million-dollar home. No one could ever take that away from him. The world was his.

* * *

A few nights later, in another restaurant in another part of town, Kyle decided to style out Cynthia, Kyp and his girlfriend Sara, and Mauricio and Lorena. The three couples were to meet up at a popular restaurant, Market, across from the polo fields of Del Mar. It was a local hotspot in the summertime during the horseracing season at the Del Mar Fairgrounds. It would be a fine celebration.

As Kyle handed over the keys to Cynthia's white Saab to the valet, he decided then and there that he was going to indulge in a few well deserved drinks this evening. If Cynthia wanted to stay sober enough to drive, well, that was up to her. But if they had to catch a cab or jump into Kyp's or Lorena's car, then he was okay with that as well. No one was going to tell him—on tonight of all nights—that he hadn't earned himself the freedom to cut loose. And that's exactly what he planned to do.

Cynthia immediately noticed his march to Market's bar area as she went to check in with the hostess. She shook her head, more for the benefit of the hostess than herself, but at the same time she couldn't help smiling a little. She'd keep an eye on his consumption, but tonight she was in agreement with her husband. He *had* earned a night to unwind.

He was on his second cocktail when the rest of the party arrived. He greeted everyone in high spirits, upbeat without being rowdy. Genuinely at ease and contented, he gave off a positive energy that soon caused everyone else to share his enthusiasm. And it wasn't hard. They had reached this point working together.

In time, the hostess sat them down and they went about ordering up multiple bottles of old world red wine, and enough starters to risk them all filling up before they'd even ordered their entrees. They came in waves: lobster-shrimp soft rolls, blue cheese soufflés, mushroom tarts, softshell crabs, yellowtail tartare, and crispy duck confit.

They were in no hurry. There was plenty of conversation to go round, and they were enjoying themselves thoroughly. The sitters at home were prepared to stay late, and the six of them so rarely got out to socialize like this these days that they were all in agreement when it came to relishing the evening and enjoying it while it lasted.

Sara, a leggy, dark brunette, hadn't been dating Kyp for long at that point, but she fell into the group's dynamic easily and comfortably. She was a little bit more quirky than Cynthia and Lorena, but she had a sweet disposition and wry sense of humor. "Well, for me the best part about having this project behind us is that I get the old Kyp back."

"Hey, hey, hey!" Kyp interjected, feigning insult. "I'm right here. I never went anywhere."

"I'm not talking about personality," she said, leaning into him and looking him in the eyes. "I'm talking about basic hygiene. It's good to see you out of that dirt-ass work uniform you were wearing every day. I should burn it."

"Well," Kyp said, grinning and addressing the entire table. He leaned back in his seat and folded his hands back behind his head. "No argument there. I didn't realize we were being strictly superficial here." Much the way Kyle had felt a few days before at Emilia Romagna, Kyp felt good being freshly groomed and washed up for the night out, a sport coat and collared shirt in place of a raggedy, grime covered T-shirt.

Cynthia backed up Sara. "Oh my God. That smell. It's actually permeated every corner of our household."

"Knock it off, both of you," said Kyle with a wave of dismissal. "You love our man scent." This got a mild laugh from everyone at the table, Mauricio and Lorena included. Mauricio hadn't said too much this evening, but he still appeared to be enthralled with the banter of the brothers, especially when drinking was involved. Lorena appeared to be having a good time as well, although most of her talking involved one-on-one exchanges with Cynthia, and a lot of them were work related. This made Cynthia uncomfortable for two reasons. For one, she didn't want to make Sara uncomfortable by having discussions that she couldn't participate in. Furthermore, she didn't want to talk shop tonight. She didn't know what was going on with Lorena, but she wished her friend would just relax and follow the social cues of the table. Tonight wasn't the night to talk about work.

"Kyp," Kyle blurted out loudly enough to take Cynthia out of her comfort zone. "What's the best supervillian plot in any superhero movie?"

Kyp glanced at Sara with an apologetic grin. The expression told her that they had in fact had this discussion before, but now Kyle was making Kyp recite for the benefit of his new girlfriend. Interested now, Sara asked, "Well, Kyp?"

Kyp played along. "Lex Luthor's master plan in *Superman One*."

Kyle, glassy eyed now, looked around the table to make sure that everyone was paying attention to this mundane conversation. "And why's that, Kyp?"

Kyp wiped his mouth with his napkin and continued, as if this had all been rehearsed. "Because it's not about global domination or subjugation of an entire population. His plan is just greedy and self-interested enough so as not to be over-the-top."

"What does he do, Kyp?"

"He shoots missiles at the San Andreas Fault, trying to cause all of California to fall into the ocean."

Kyle was certainly entertaining himself. "Why in the world would he do that?" he asked as if he didn't already have the answer.

Kyp chuckled and gave Sara a look that said, *You see what I mean about Kyle?* "Because he's already bought up a bunch of real estate just east of the fault line. Once California falls into the ocean, he'll own all of the oceanfront property on the new West Coast."

Kyle laughed with satisfaction at the explanation, and Cynthia was steadily becoming more aware of the onlookers at the other tables. She opened her mouth to tell Kyle to tone it down a few notches, but then closed her mouth and said nothing.

"Damn right!" Kyle persisted. He was addressing everyone at the table now. "Genius in its simplicity. No conquering or enslavement. Just a simple get-rich-quick scheme."

Sara had sat through this exchange, and apparently the explanation at the end hadn't been the payoff she'd been waiting for. To Kyle she said, "And the point to all of this is . . . ?"

Kyle's smile vanished and he stopped dead in his tracks. He scrutinized Sara for a moment, but both Kyp and Sara knew it was all in good fun. "The point, Sara," Kyle began slowly and deliberately, "is that Lex Luthor could have used his criminal mastermind to hatch a lot of plans involving global domination. But he was smart. He kept his eye on the prize that was just big enough without being too big."

"What's that?" Sara asked while arching an eyebrow. "West Coast real estate?"

"Exactly," Kyle said smugly, and Cynthia was now embarrassed, both for him and for herself. In her opinion, Kyle was overdue for a little dose of humility. She didn't like how full of himself he'd become in the last few days.

The entrees were due to arrive shortly, and Cynthia excused herself to use the ladies' room. Once inside she wrestled with the idea of telling Kyle to lay off the booze. He was starting to get obnoxious. But she'd told herself earlier that she'd let him have his night, and so she resolved once again not to interfere with his good time. And anyway, he wasn't being mean this time, just loud.

Coming out of a stall, she encountered Sara, whose face was only a few inches away from the bathroom mirror as she was reapplying her mascara. Cynthia joined her at the sink, and talked to Sara's reflection in the mirror. "Sorry about Kyle."

"What for?" said Sara with authentic surprise. "He's totally harmless."

"He's got this East County redneck persona that seems to have passed over Kyp. We don't think it's genetic."

Sara laughed heartily at this remark. "Seriously, Cynthia. He's really sweet. You did alright."

Cynthia turned her body and leaned against the sink so that she was now looking in the eyes of Sara, and not merely her reflection. "So did you. Kyp is my brother-in-law. I've known him a real long time. He's a great guy, Sara. He'll treat you right."

Sara stood up a little bit straighter and put her mascara back into her hand bag. Returning Cynthia's gaze, she said, "Oh, I know. Believe me, I've seen how preoccupied he's been all of these months, and he's still managed to lavish plenty of attention on me."

"Like that necklace he bought you last month?" Cynthia asked.

"That, yes, and then . . ." she trailed off. She looked like she'd spoken out of turn.

"And then what?" Cynthia said, truly curious now.

Sara hesitated for only two seconds before she said, "Kyp sprang two tickets on me today. We're going to Oahu for two weeks next month." Sara tried to restrain her excitement as she clapped her hands together, as if in prayer, and lightly bobbed up and down. When she realized that Cynthia wasn't immediately sharing in the excitement, her first inclination was to assume that Cynthia was perhaps jealous, that maybe Kyle wasn't rewarding his wife with some kind of getaway after so many months on the job. But then she remembered that all four of them would be heading down to Mexico at the end of next month for Kyle's thirtieth birthday. Sara put her hand on her hip. "What? What is it?"

"No, nothing," Cynthia insisted. "That's great."

"CC?" Sara said dubiously.

"Really," Cynthia said, lightly touching Sara's arm. "A Hawaiian trip sounds lovely. You both deserve it."

"But?" Sara asked, turning her head to the side an inch.

"It's not my place to say, Sara. But I know Kyp, and sometimes I worry about him. I've noticed that he's been throwing a lot of money around lately."

Sara looked relieved. "Is that all?" She leaned forward and put her right hand on Cynthia's shoulder. Cynthia looked into Sara's big brown eyes. Such a beautiful, youthful complexion this girl had. And a personality to boot. Kyp had discovered a real gem of a woman. "If that's what you're worried about, then don't. I think about it too. Trust me, I've seen money just slip right through his fingers. But let's face it; He's definitely earned himself a holiday. All three of them have. And that bonus was such a pleasant surprise."

Cynthia's cheerful expression fell instantly, and she turned stone-faced. Sara knew immediately that she'd said too much.

"What bonus?"

* * *

Lorena was glad to see Cynthia and Sara return to the table. Kyle had been dominating the conversation in their absence, annoyingly vocal and flushed with wine. There was no hope of grabbing her husband's attention while Kyle prattled to him and Kyp. Mauricio tended to soak up everything Kyle said the way an undergrad listened to a professor's lecture. She'd welcome an escape to a side conversation with one or both of the girls.

"—because I don't know shit about betting on horses," Cynthia heard Kyle carrying on as she returned and took her seat. "Just get me to Vegas and put me at a craps table. You can bankroll me if you want. I'll only take a small percentage. You *will* see a hefty return on your investment." He looked over at Cynthia and immediately took notice of her facial expression. She looked like she'd just taken a bite out of a lemon. *Goddamnit. What now?*

Kyp, too, was assessing the situation. Sara sat down, and Kyp noticed how she was avoiding eye contact with the others at the table.

She looked up at him and smiled weakly, then broke the contact while reaching for the bottle of Tempranillo in front of her. She was pouring herself another glass when the entrees arrived.

When everyone had gotten a plate, Kyle demanded one more toast before he went to work on his braised short ribs. He ate ravenously, and the conversation at the table returned to a socially acceptable norm, at least in volume. He didn't know what was nagging Cynthia, but it could wait. He wasn't going to validate her negativity at the dinner table. Not tonight.

The conversation continued to flow with the wine. Sports. Politics. Outdoor life. Kids. Perhaps the food settled Kyle down a little, but he was less boisterous now than he'd been when he only had two whiskeys in him. He no longer demanded command of the conversation as he had before, and he sat and listened earnestly to Kyp, Sara, and Lorena as they opined on social issues and regaled the table with amusing anecdotes from the past. Mauricio was quiet mostly, listening attentively. That was typical. Cynthia chimed in every now and then, but Kyle could tell that whatever it was that was irking her was keeping her from contributing to the table-talk wholeheartedly. No matter. *He* was having a nice time.

He was about to take his last delicious bite of cabernet braised short ribs when he happened to steal a glance across the dining room at a couple at another table getting up and preparing to leave. He'd been about to spear the meat with his fork, but he stopped short, the fork in his hand just wavering over the plate. "Oh, fuck me," he groaned.

Cynthia, mortified now, watched Kyle raise his left hand and cover his eyes. "What?" she almost hissed. "What is it?"

"Please, please, please tell me that's not Blain Lindeman over there. Not tonight."

Cynthia leaned forward a little and craned her neck so that she could see past Mauricio and Lorena. She squinted so she could see better in the dimly lit dining room. "Yeah, that's him. And Regan."

"Are they coming this way?"

Blain must have felt like he was being watched. He found Cynthia's gaze. "He is now," she regretfully informed Kyle.

"Tonight, of all nights," Kyle muttered with a keen appreciation for nature's sense of humor. Taking his napkin off of his lap and tossing it on the table, he leaned back in his chair and crossed his arms over his chest, awaiting the inevitable.

Blain Lindeman, a late thirties man of solid build, with golden hair and a tan that suggested long hours spent in the sun either working or surfing, approached their table with his hands in the pockets of his black slacks. He surveyed the table, taking in each individual face, before his eyes rested on Kyle. Even Blain's greeting was enough to get under Kyle's skin. "Well, hello there. Look who it is, Regan. The prodigal son who never returned."

Blain's girlfriend, Regan, who hadn't cared much for Kyle even before he and Blain had had a falling out, remained a few steps behind her dinner date. She was curvy, with wavy light brown hair and a pearly white smile. She looked stunning this evening in her low-cut emerald dress and white pumps, but looks alone weren't enough for Kyle to disregard the unchecked malevolence he knew was lurking just beneath the surface.

"Hello, Blain," Kyle began carefully. "Good to see you."

"And what are we celebrating this fine evening?" Blain asked. Everything he said seemed to drip with condescension.

Kyle *did not* want to have this conversation. "Nothing in particular. Just a night out with friends." Everyone else at the table sat there in silence, watching the male posturing and wondering how it would unfold.

"Really?" said Blain, not believing a word of it. "I would've thought you'd all be out celebrating your latest milestone." Blain appeared to be relishing the fact that he was making Kyle uncomfortable. "The whole town's been talking about your rising star."

Kyle could think of about three different directions Blain might try to steer the direction of the conversation. He liked none of these options. And he didn't want to be forced to put Blain in his place if he stepped out of line. He would not make a scene on this occasion. "I'm sure anything you've heard has been exaggerated," he said politely. "Thank you just the same, though."

This was the point where Blain should have graciously bid them all farewell. But apparently he still held a grudge. "No, seriously though," he said while removing his hands from his pockets and gesturing palms upward, "I know the secret now, Kyle. You tried to tell me all those years ago, but I just didn't want to listen."

Kyle's complexion flushed a few shades redder. He knew this territory Blain was entering; he knew it well. Blain hadn't said anything untoward yet, but like someone bracing for a physical impact, Kyle readied himself for some kind of verbal onslaught disguised in pleasantries. And then something else dawned on him. If Blain had indeed heard things about the Point Loma house, then there wouldn't just be bitterness about the split. Blain might be having a serious gripe about the fact that Kyle and his younger brother had actually surpassed him. Blain looked Kyle right in the eyes. "You've got to cut corners if you want to get ahead in this town. That's what Kyle always wanted me to see, but I just couldn't."

He was fooling absolutely no one at the table. No one believed he'd had some kind of revelation. They knew he was setting himself up for some kind of attack, all sauced up, and they were embarrassed for him. "Taking risks is what it's all about," he continued, sounding entirely too forceful to be convincing. "Like, say, sneaking a baker's dozen of undocumented workers onto a site to get it done faster and cheaper; now that's a worthy gamble. I mean, sure, you might be endangering your contracting license, and basically your whole livelihood, to get the work done in half the time and less than a quarter the cost. But hey, it's risky business like this that put Kyle and his bro right at the top of the food chain." He inclined his head and actually bowed slightly to Kyle, keeping the bit going. "So thank you Kyle, for showing me the way. From now on I throw business ethics to the wind."

Regan rolled her eyes and sighed, and actually looked apologetic to the friends at the table. Her expression seemed to say, *Sorry. He's been drinking. If he's trying to impress me, he's not. I've got better things to do.* But Mauricio, Lorena, Cynthia, Kyp, and Sara were all looking nervously at Kyle, curious to see how he would respond to the goading. But Kyle simply folded his hands on the table and held Blain's gaze. He wouldn't play Blain's game. Blain was hoping for a pissing contest; Kyle would give him a staring contest.

Blain plunged boldly ahead. "I hope you're not hard on your people the way I was hard on you, Kyle. I would hate to think . . . "

He glanced to his left, at Mauricio sitting silently and not know-ing what to think. Blain narrowed his eyes as he was just now noticing Mauricio. "Well, hello there. And who might you be?"

Mauricio knew the man was drunk. Drunk and obnoxious. But he still offered his hand to Blain and introduced himself. "My name is Mauricio Solares. I work for Kyle and Kyp."

Kyle secretly wished he'd said work *with* Kyle and Kyp.

"Mauricio. *The* Mauricio?" Blain looked genuinely taken aback this time, and Kyle wasn't sure if his reaction was part of the act. Blain took Mauricio's outstretched hand and shook it. "Well, pleased to meet you. I've certainly heard a lot about you. You're their secret weapon."

Mauricio didn't know whether to receive this as a compliment or an insult. He simply smiled and waited for Blain to say something else foolish. Blain didn't disappoint. "Amazing for an alien to have made such a name for himself in this often dirty business." Condescension again. "You should be very proud."

This, too, Mauricio was willing to let slide, even if Blain was start-ing to irritate him. Out of nowhere Lorena spoke up, "I'll have you know that my husband is an American citizen, and does, in fact, hold a certified contractor's license." There was venom in her voice. "So it's really not that amazing."

Blain looked falsely taken in. He stepped over behind Mauricio and gently rested his hands on the top of his chair. He had to look down to see Mauricio, and Mauricio would have to look up over his shoulder to look at Blain, if pride hadn't kept him from doing so. But Blain was put-ting on such a show for himself, his bitterness presented as satire, that he wasn't really addressing Mauricio. And as Kyle looked up at Blain, and at his incredibly rude body language and posture, he knew that he would soon reach his boiling point. He didn't want to, and he could just feel how tense Cynthia was sitting next to him, just waiting for him to blow up.

"Oh, I'm sorry. How rude of me," said Blain, not sorry at all. "Well then, that must mean you've made partner by now. There's no way a man with your reputation would be kept down after so aptly proving yourself."

Kyle couldn't take this. He was trying so hard, so goddamned hard, not to lose it on Blain. He reached down and picked his fork back up, ready to take that last bite of braised beef and hope that by the time he looked up from his plate that Blain would be gone.

Mauricio, too, had had enough. He wouldn't dignify Blain's attempt to lash out at Kyle by looking up at the man. When Mauricio didn't answer, Blain said, "No? Oh, my mistake. Well, I'm sure Kyle takes good care of you. I mean, these guys just cleared over a million for their latest venture. If he's generous enough to swing the usual two-percent your way, you're looking at about twenty-grand." He strong-armed the chair top and addressed the whole table. "Not bad, huh?"

Kyle dropped his fork, and it hit his plate with a loud enough clanging noise to draw the attention of everyone at the table. But it was when he spoke that the people at the nearby tables halted their conversations and listened in. "All right, that's enough!" he spat. "My friends here might not know when you're being a patronizing douche bag, Blain, but I do. Now we were thoroughly enjoying ourselves before you came over and started being an asshole. I'm sorry it didn't work out between us, but I'm asking you to push on."

It seemed that Blain was only content with his display as long as he had the exclusive attention of Kyle and his people. And now that he knew he had onlookers to his masked tirade, he had trouble hiding the sudden shift from nonchalance to superciliousness, as if his cover had been blown. Years of bottled up resentment resurfaced in an instant, and Kyle wondered if he was the only one at the table who noticed it. Glancing at his dinner companions, he realized that he wasn't.

This was all too much for Regan. Her evening had been ruined. She aggressively took hold of Blain's arm and began to usher him away from the table. Trying to save face in light of her mortification, she humbly said, "We're sorry to have bothered you. It really was nice to see you. Good luck, and have a wonderful evening." Blain didn't say another word. Perhaps he was trying to play the drunk guy who really didn't know what was going on card, but he wasn't fooling Kyle. All six of them heard Regan hissing in Blain's ear as the couple left the restaurant.

Their post-conflict return to celebration began awkwardly, but Kyp and Sara did their best to lighten the mood with pleasant and light-hearted conversation. To the credit of his companions, Kyle noted that everyone did their best to put the recent unpleasantness out of mind. But when the dessert course was offered, he politely declined, speaking for everyone. No one seemed to object.

As they waited outside for the valets to bring their cars, they bid each other heartfelt farewells. It wasn't as if they were parting ways for an extended period of time, but the men had all been working closely together around the clock for months now, and the women had lived with the tension of the project's demands. Now that it was behind them, the couples would be spending time apart from each other, trying to regain some semblance of normalcy in their schedules.

The ladies hugged and kissed, and for some reason when Cynthia and Sara bid each other farewell, Kyp thought he saw an expression on Sara's face that registered with him as contrition. He knew that his girlfriend was outspoken, and he wondered what the hell she might have blurted out this time. However, he was easily pacified by his own laid-back nature, and he didn't dwell on it for very long.

As the valet brought up Mauricio and Lorena's Buick, Kyle took a step forward and kissed Lorena on the cheek. She thanked Kyle for picking up the tab at dinner, but he couldn't help but think that she'd been somewhat distant lately, and their parting here and now was no different. He wondered if she was being this cold to everyone, or just him. And if it was just him, then why?

He next clasped hands with Mauricio. Mauricio too thanked Kyle for a nice evening out, and Kyle found that Mauricio also appeared as if something was bothering him. Whatever it might be wasn't made apparent, for Mauricio was pleasant and cordial as always. But there was something lingering just beneath the surface, an unidentifiable negative emotion that he was doing his best to keep hidden. Kyle had no idea what might have changed his demeanor over the course of the evening. The group had held a unified front against the spectacle Blain had made at dinner, but then Kyle wondered if perhaps Blain's erroneous comments about how he was shortchanging Mauricio had gotten under his skin. Perhaps Mauricio had taken it to heart. Maybe he truly believed that Kyle was cheating him in the long run.

Blain had attempted to humiliate Kyle by insinuating that Kyle exploited cheap Mexican labor to line his own pockets. He'd made Kyle out to be the bad guy. But what had really gotten to Kyle—what he had trouble reconciling with himself when he was alone with his thoughts— was that even after all he had accomplished in such a short period of time, the men who knew the business and openly competed with him still whispered behind his back that he was a man who didn't play by the rules, a man who would take advantage of hard working, illegal day laborers in order to preserve his own interests. Even if that were true— and Kyle wouldn't even consider that notion—couldn't Mauricio see that he wasn't one of the men Kyle allegedly low-balled, that he was in fact *family*?

He would have to have a long talk with Mauricio when the opportunity presented itself, but now was not the time. He'd make Mauricio see that he and Kyp needed him, that he was an essential fixture of Conway Brothers Construction Company.

"Have a good night, man," Kyle said softly. "I'm really proud of you."

"Thanks, boss," Mauricio replied meekly, and then he got into the car with Lorena and drove off. Kyle sighed and waited for his car to arrive.

He and Cynthia rode home in what he perceived at first to be comfortable silence. He drove with the stereo turned up loud, and was singing along to Neil Young when he glanced at his wife and saw that she was wearing a sourpuss look on her face. He turned the knob on the radio, reducing the volume, and turned toward her. "What? What's wrong now?"

"Let's just wait until we get home please," she pleaded.

"No, CC, what's eating at you this time?" She shook her head and gazed out the window. Discontent settled in, and he grew extremely frustrated that she was giving him the cold shoulder after he'd gone to such lengths to create a nice, relaxing evening out for his friends and family. "Look, if this is about the way I handled myself back there with Blain—"

"No, Kyle. It's not."

"Because if you ask me, I think I handled myself pretty damned well, all things considered."

"It's not that at all."

"Then what? What have I done to deserve this stony silence?" Then he remembered the look on her face when she'd returned to the dinner table with Sara. "What happened in the bathroom with Sara?"

Having been called out, and perhaps not wanted to hold it in anymore, she came right out with it. "Sara and I had a very interesting discussion in the ladies room."

He had no idea what might have transpired in that female sanctuary. "And?"

She turned to face him. "And as it turns out, you haven't been working your team like a plantation owner because you were worried that you were going to go over the deadline. As it so happens, you were working so hard this whole time, putting your obligations to your family on hold, because there was a big, fat bonus check waiting for you if you finished the work a couple of weeks early."

Kyle grunted. *Goddamn, gossipy Sara and her loose tongue.* "Unbelievable," he muttered with disgust.

"So it's true."

"Yeah, it's true. It was also supposed to be a surprise."

"I don't need any more surprises, Kyle. And I don't want any more money. I want my husband back."

"You've got me back. The project's finished, remember? And a whole two weeks early."

"Some tradeoff," she barked. "You worked yourself and your people half to death chasing after that bonus. The boys and I haven't seen you."

"Enough already," he cried with exasperation. "It was worth it."

"How much?"

"CC, please, don't make this evening end on a bad note."

"No, really. How much was the bonus?"

"Stop it."

"Okay. Fine, don't tell me. I don't really care," she said dismissively, because truthfully the exact figure didn't matter to her in the slightest. "Last question, though. How much of that bonus are Mauricio and Lorena going to see?"

"I am not going to do this with you right now," he growled. "I have their best interests at heart."

She remained steadfast, and repeated, "How much of that bonus are Mauricio and Lorena going to see?"

"Please stop asking me about my business affairs."

She narrowed her eyes to slits. "Would you come off it? Stop acting like you're Don Corleone. You're my husband. We're supposed to be a team. We have a joint bank account, for God's sake."

"I told you once before: This is a business you know nothing about, and it's not for you to say where and to whom I allocate my earnings."

Her revulsion at her husband's clandestine dealings and the way in which he was so quick to dismiss her opinion intensified, and she found she had nothing more to say. She thought about how embarrassed Lorena had been when her card had been declined that day at lunch, and how let down Lorena had appeared on the day of Franco's First Communion. She resumed staring out of the passenger-side window and watched the rolling, silvery fields illuminated by the moonlight pass her by. It broke her heart sometimes to come to terms with the fact that she very often felt like she didn't really know the man sitting next to her, the father of her children.

Part Two

"Powerful push-pull factors are driving undocumented migration from Mexico to the United States, i.e. the lack of economic opportunities in Mexico and the growing demand for low-cost unskilled labor in the U.S. market."

—Carol Wise
2007

Kyle was convinced that you could actually feel the atmosphere change as you stepped over the United States/Mexico border into Tijuana. The air seemed to thicken, and it had a stale smell to it. *Like an old diaper,* he thought to himself. Nevertheless, he wore a grin on his face as he and Cynthia strolled down the cement walkway covered with colorful Mexican mosaics. It was good to be back. He glanced at Cynthia and raised his eyebrows. She returned the smile. Although she hadn't come down south of the border in search of fun as often as he had back in high school, she was no stranger to TJ. There had been wild times here for the both of them when they were younger. And perhaps when they had looked at each other and exchanged smiles, they'd both been thinking about just how ridiculous nostalgia could sometimes be. But here they were, and they were going to make the most of it.

The disagreement had arisen back at the house while the trip was still in the planning phase. He had flat out refused to buy the Mexican car insurance needed to drive your car legally once you crossed into Mexico. People drove like maniacs down there, and he wouldn't want to find his wife's beloved Saab at the mercy of the architects of some complicated scam. Cynthia had thought that the matter was settled. They'd wait a couple extra days and drive down with Kyp and Sara in his Chevy

Tahoe. He'd immediately objected, stating that he and she needed to have a couple of days to themselves before his brother and his girlfriend arrived and commenced the celebration.

It was the weekend of Kyle's thirtieth birthday, and Cynthia knew that when he and Kyp got together with their country-boy antics, there would be heavy drinking and partying involved. She wouldn't begrudge him his fun. Thirty was a big one, and the man she'd chosen to be with had been highly spirited and animated when she'd first known him. It was only fitting that he give his twenties a send off when their sons were in another's care for the weekend and he was vacationing in a place that had been special in his youth. Anyway, that was the way she saw it, and that was the *only* reason she'd allowed him to talk her into parking their car stateside and then walking into Tijuana where they could catch a cab to their rental house in Rosarito.

Kyp, if he was foolish enough to ignore Kyle's advice and drive into Mexico, would bring them all back in four days at the end of the weekend. That gave him and Cynthia two days to enjoy each other's company alone. And having just stepped over the border seemed to make their long-awaited vacation more real, as if the formality of the planning it had diminished its therapeutic value. They were here now, and they couldn't simply turn around and walk back through the gate into San Diego. The long weekend was upon them.

He was donning a gray North Face camping backpack that was just big enough to make her uncomfortable. She too, carried a backpack with enough of her clothing and toiletries to tide her over for the few days until Kyp and Sara arrived. But the sheer size of Kyle's backpack, the way it loomed so large over the back of his head, worried her that it might be an invitation for theft.

There were several eager cabbies awaiting them when they'd cleared the entrance corridor, but they politely declined their services and turned right to head into the city. They slightly hastened their pace as animated men lurking in the doorways of the local bars and restaurants began to accost them.

"Hey, amigos, come on in over here. We have happy hour all day long. Best Margaritas in town."

"Hey, honeymooners, you come have a drink with us. We have five dollar buckets of beer."

"Come try our carne asada. On special. You look hungry."

As Kyle politely attempted to ward off their entreaties, he nearly knocked over a little girl who'd placed herself in his path. "Whoa!" he cried out. He looked down at the dainty child, who was carrying a cardboard box full of packs of gum.

"Chicle," she declared, holding the box up a little higher. Her hair was filthy, and she had dirt smudged on her young face.

"No, gracias," he said with a sympathetic smile. "No necesito chicle."

"Chicle," she repeated more adamantly.

Before he could decline for a second time, Cynthia bent down slightly and asked, "¿Cuanto cuesta?" Kyle sighed and shook his head.

"Un dólar," the girl stated hopefully. Cynthia reached into her purse and retrieved a dollar bill. She placed it into the girl's waiting hand, took the gum, and then patted the girl on her head to send her on her way.

They resumed their walk, and while smiling as if she'd just done a good deed, Cynthia looked over and caught the exasperated expression on Kyle's face. "What?" she asked.

"We've been here less than five minutes. You start that now and there'll be no end to it."

She wasn't naïve, but she felt good about helping the little entrepreneur. "It's a dollar, Kyle," she said with an incredulous smile. "We can afford it."

"Give me the gum," he commanded her.

"Why?"

"Because there's no way in hell I'm going to let you chew it."

"Oh, gimme a break," she said with a laugh. She deposited the pack of gum into her purse. "This goes in here."

"Whatever," he said dismissively. This wasn't a battle he was going to engage in. As they continued along the wide open thoroughfare, she took in her surroundings. Everyone was selling something, looking for that American dollar. There were Mexican wrestling masks, plush toys of Spider-Man and Spongebob Squarepants, plastic statues of the Virgin Mary, and carved wooden jewelry. Other tourists who'd crossed over with them were being approached by proprietors just as they were. As she scanned the crowd and ran her eyes over the sea of faces, she noticed a Mexican police officer, a Federale, staring at them.

He had the faintest hint of a smirk on his face. His eyes were indiscernible through his wide aviator-style sunglasses, but she had no doubt that he was staring right their way. She and Kyle weren't walking close enough to any other visitors for her to be mistaken. The man was of average height, with a stocky build and broad shoulders. He had his thick arms crossed over his bullet-proof vested chest, and as she and Kyle continued on toward the winding walkway that would take them to the bridge that crossed the Tijuana River, his gaze followed their movement. Fedarales represented law and order down here, but as she continued to stare at the man's bald pate and mustachioed face, she couldn't help but think that something about this peace officer seemed . . . what? Malevolent? Whatever it was, his gaze made her uncomfortable. He did not stop staring as he lowered his arms and rested his hands on the loaded cartridge belt that circled his waist. They were almost to the enclosed walkway, but then he broke off his gaze as he took a call on his two-way radio. She took Kyle's arm as they started up the ramp. He hadn't noticed a thing.

"What crap," he said, nodding towards all the novelty trinkets being sold.

"They have to make a living too," she replied, trying to be a beacon of positive energy and empathy that he might hopefully respond to.

"It's all so damned tacky here," he plunged ahead. "None of this stuff is indicative of what really is a rich Mexican heritage. I can't wait to get down to Rosarito."

"Then maybe we should just get in a cab and head there now," she suggested.

He turned to her with a devilish grin and arched eyebrows. "And skip our date at AnimalE? I don't think so."

* * *

The entreaties from cantina proprietors to join them at their establishments did not cease until they'd reached their destination. Impatient from being repeatedly approached on the streets, Kyle hastened his pace leaving Cynthia little choice but to speed up and fall in step with him. The two finally reached AnimalE, and a host took them upstairs to the balcony and seated them at small circular table alongside the railing, giving them a full view of the bustle of Avenida Revolución. The lure of the street was evident from how populated it was by American tourists. Running adjacent to Zona Norte, Tijuana's red light district, Avenida Revolución had been a hotspot for thrill seeking and debauchery since the days of American prohibition. Kyle had been coming down with his friends here looking for trouble since he was seventeen, and had started bringing Kyp along for the ride once he'd established himself as a seasoned veteran. Cynthia, too, had come down here in her teens with her girlfriends, although her good times had consisted of entering dance contests and flirting with military personnel on leave, while Kyle and his buddies had drunk themselves into such stupors that they were lucky if they made it back across the border before they fell face-first into the gutter. Both had come here, to Club AnimalE, an upbeat party spot that had never been intended to cater to the conservative.

Those days were behind them both; they had careers now and children to think about. But this little revisiting of the past while passing through was a way for them both to unwind and acknowledge that they were both still young. It was symbolic of what they were trying to encapsulate with this trip. Kyle had entered Mexico as a twenty-something. He would leave as a thirty-something.

Husband and wife were bombarded from sounds all around them. There were cries and shouts from the street below, electronic music from the stage behind them. Perhaps they'd both changed more in the last twelve years than they would like to admit. They were now both thinking along the same lines: seaside relaxation is what they desired more than anything else at this moment; the hubbub of this carousel wasn't nearly as appealing as it used to be. In recognizing this, they both knew that they could loosen up over a few beers and be on their way shortly. It would be a good start to the weekend.

The server brought them a bucket of beers chilled in ice, then cracked a Tecate for each of them and placed a plastic ramekin of limes and a shaker of salt on the table. After he moved on, Kyle raised his bottle to toast Cynthia. She clanked bottles with him. The two sat in silence for a few moments as they absorbed the scene around them. The scantily clad girls on stage were drawing quite a crowd—even this early in the daytime—with their sexually suggestive dance moves. As the whistling and hollering of the men intensified, Kyle pretended to rub his eyes or massage his forehead, as he stole glances over Cynthia's shoulder. She reached over and gave him a love-tap to his forearm. "Stop it," she said smiling. "You can look. You don't have to hide it."

"Ah, they're trashy," he said dismissively. "They have no class. Not like my CC."

Her smile broadened and she reached out and took his hand in hers. Her eyes seemed to brighten as her face softened. "This is nice."

His façade of smart-mouthed, quick-witted companion fell away, until all that remained before her was the hopeless romantic she'd always known him to be. "It is," he agreed.

"Look, I know that these last few months have been crazy. It's been a taxing time for the both of us. But I need you to know just how proud of you I am. I hope you know that."

He exhaled as if he'd been holding a long breath. "Thanks. I know I've been difficult to deal with. These projects bring out the worst in me." He gave her delicate hand a gentle squeeze. "But we're over the hump now. I think we can all breathe a little easier. So let's just try to enjoy ourselves while we're down here and put the trials of the recent past behind us."

"I'd like that," she said smiling.

They tossed back the remainder of their first beer and then popped open a new one. They would split a six-pack before they left. He poured salt into his bottle and dropped in a wedge of lime. He sealed the lip with his palm and then flipped the beer upside down, letting his lime rise to the bottom. When he put it back on the table it began foaming up through the neck until it was overflowing. "Goddamnit," he muttered. She laughed as his misfortune. "Oh, you think that's funny, huh?"

"I'm sorry," she said, grinning. "I thought you were a pro."

"Yeah, well one time when Kyp and I were down here, we—"

He was cut off by an intense shrieking in his left ear. It startled him so much he nearly jumped off his chair. Before he knew what was happening, and arm wrapped itself around his head, tilting it back so hard that it put a strain on his neck. He saw a paunchy Mexican doing the same with Cynthia. Even though he was aware that this was a standard initiation for tourists, he was angered to the point of being livid as the server tried to pry open his mouth and pour tequila into it. The man did not stop blowing into the whistle around his neck, even when only a few centimeters away from Kyle's face, and the piercing sound at such close range after being so startled made him tense up as if he was about to throw a punch. But when he looked across the table and saw Cynthia getting the same treatment, he noted that she had decided to just go with it. In that instant he decided to follow suit, going against his initial gut reaction to resist this supposedly amusing treatment. The distilled blue agave was low quality, but not too strong, and as patiently as he could, he waited out the obnoxious waiter as the man continued to pour the liquor down his throat. Then both men ceased with the bottles and Kyle felt a slap on his back. He coughed a little and then reached for his beer, chasing the foul liquid and eradicating that taste from his mouth. Cynthia wiped her mouth and then thanked the men graciously.

"The party's just getting started, amigo!" Kyle's new companion cried. Kyle put on a false smile, but raised his hand up, palm outward, to ward off this most unwelcome presence.

"Alright, alright," he said. "Muchas gracias." He turned his attention back to Cynthia, and assumed the two men would just walk away. But they remained fixed right where they were. Kyle gave them both a suspicious up-and-down. "Gracias," he repeated.

"Three dollars," Cynthia's private bartender said.

Kyle squinted as his mouth fell open a little. "What?"

"Three dollars for the liquor," the man elaborated, although Kyle had understood exactly *what* was being asked of him, he just didn't know *why*.

"Three dollars? Are you kidding?"

The men looked at each other uncertainly. "No. It's three dollars for the shots."

Kyle glanced at Cynthia to make sure that she was witnessing this scam as well. "I've been coming here for years, and never once have I been shaken down like this. You really expect me to pay for that?"

Cynthia began to reach into her purse. "Kyle, it's fine. Let's just pay the men and—"

"No," he cut her off, "it's not fine. Put your wallet away." He turned his attention back to the two men. "My wife and I were enjoying ourselves before you came over blaring whistles and putting your hands on us. We didn't ask for it. I didn't even want it. We just assumed, as we always have, that it was on the house."

Kyle's pourer looked at him incredulously. "You're not going to pay?"

This was the point where Cynthia smelled trouble, and she was about to insist to her husband that they pay immediately, when Kyle blurted out, "Get that watered down shit out of my face." The two men looked at each other for a long moment, the one closest to Cynthia shrugged, and then they left them alone.

Cynthia followed their retreat with her eyes, pleading to God that they weren't heading right over to management to make an issue out of it, but then the two men began blowing their whistles again as they approached the people at another table. As she watched them go, she spotted a young man, slight of build, who looked to be in his late teens or early twenties, watching her and Kyle much in the same way the Federale had been earlier. He wore jeans and a navy blue polo shirt, his hair was cropped very closely to his scalp, and he had a wispy mustache and goatee. Unlike the Federale, though, when Cynthia held his gaze he looked away and quickly retreated down the stairs. This unnerved her a little, but she put it aside as she turned her attention back to Kyle.

"Can you believe that?" he asked, assuming that she was in total agreement. "Everyone down here is a goddamned grifter."

She simply stared at him. He knew that look of disapproval. It did not sit well with him. "You're unbelievable," she finally said.

Oh, no, no, no. Not now. Not after everything was going so well. She can't be serious. We're going to let those two nickel-dimers spoil our good time? "I have never, ever, paid one of those guys for that inconvenience. And I'm not about to start. I'm sorry I even opened my mouth."

"What if those two had made a big stink? Would it have been worth it? We could've at least tipped them."

"Everyone's trying to dip into our wallets, CC. The girl who sold you the gum. Those guys. I won't be taken advantage of. Not by them."

"It's their job, Kyle. It's meant to make us feel welcome here. And you talk to them like they're second-class citizens."

"They're not citizens at all. Not American citizens."

"You want to get technical? Fine. You're right. They're Mexican citizens, and we're guests in their country." She leaned over the table. "You would never talk to a waiter like that back home."

He rolled his eyes in exasperation, not wanting to believe that they were actually having this conversation. "Do I really need to explain the difference to you? Would something like that ever happen back home?"

She grew frustrated at his inability to grasp what she was getting at. "It's not about that. It's about you, and the way you talk to people. The way you talk to . . ."

He didn't like the way she had trailed off. "What?" he queried. "Mexicans?" She didn't want to come right out and say it, but her silence told him everything. "Is that what you think?" he said, disbelieving. "After everything I've done? For Mauricio? For his family and friends? After all that, you're going to sit there and call me a bigot in so many words?"

She tried changing tack, desperately trying to get him to see himself the way she, and others, often saw him. "It's not that simple. Yes, you helped him and many others like him. And I love you for it. But I've heard you say things in passing. Belittling things. Sometimes I don't think you even know you're doing it. It's like you can acknowledge how far they've come and all that they've accomplished, but they'll never really be like you and me. It's like . . ." She searched for the right words. "It's like you draw these lines, Kyle. These lines in the sand. Us and them. And no matter how closely aligned they are to us and what's important to us—like family, or values, or work ethic—all you're ever going to see is the line that seems to divide us. And it's hurtful. I've seen it in Lorena's eyes."

This was all too much for him. He had trouble processing it. He wondered how long she had felt this way and why until now he had never recognized the extent of her feeling. He knew that people had always perceived him as somewhat of a roughneck from East County, but he'd always assumed that he'd evaded the negative stereotypes that sometimes came with it. But here his wife—his wife of all people—was telling him in no uncertain terms that he exuded an air of superiority over the very Latinos he called friends. And it *hurt* him to hear this. He wasn't even sure he could deny it. He knew what was in his heart, and he'd never once considered that it might be ugly. And maybe he did make culturally insensitive remarks from time to time, but it shocked him to learn that his own wife, the one who should know him better than anyone else on earth, perceived him this way. It shook him a little. "I . . . I never knew you felt this way."

"Don't take it the wrong way, baby." She took his hand again, fearing she'd overstepped her bounds, and yet glad she'd gotten through to him. "I know you're a good person. You just come off as a bit gruff sometimes. And you're still the man I married. I would never try to change you. That's not what this is about. *We're* changing. Both of us. We're growing as a couple. And now there are kids involved. We've got to use compassion to set a good example. Does that make sense?"

He nodded, but he said no more. He wasn't giving her the silent treatment, but this was all a lot to take in, and he wanted some time to reflect on what he'd just been told.

"C'mon," she said softly. "Let's pay for these and get out of here."

* * *

They walked Revolución in silence for a few minutes. She was still second-guessing her decision to come at him like that so early into their trip, but it was he who took the initiative to lighten the mood. As they walked, they came across a live burro painted in the black-and-white stripes of a zebra. It was harnessed to a wooden cart adorned with Mexican blankets with bold colors, and wide sombreros with varying brightly colored patterns and straw tassels.

He recognized what the display represented, and grinning slyly, asked, "Are you sure you don't want to stick around for a donkey show?"

The revulsion that swept over her made her wince. But at the same time she couldn't help grinning in spite of herself. He was showing her that he wasn't going to dwell on the recent unpleasantness. He would quickly move past it and enjoy himself before he bid his twenties farewell.

"There are some cabbies down here," he said while nodding toward a downward sloping side street. "Let's go talk to them." They walked down the street passing pharmacies and shops with gaudy displays of costume jewelry. The cab drivers were gathered on the corner of the next intersection, but they were leaning against their cars with their arms crossed over their chest in relaxed postures. Watching them engaged in their leisurely conversation, Kyle couldn't help but think that this group was far more passive than the ones who'd made their pitches back at the border. "Hola," Kyle greeted them as he and Cynthia approached.

The pudgy man who was closest to them gave them a casual nod in response. Kyle was surprised by the drivers' indifference to their presence; a young traveling gringo couple with oversize backpacks should have had them scrambling to see who was the quickest at elbowing his way to the fare. But instead the man who had nodded to them walked to the back of his cab and popped the trunk open, apparently not the least bit interested in where they might be going. Kyle suspected that if he told the man that their destination was Cabo San Lucas he would simply shrug and wait for Kyle to suggest a reasonable price. Kyle's first bid was an attempt to lowball the driver. "We need to go to Rosarito. ¿Veinte dólares?"

"Si," was all the man said. He then reached out with both hands and gestured for them to hand over their backpacks so he could place them in the trunk. Kyle tossed Cynthia a look. *Well, that was easy.*

He was just starting to comply when he and Cynthia heard a voice call over their shoulders. "Un momento," They both turned and saw a barrel-chested man coming toward them. Whether it was nature's generosity or the bulk of his bullet-proof vest that gave him the appearance of physical intimidation, Kyle couldn't tell. The man carried himself authoritatively, but even if he hadn't, the navy blue uniform of the Mexican Federales gave him all the air of authority he would ever need to make a couple of tourists stop dead in their tracks. When he came within a few feet of them he gave them both an up-and-down. Kyle, in turn, took stock of the man before them. He had a hand gun holstered at his side, and Kyle noted the barrel of some kind of semi-automatic rifle protruding from behind the man's back. He had a two way-radio held in his black gloved hand, but he didn't seem to be communicating at the moment. The man's sudden appearance was enough to make Kyle's pulse quicken.

But it was Cynthia who'd gone white in the face. The man looked different than he had before. Previously he'd been wearing the aviator sunglasses, but not the bulky vest or his navy blue cap. But there was no mistaking the thick neck and mustachioed face of the Federale who'd been watching them when they'd first come across the border. Her heart rate began to pick up. She wasn't much of a believer in coincidences.

The man addressed the cabdrivers. "Voy a necesitar un minuto con ellos." The cabbies shrugged it off as if it was of no consequence. The paunchy one who had been about to load up Kyle and Cynthia's gear simply returned to the conversation he'd been having with his associates only a moment before. Perhaps a Federale swooping in on American tourists was a more common occurrence than Kyle had realized; the men paid very little attention to Kyle and Cynthia after that. If and when the Federale was finished with them, their fare would be waiting.

Kyle turned his attention to the officer. "Yes, can we help you?"

The man's English wasn't perfect, but he could communicate effectively enough. "The manager at AnimalE, he say you no pay the bill."

Kyle tilted his head back, groaned audibly, and stared at the blue sky. *Why is this happening?* He looked over at Cynthia, who wore an expression on her face that read: *Look where your principles have landed us now.*

He responded to the challenge in her look. "Just let me do the talking," he bluntly told her. Back to the Federale now. "Look, there's been a big misunderstanding. We paid for everything we ordered."

"Not the shots of tequila."

"Like I said, we paid for everything we *ordered*."

"So you leave and you no pay for the tequila you drink?"

Kyle thought he might actually be able to feel one of the veins in his forehead bulging. Everything leading up to this trip had been so goddamned stressful. And now they were *here*, and this was happening barely an hour after crossing the border. It was too much. He knew how this game was played, and yet he didn't have the energy for the back-and-forth that was surely about to commence.

Cynthia misunderstood the look of consternation his thoughts were creating and went to his side in two steps. She stood up on her tip-toes and said into his ear, "For God's sake, don't even try to match wits with this guy. Just give him whatever he wants."

He looked down at her with annoyance. "Actually, I was just about to agree with you." From past experience he guessed that the starting bid was going to be about five-hundred dollars. He knew this amount was usually enough to appease these crooked bastards. Also, five-hundred was typically the maximum amount one could withdraw from a Tijuana ATM in a single day. Kyle was ready to pay off this corrupt official—assuming the amount wasn't too absurd—just to have this whole affair over and done with. He came right out and asked, "How much?"

The big Federale seemed amused. "¿Que?"

Goddamnit, I will not do this right now! "How much do you want? Dinero. How much for us to be on our way?"

The imposing figure took another step toward them. "You think it's that easy, heh?" he looked over at Cynthia, who couldn't bring herself to hold his gaze. "You come down here, break our laws, and then just be on your way?"

Cynthia, like Kyle, recognized this for exactly what it was. It unnerved her to think that this man had zeroed in on her and Kyle the very minute they'd stepped onto Mexican soil, just waiting for them to slip up. What she couldn't figure out was how this guy had become wise to the tequila incident and then moved to intercept them so quickly. *We were almost in the back of that cab.*

Kyle thought he understood the act. All of this was happening within earshot of the cabbies gathered on the corner. He realized this dirty Federale probably had appearances to keep up. Kyle glanced at Cynthia again. He knew they both had cash for a payoff, and then hopefully they could be on their way to Rosarito and then the closest ATM. With discretion, and not wanting to anger this guy, he leaned in and said, "So what happens now?"

The Federale surprised them both. He reached for the handcuffs on his belt and said, "Both of you, against the wall."

Cynthia gasped. She wasn't prepared for how quickly this was escalating. Kyle took his backpack off and told Cynthia to do the same. "It's okay," he said. "It'll be fine." He didn't want her to start panicking. He knew they were both about to be handcuffed, but down here that was no guarantee that you were going to jail. They both needed to play it cool. Cynthia simply didn't have the experience that he did with this. Not that it was anything to be proud of, but at the very least he knew how to deal with a situation like this one in a calm and collected manner. He walked over to the wall, spread his feet, and placed his palms on the stone. He gave Cynthia a look over her shoulder which told her to do likewise.

She was shocked that this routine seemed so familiar to him. She was scared, but she did as he did. She was dreading the frisking, and the possibility of her hands being brought behind her and cuffed together with hurried, forceful motions.

Kyle was patted down first. He knew he had nothing to hide, but that in no way assuaged his tension. At any moment he expected a bag of cocaine—having materialized out of nowhere—to hit the ground by his feet. But then he dismissed the thought. It didn't matter if this guy really was as on the take as much as Kyle suspected. Because of what had happened at AnimalE, this guy now had him in an extremely vulnerable position. When the big man was satisfied that Kyle wasn't carrying any contraband, he moved on to Cynthia. Kyle, now very alert, watched the Federale's movements with intense scrutiny. But the pat-down she received was no more hands-on then his had been, and for that he could sigh with relief. Then Kyle felt his left wrist being seized and then cold, hard metal biting down into it. The man jerked Kyle off of the wall, and Kyle tried to suppress a momentary flash of rage. Cynthia fared no better when her right wrist was bound in a similar fashion, but her look was one of pure fright, and her lip trembled a little when she and her husband were handcuffed together.

"Is this really necessary?" said Kyle while trying to keep his rising anger in check. He had been willing to play along, at an expense he wasn't even going to waste his breath objecting to. And now the handcuffs had been brought out; not to tether him to one of his buddies from high school, but to his own *wife* of all people. The implications of his situation began to sink in, and he felt both guilt and shame wash over him at the same time. He looked Cynthia in her bright hazel eyes and knew what she was thinking: *he* had landed them in this situation. "We have money," he pleaded.

The Federale seemed to consider this, but Cynthia feared he wasn't entertaining the offer even in the slightest. And what troubled her about this—aside from the fact that this man had already been running surveillance on them—was that she couldn't figure out his angle. If he wasn't interested in money, then what could he possibly want? "How much you have?" he asked.

"Five-hundred dollars," Kyle said while trying to pour the confidence into his voice that might suggest that this was more than enough to make the man forget about this little incident. And Kyle knew that he and Cynthia had that much cash on hand between them.

The Federale stared at Kyle while a bemused smile slowly spread across his face. "We not talking about too much drinking or pissing in the street," he stated in a patronizing manner. "We talking about *stealing*. Very serious down here. Big problem with you Americans."

Bullshit! Kyle thought. *You'll say anything to drive your price up, won't you?* Kyle was reaching the point where he could no longer pretend to appeal to this guy's false sense of civic duty. He took a chance. "That's all we have." He wasn't going to play this game anymore.

All of this was happening with Kyle and Cynthia regarding the Federale over their shoulders with their feet still spread. The man clipped his two-way radio to his belt and reached out with his two meaty hands. He took hold of Kyle and Cynthia's arms and began to lead them away, back up the street they'd come down.

"Hey, what the hell?" Kyle blurted out. "Where are you taking us? What about our bags?" But the Federale remained silent as he marched the two along with increasing force. "Hey, take it easy," Kyle demanded weakly. But instead of taking them back all the way to Revolución, the Federale halted them at the mouth of a sunlit alley. The man brought both his index and middle finger to his lips and let out a whistle that echoed off the stone walls. Kyle squinted as he gazed into the rays of sun that bathed the alley, and thought that he saw the silhouette of a parked car. He heard an engine sputter to life, and a navy blue sedan came roaring out of the alley, and came to a stop right in front of the three of them. The Federale turned and went back to the cabs for their backpacks.

Cynthia watched with disbelief as the trunk of the squad car was popped open from the inside. She glanced over her right shoulder and saw the Federale scooping up both of their backpacks. "Oh my God," she said with a feeling like her chest was tightening. "Oh my God. I don't believe this is happening."

Kyle needed her to know that this wouldn't go as far as she feared. "Cynthia, listen to me. Here's what's going to happen right now." He said it with conviction, an experienced veteran who had been in a scrape like this before and knew exactly what to say and do. "He wants more money. This is one of the greedy ones. So their plan is to throw us in the back of the car and then drive us past the local jail to scare us into forking over more cash. Then they'll take us to an ATM." He needed her to know he had this under control. He needed her to know it was going to be okay.

The Federale threw their gear in the trunk. Then he opened the back passenger door and started to usher Cynthia in. She knew that good sense required her to put aside any thought of resisting: this Federale could arrest them both if he pleased. But her instincts kicked in, and her reflexive response was to squirm against the man's arm as he tried to shove her into the car, as if there was some terrible event awaiting her if he were to succeed in planting her there. Kyle, already attached to her and afraid that she might be worsening their situation, put his free hand on her shoulder and whispered in her ear, "It's all right, sweetheart." He poured every ounce of calm he could into his voice to soothe her fears. "It's going to be all right."

The Federale continued to prod Kyle into the squad car, putting his hands on Kyle's right shoulder rather than his head. He gave Kyle one last push and then slammed the door. Kyle's first instinct was to reach over and take his wife's hand, the hand he was cuffed to. He tried to look her in the eye, to keep reassuring her, but her eyes were busy wildly scanning their immediate surroundings. "Is this even a real police car?" she asked, perhaps just to herself, in a voice that cracked. Kyle's heart sank when he realized she wouldn't meet his eyes, and that her lips were visibly trembling. She cast her glance forward and gazed through a steel mesh barrier at the driver. She couldn't see much. When she craned her neck in attempt to take in his profile, she realized the man was wearing a black mask underneath his shiny and goggled black helmet. The image was menacing, and she found herself involuntarily gasping. She tried to lock eyes with the masked man in the rearview mirror, but the man must have sensed her attempt. He reached over and bent the mirror to an angle where Cynthia couldn't see him. *This isn't right,* she thought to herself. *This is overkill.* She knew that the Federales were the law down here, so why were alarm bells going off in her head if she knew that they had been caught doing something illegal? Was it because Kyle had already called the Federale on his scam? *And now this, this fearsome looking ninja driving the car.*

The Federale opened the front passenger door and plopped down in the seat heavily enough to rock the car. He took his hat off and glanced over his shoulder at his prisoners, but he said nothing. The masked driver, whose appearance suggested membership in a specialized Mexican task force, put the car into gear and turned from the alley into the road.

Kyle had dreaded this. He had had such hopes a mere moment before, hopes that he had it within him to diffuse this situation before it turned into something worse. But the big man hadn't budged at the offer of five-hundred dollars, and it troubled Kyle to think that the man had yet to show that he was receptive to a larger payout. The Federale and his partner had yet to make any monetary demands, but Kyle couldn't believe that these two had the intention of booking them over a misunderstanding about tequila shots. No, these men were looking for a bribe; there was no other explanation for them having tracked him and Cynthia down like this.

He looked back to Cynthia, and she was finally looking at him. The fear in her glistening eyes was palpable, and his guilt resurfaced. "I am so sorry, baby," he said weakly. "I'll get us out of this, I swear." She said nothing in return, only bit her lower lip.

Kyle was now angry it had gone this far. As they continued to speed on side streets, steering clear of main roads, he held out hope. More boldly now, he leaned forward and addressed the Federale in the passenger seat. "Look, there's no reason to drive by the prison. Just take us to an ATM and we can get more money out." He calculated how much more of a payout they could come up with. They could probably each take out another five-hundred from their joint checking account, but then their bank would issue a cutoff for any more transactions that day. If these men weren't satisfied with a quick grand to split between them, then he didn't know what he would do. But the two men in the front didn't respond, and the masked driver continued to barrel down side streets. Kyle was growing more confused with each passing moment. He'd been down here plenty of times before, but he had no idea where they were except that they seemed to be getting farther away from Tijuana's business district and heading into residential areas. Finally the car peeled out onto a main road and just as quickly jumped onto the on-ramp for the southbound federal highway 1D. Almost forgetting about Cynthia sitting next to him, he placed his head against the glass and stared out the window in disbelief. "Hey, where are you taking us?" He looked at the two men in front of him, who didn't budge an inch, and slapped his hand against the steel mesh. Cynthia started. "Hey, TJ's back that way." He tried to keep the fear out of his voice for Cynthia's sake, but his growing trepidation was showing. "C'mon, man. What is this? Just take us back and we'll give you however much you want."

For a split second the driver glanced in the rearview and locked eyes with Kyle. To Kyle's surprise he thought he saw what might have been construed as anxiety in the man's eyes. That certainly didn't add up. "What the hell is going on?" Kyle demanded, his voice rising. "Where are we going?"

Cynthia realized now why she was so terrified. They were obviously in the hands of truly corrupt officials who apparently weren't interested in a cash payout. As they sped along southbound, the urban landscape was quickly giving way to a more rural, desert one. She realized that these two were now acting outside of the routines that Kyle had anticipated, and neither she nor Kyle had any idea what was happening other than that they were quickly leaving civilization and the American border behind them.

Kyle turned around and watched through the rear window as Tijuana grew smaller and smaller. He looked back to Cynthia, and the uncertainty written on his face made their situation seem increasingly hopeless. He banged his hand more forcefully on the steel that separated them from their silent captors. "What is it you guys want?" he pressed, fighting down the desperation that was threatening to surface. More silence. "Hey!" He banged his fist again. "I'm talking to you!"

"Kyle, stop!" Cynthia pleaded. "You'll only make it worse."

Kyle leaned back against the seat and sagged down a little. This was *very* bad. They continued down the highway as the late afternoon sun moved toward the western horizon. Buildings became sparser. Eventually the car got off at an unmarked exit and headed east for a few miles. Kyle said nothing to Cynthia, but continued to hold her hand in a firm grip. The car slowed and he wondered if they were arriving at some hidden destination, but the car made a sharp right onto a dirt road and began to pick up speed. It started to bump up and down on the uneven surface, and Kyle and Cynthia were now being tossed around violently in the back. The driver applied more gas as the car continued to accelerate, and with his free hand Kyle wrapped his arm around Cynthia's head in an effort to protect her, growing more fearful as they continued to disappear off of the grid. Cynthia's whole body was trembling now, and with her free hand she dug her nails into Kyle's arm so deeply she nearly broke skin.

There were no further soothing words of reassurance from Kyle. He had gone beyond mere anxiety. He was now experiencing pure dread, mainly a result of the fact that he knew he couldn't protect his wife from whatever might lie ahead. The car's shocks strained under the pressure being exerted on them, and Cynthia cried out a few times as their bodies lurched back and forth whenever they hit a bump. There were tall cacti on either side of them, creating a narrow corridor for the vehicle to travel through. And then they sped into a clearing far out from the main road, and the driver hit the brakes abruptly enough to cause the rear end to swerve, kicking up a huge dust cloud in its wake. They were stopped.

In a moment both front doors flew open as their captors jumped out. Kyle lifted his eyes up from the nape of Cynthia's neck and saw the driver move around the rear of the car to join his partner. Then his eyes went wide as both men drew their side-arms. The man who'd arrested them took careful aim at the window as the driver went to open the door on Kyle's side with his free hand. Cynthia didn't know what was happening yet, but Kyle exploded into action when he saw the men's guns come out. As the driver reached for the door handle, Kyle reached over with his right hand and firmly pulled on the door's armrest. The driver pulled more forcefully, and Kyle leaned back into Cynthia and redistributed his weight in a futile effort to play tug-of-war over the door. With only one hand free to pull back on the handle, the masked man tried to apply more leverage by placing his booted foot against the rear tire. He succeeded in prying the door open, taking Kyle with him, who fell forward out of the car and hit the dirt hard. Cynthia was partially dragged out with him, and she let out an unintelligible yelp as she nearly fell on top of Kyle. The driver took a few steps back, leveling his pistol at them, and the big, bald Federale moved in and pushed him out of the way. Having freed his assault rifle during the ruckus, he leaned forward and pressed the gun's barrel to Kyle's temple, pushing his cheek forcefully into the dirt. Cynthia cried out again and went to shield Kyle with her body, although she sensed it was a useless gesture.

"No!" she screamed, as if effective words of entreaty suddenly eluded her in her terror. But apparently immediate execution wasn't what the men had in mind. The masked man hastily turned and ran back around the car while the burly bald one took a step back and pulled the muzzle away from Kyle's head. Pointing the rifle up to the sky with his thick right arm, he knelt down and used his left hand to seize the chain links between their cuffed hands. He yanked forcefully, and Cynthia cried out in pain as Kyle, face still in the dirt, realized that he meant for them to stand up. Propping himself up on one elbow, he knew now that their situation had just been altered, and he saw with clarity that these men did indeed intend to do them harm unless he and Cynthia went along exactly with whatever their designs were. And looking at Cynthia sprawled on top of him in hysterics, he also knew that he would need to reverse his and her usual roles if they were going to play this right: he needed to approach this situation logically if she surrendered to emotion. He gently pushed Cynthia off of him and stood up as quickly as he could without spooking the man into opening fire. Without speaking Cynthia followed suit, and the Federale retreated a few steps and once again leveled his gun at the both of them. Kyle scowled at their abductor, and then slammed the car door they'd just fallen through. He leaned against the squad car, breathing heavily, mind racing. Cynthia leaned against him and then began sobbing. Kyle stared the Federale down with hatred in his eyes.

The Federale glanced to his right, and then as if on cue another engine roared to life, and Kyle turned his head to see what the source was. An old, rust-brown van was backing toward them, and it came to a stop just a few feet away from where they were standing. The masked driver didn't kill the engine, but threw the van in park and then jumped out.

Kyle's hopes for some kind of resolution to this unthinkable situation evaporated when he saw the van. From the moment they'd been stopped by the first Federale until now events had been happening so quickly and in such rapid succession that he'd had trouble processing just what they were experiencing. But now it seemed real, and yet he still couldn't believe it. He felt queasy as the thought took hold in his mind. *We're being kidnapped.*

The second Federale threw open the rear doors of the van. Cynthia looked over Kyle's shoulder and saw the dark maw that she guessed awaited them both, and she began to shudder even more violently.

Kyle stared at the open van, and then looked back at Federale 1. His rational thought didn't serve him well at this moment, because right now it was telling him that if he and Cynthia stepped into the van they'd never be seen again. "Please," he managed to choke out, as if he'd swallowed some of the sand. "We have children." He held Cynthia close.

"Gire alrededor!" Federale 1 barked. When Kyle didn't understand right away, the man repeated his command in English. "Turn around!" Kyle released his one armed-hold on Cynthia and slowly maneuvered his body so that he was facing east. Cynthia glanced over her shoulder, tears streaming down her face, and then did likewise. There was an agonizing moment of waiting, and then Kyle heard footsteps behind them approaching cautiously. He contemplated whirling on whoever was closing in when Cynthia's head jerked back as a cloth rag wrapped around her head, blindfolding her.

"Hey!" Kyle cried as Federale 2 went about tying the knot on the rag, but Fedarale 1 was there too, and now Kyle once again felt the pressure of the assault rifle's barrel pressed firmly against his skull. Kyle's last thought before his vision too was cast into darkness was how utterly powerless he felt. The cloth that blindfolded him was tied crudely and rapidly, and then a hand like a vise grip took hold of his arm and led him away from the squad car that had taken them here. As they were pulled toward the van, one thought kept repeating itself over and over in Kyle's mind: *It's not too late; there's still a way out of this.*

Kyle and Cynthia were roughly shoved onto the waiting bed of the van, and as the door slammed shut and their darkness became even more absolute, Kyle now repeated the thought to himself as if it were some mantra that just might save them. *It's not too late; there's still a way out of this.*

* * *

The length of their journey was hard to judge, but long enough for Kyle to contemplate just how vast the deserts of Mexico were, and just how much distance their captors would be able to put between themselves, Tijuana, and the United States border.

Cynthia had settled down a little. She quietly continued to sob from time to time, but she didn't speak to Kyle. He knew that they were well past the petty stage of her blaming him for their current predicament, but her silence troubled him. And it continued to drag on and hang foully in the air between them. The problem was that he needed to choose his words precisely, make every word count, when conveying to his wife that all hope was not lost. But how could he tell her that when he scarcely believed it himself?

He'd taken only cursory glances at the headlines that were shedding light on the recent and alarming rise of both kidnappings and cartel violence in Tijuana. He'd known it was real; he'd known it when he and Cynthia had made their initial plans to travel down here. But it hadn't seemed real for *them.* Mostly the cartel members seemed to kill each other, and the kidnappings were typically either politically or financially motivated. He'd never have thought that a couple like them would end up as potential targets, with their simple attire and mountaineer backpacks, not to mention that they'd walked across the border and not driven into Mexico. He now felt guilty for a thought he'd had back when they'd been parking back in San Ysidro. He'd glanced at a Subaru Outback parked with a bright yellow boot fastened to the front driver's side wheel, and thought to himself: *Looks like someone did something wrong in TJ.*

Now he wondered where the missing driver of that car was, why he or she had never returned. How many people had ridden down here in that car? Were they in a Mexican jail? Kidnapped as he and Cynthia were? Dead?

He'd always assumed that if you remained in busy public places, especially tourist traps, you could avoid trouble and all the seedy characters that came with it simply by keeping a low profile. Even the incident with the tequila shots should not have brought them to *this.* It had seemed unthinkable that he and Cynthia should have been scooped up barely two blocks away from Revolución by two men posing as Federales.

For that's what Kyle had decided they were—imposters. It wasn't much of a stretch to imagine that two Federales on the take would abduct two unsuspecting Americans and ransom them. But there had been something so unpolished, so haphazard about their capture and expedition that Kyle, mind frantically trying to examine every mundane fact in order to increase their chances for survival, decided that these two men were no Federales.

The smaller one didn't fit. A ski mask was something one wore when a task force was about to hit a major cartel compound, not when about to whisk up two unarmed and unthreatening travelers. If only he'd followed his instinct then and somehow tried to raise the alarm before they'd been cuffed and thrown in the squad car. Would their situation be different right now?

Listening to Cynthia's sniffles pained him more than anything else. His life had never really been threatened before, and he had absolutely zero experience in hostage crisis situations. And yet he *needed* to take the lead on this one. No amount of Cynthia's trademark diplomacy would bail them out of this, and that's why Kyle needed to handle this his way. Not because he had a plan. Not because he knew what to say or do. And it wasn't because he suspected that she failed to grasp the direness of their situation, and that they would both surely be murdered if they didn't play this *exactly* right.

No, it was because he had to act like a man. He was her husband, and there wasn't the slightest trace of doubt in his mind that he would lay down his life in a second to guarantee her survival. That thought actually brought him some semblance of peace within the confines of the pitch black van. He needed to man up for his wife.

"Cynthia," he muttered weakly. "Baby, can you hear me?"

"Y-yes," she replied, trying to pull herself together.

"Whenever we get to wherever it is we're going, don't say a word. Okay?"

"Kyle," she tried to keep from moaning. "What is this?"

"Baby, we've got to keep it together. Just keep quiet when we get wherever we're going. Don't say a word. Alright?"

"Alright," she agreed, and Kyle though he heard a spark of hope in her voice, like he might actually have a plan. But he had no plan. He was as terrified as she was, and he had no idea what the two men in the front of the van intended to do with them. *Don't say a word.* That's all he had to offer her at the moment.

* * *

The van came to an abrupt stop in the dead of the night. Cynthia heard the two front doors groan open on rusty hinges. Her terror, which she'd managed to hold somewhat at bay for the last hour or so of travel, resurfaced anew as she listened. The back two doors were yanked open again and a cool dusty breeze overtook the interior.

Their captors clamped rough hands on their biceps once again as they were dragged out of the van. Then she felt the pressure on her wrist as one of the men took hold of the handcuffs that bound her to Kyle and yanked both of them forward. She faltered slightly and was then prodded forward by what she guessed had been the assault rifle that had been pointed at them mere hours before. They marched. Twenty feet. Sixty. The distance on foot became as indeterminate as their travel time in the van had been, and this disorientation of time—when added to her current blindness—only added to the uncertainty of their situation. The control that these men had over her and Kyle was so absolute that she feared she would say or do *anything* just to get back to her two boys.

Then came the guilt. What were she and Kyle doing down here, playing college spring break, while she had two sons who needed her back home? Look at this horror she and Kyle had landed themselves in by selfishly abandoning Cameron and Cal, and for what? A hopelessly romantic weekend intended to close a widening chasm between her and her husband? And a weekend getaway in—*let's face it*—a third world country where violence and corruption were running rampant. How irresponsible she felt; this was the guilt of a failed mother.

The darkness was pitch black once again, and as she bumped her shoulder into a blunt object that felt like a doorjamb, she felt the air around her become still and heard her footsteps echo. They'd been brought indoors.

She heard the unmistakable sound of a match being struck, followed by a rattling of metal against glass. A soft light attempted to penetrate the cloth that blindfolded her. Then the blindfold was briskly yanked off of her head, and what was still a soft glow from an oil lantern made her squint. It took a moment for her eyes to adjust to the light in the room, and she looked over to see Federale 1 removing Kyle's blindfold. She turned and looked over her shoulder to see Federale 2 closing a flimsy wooden door behind him, the glock still in his right hand. He took a step toward her and she started, moving closer to Kyle and trembling.

Her eyes scanned her surroundings, and what she saw was the skeletal remains of some long abandoned and insignificant structure made of concrete. It reminded her of some fallout shelter she'd seen from those reality shows about survivalists. There were old newspapers on the floorboards scattered everywhere, as well as both intact and shattered beer and liquor bottles. The windows were boarded up tightly.

Kyle was panting lightly, but he took a deep breath to collect himself. "Okay," *huff, huff, huff,* "We're here now." *Huff, huff.* Deep breath. "Just tell us what you guys want."

The big man arched an eyebrow at Kyle as if to suggest how ludicrous it was for Kyle to make any demands of them. Still looking Kyle right in the eyes, he used his big bald head to gesture toward another doorway, another room. "Andale," he said.

Huff, Huff. He took Cynthia by the hand, the hand he was chained to, and led her through the doorway. It was dark in the next room, but the Federale followed them in, holding up the lantern. The next room was just as unimpressive, but on the far side it had a filthy and torn cloth couch that might have once been beige, with an equally worn-out patterned blanket draped across it. In the center of the room was a mockery of a coffee table, a piece of plywood lying across four cinderblocks. "Sientense," Federale 1 commanded. Keeping her eyes on their abductors, Cynthia let Kyle lead her around the makeshift table, and they both sat down on the couch. Federale 2 came up to the door jamb and leaned against it with his gun in both hands. He remained standing there as Federale 1 leaned his assault rifle up against the wall and then set the lantern down on the plywood. Against the wall near the rifle leaned a rusted metal folding chair, and their host wrestled it open as he placed it down on the floor opposite them. He slowly and deliberately sat down on the chair, removing his sidearm from its holster, first pointing it up at the ceiling, and then slowly placing it down on the plywood next to the lantern. He took his hand off of it, eyeing Kyle and Cynthia as he took keys from his utility belt and reached across the table to uncuff them. After returning the handcuffs to his belt, he leaned forward and rested his elbow on his knee and began to stroke his mustachios. The look he gave them unnerved Cynthia, as if he was realizing for the first time since capturing them that he now had no idea what to do with them. The seconds ticked by as the two Federales watched Cynthia and Kyle, one's face half cast in shadow and the other's still hidden behind his mask. The silence unnerved her more than the jerky movements of the car had.

The big man took in a deep breath, held it in a moment, and then let out a long exhalation that told Cynthia that perhaps he'd reached a decision concerning their immediate fate. "The sun comes up in a few hours," he finally said. "We talk then." And then he shot up out of his chair, grabbing his gun in the process. The Conways both started. Federale 1 turned to exit the room and his partner turned to follow him out, but he faltered at the doorway and turned back to them. He gestured toward the lantern. "I'll leave this on so you can see, but don't get any loco ideas." He pointed at the ceiling. "This won't burn." He pointed at the both of them. "But you will."

* * *

As the first hour passed, Kyle and Cynthia exchanged looks of concern but remained silent. A thick, unhinged wooden door had barricaded them in the room, and Kyle suspected that their only exit out this enclosed area was barred by a heavy wooden plank he was sure had been placed just on the other side. The only things to look at were the burning wick of the lantern and each other. Every time Kyle thought Cynthia was about to speak, he quickly put up a finger to his lips. *No talking.* Federale 1 was whispering in rapid Spanish to his partner, and Kyle was straining his ears with the hope of picking something up. But it was no use; he couldn't hear what was being said. After another few minutes, he heard the frequency of the hushed tones increase into the hissing chatter of a voice escaping through clenched teeth. Then, as if sensing his attempt to listen, Federale 1 stopped. Kyle heard the creak of the outer door opening, and the night wind whipping through the building as the men stepped outside.

"Can we talk now?" Cynthia pleaded with him weakly, the heavy lump in her throat making her voice hoarse.

He needed to reassure her somehow, and convince her to follow his lead and let him do the talking. "Okay, fine. But keep your voice down."

Whatever she'd been holding back for his sake came to the surface full force, and the tears welled up in her eyes as it all came out. "Kyle, why is this happening? Why is it happening, baby?" *Sniff, sniff, sniff.* "Why is this happening? Why? Why?" She sobbed uncontrollably, and she pulled her knees up onto the couch and against her chest, her face now hidden behind the tangled blonde hair that cascaded down her shins, as if she could hide her desperation from him. He took her in his arms and rocked her gently back and forth.

"I don't know, baby," was all he could say, trying to keep the tremors out of his own voice so that he could remain strong for her.

"I saw him, Kyle," she said through sobs, and she lifted her head to meet his eyes. "I saw the big one when we crossed the border. He was watching us. They were watching us the whole time."

This was news to Kyle. Perhaps everything had happened so fast that she hadn't had a chance to tell him. A pathetic and shameful thought of relief surfaced, a thought that told him he was not to blame, that his actions at AnimalE had not, in fact, gotten them into this mess; but he quickly seized it and extinguished it. The implications of their being targeted at the border crossing were far more troubling. He still had no plan, but it was time to tell her the truth about what he suspected. "Cynthia, I think we were randomly picked out of a crowd of American tourists. I think these guys are planning to hold us for ransom. That's the only thing that I can come up with that makes any sense."

"What—what do we do?" she croaked. "What can we do?"

There was nothing reassuring he could tell her. He knew that even if the two of them did exactly as they were instructed, if their kidnappers were somehow able to get their hands on the family's life savings, he and Cynthia might still be murdered. He'd read about such things in local columns all too often, and the fact that they'd both seen Federale 1's face was a thought that terrified him.

He stroked her greasy and matted hair. "There's nothing we can do, CC." *God, why can't I ease her suffering just a little?* "We just have to wait and hear what they have to say."

That's when the beams from an approaching car's headlights pierced the cracks in the boards that covered the window on their right. Before Kyle could process what was happening, he heard the outer door open and the heavy tread of boots on broken glass rapidly approaching. The plank on the other side of the door was removed, and Federale 2 took a wide stance in the doorway to bar their passage. He had a new gun now, a shiny, old Colt revolver, a gun that to Kyle seemed mismatched with the task-force uniform. Federale 2 kept the pistol pointed at the ground, but as he brought his left index finger to where his lips would be behind the mask, he used his right thumb to cock hammer on the colt. He wanted silence, and he was dead serious about it. He glanced at the boarded window to his left and noticed that the headlight beams were peeking through the cracks. He bent down carefully and used his left hand to remove the bulbous, cylindrical glass that encased the wick, and then used his gloved fingertips to extinguish the flame. The room went dark again, and in observing Federale 2's silhouette, Kyle could see by the man's profile that he was keeping his gaze fixed on the boarded window. Federale 1 was nowhere to be seen. They waited.

* * *

A car! A car! Ohmygod, ohmygod, ohmygod, we're saved. Thank God, they're going to come save us. They saw us get taken in TJ, and they followed us here. They're going to surround this place and kill these two thugs and rescue us and take us away from here, back home, back to the boys. Thank God!

The thought went through her head in mere seconds, and she was sure the vehicle outside must have been transporting her saviors, for there was no other explanation for their captor's sudden and erratic behavior. He was concealing them from whatever prying eyes lurked outside.

Just as quickly as thoughts of salvation passed through her mind, there came the harrowing realization that the situation might quickly escalate into violence and death. The bogus Federales were cornered now, and who knew what they might do in some desperate attempt to preserve their own lives? There might ensue some terrible standoff where she found herself and Kyle caught in a crossfire, and, try as she might, she found it difficult to envision any possible scenario that didn't end in a shootout.

Maybe they'll use smoke. Maybe they'll use gas. Maybe they'll use those—what were they called?—flash-bang grenades. She and Kyle might be injured when the law men outside stormed the building, but at least they would leave this place with their lives intact. But no, her doubts weighed heavily upon her. They weren't holed up in some office building in a busy urban plaza by militants with no hope of escape, a helicopter circling in the air, seeing everything. They were in the middle

of the desert, in the middle of God only knew where, and their libera-
tors were an unknown quantity who, for all she knew, had no experience with hostage negotiations and extractions. The newcomers outside
might get her and Kyle killed faster than their kidnappers would have.

* * *

Kyle kept his mouth shut as he'd been commanded to do. The approaching car had come to a stop. He needed Cynthia to somehow
control the rate of her breathing, for she was keeping him from hearing
what was going on outside. Judging by how bright the beams on the vehicle had been when they'd ceased brightening, he surmised that it was
only about a hundred feet or so from this shack. He could hear voices
now, and he was grateful for the knowledge of Spanish that he had
acquired from the Mexicans with whom he had worked over the years,
and he understood the gist what was being said. Perhaps neither of the
two men speaking outside knew this about him, nor the man crouching
right across from him, but he understood. And his heart sank when his
fears were confirmed; the arrival of the strangers outside did not mark
the rescue of the Conways. When he looked at his wife he saw the de-
spair that told him she'd reached the same conclusion.

"Hola, Jefe," said the first voice. Kyle recognized it as Federale 1's.

"Nunca hemos oído de usted," said an unfamiliar voice that carried
an air of authority. *We never heard from you.* "Se suponia que me llama-
rias." *You were supposed to check in.*

"No hay tiempo hasta ahora. No pudimos conseguir una señal."
There was no time until now. We couldn't get a signal. Federale 1's voice
had lost its edge; it had none of the previous menace to it. He was being
cowed by the newcomer.

There was a long silence, and then Kyle heard the new speaker say,
"¿Dónde está tu niño?" *Where's your boy?*

A moment of hesitation, then Federale 1 responded, "Él está dentro
vigilando la pareja." *He's inside guarding the couple.*

Kyle detected a deepening of the newcomer's voice, an indication of
displeasure. "Saquenlo de aqui ahora." *Get him out here right now.*

"Pero Jefe—"

"Ahora!"

Kyle felt, not so much as saw, Federale 2 visibly tense, and then he heard a high decibel whistle identical to the one Federale 1 had used to summon the imposters' squad car back in Tijuana. Federale 2 stood up to his full, unimpressive height, seemed to hesitate, and without acknowledging Kyle or Cynthia, he left the room and boarded it back up. When Kyle heard the outer door open and close, he shot up off of the couch and moved to the boarded window.

"Kyle, don't—"

"Shhhhh!" he hissed over his shoulder. He peered through the thin cracks in the board and took in the scene just beyond the wall. What appeared to be an SUV in the darkness was shining its headlights not directly on the boarded window, but on the wall just to the left, and in that light Kyle saw Federale 1's broad backside. Facing him was a shadowy figure in the headlights flanked a few feet on either side by two more men of similar height and build; and although Kyle couldn't be sure, he thought they appeared to be armed. Just then Federale 2 came trotting up from the entrance side of the building. He came to a stop when he reached his partner. The newcomer, the one who was apparently now calling the shots, turned his head slightly to study the little man who'd just joined them. Federale 2 lowered his head ever so slightly.

"[You bring your boy to me in a mask?]" *El Jefe* asked incredulously.

"[Please, boss, there's a reason]—"

"[Take it off!]" *El Jefe* shouted with outrage. He didn't wait for compliance, for as he said it, he reached over and roughly grabbed Federale 2's head, yanking the facemask off and leaving the smaller man visibly startled.

Federale 1 plunged ahead. "[Boss, we meant no disrespect. It's only that]—"

"Callate! [Now you listen to me. I didn't like this idea from the very beginning, and now I know I'm going to regret having agreed to it. Too many people saw you in Tijuana. Do you know what that means?]" Federale 1 must have suspected that he was not supposed to answer; he said nothing. "[It means]," *El Jefe* continued, "[that I now have to open my wallet. Is this all starting to sink in?]" Kyle saw Federale 1 nod meekly. "[Too many people saw you, and then you fail to check in. This does not sit well with me.]"

"[I apologize]," was all Federale 1 muttered.

El Jefe put his hands on his hips, looking back and forth between the two impersonators, as if deciding what was to be done with them. With finality he said, "[Here's how it's going to go from here on out: You two have two days to wrap this all up. Once you've collected the money, get rid of them, give me my cut, and I'll pass your tribute up the line to the chief. If everything goes according to plan, you two will have a nice payday, and maybe one day soon you]," he pointed to Federale 1, "[will find yourself a central, and you]," he pointed to Federale 2, "[will have worked your way up to an H. If you ever learn to speak, that is.]"

"[Thank you, boss. We]—"

"[I'm not finished!]" *El Jefe* shouted over him. He took a step toward Federale 1 so that they were almost nose to nose. The body language of his companions behind him remained casual, as if they knew Federale 1 wouldn't dare backtalk his superior. "[If . . . if this whole thing goes south, you two are on your own. Do you understand me? I never knew about it, I never sanctioned it, and I will personally find you, shoot you, and bring your headless bodies to the chief's feet. Do I make myself clear?]"

"[Yes, boss]," Federale 1 said for the both of them.

"[No more fuckups, Cobo]," *El Jefe* spat with reprimand. And with that he spun on his heels and headed for the back of the SUV. His companions followed suit, opening and slamming the doors on both sides of the front of the vehicle. Its tires spun as the large car kicked up a dust cloud, and the SUV backed up and turned into the beginnings of a wide K-turn.

What hope Kyle had allowed himself to entertain now evaporated as the headlights turned away from them, and the SUV began to speed off. A cartel was at the center of all this. Their captors' lives were as much at stake as his and Cynthia's. This made them desperate. There could be no further mistakes. No chances taken. He and Cynthia would never be allowed to simply just walk away from this. They would be murdered for sure. He panicked.

"Cynthia, get ready to run."

"What? Wait, Kyle—"

He made his way from the couch and kicked the plywood at his knees off the cinderblocks. He ran at the door in front of him full speed in an attempt to ram it with his shoulder. His whole body bounced off it, but he had definitely felt it give a little as he fell to the floor.

"Kyle! Don't! They'll kill us." As he picked himself back up, he found he wouldn't dare voice his thoughts. *They're going to kill us anyway. No matter what.* He repeated the process, and this time his shoulder partially burst through as the board cracked open. He pulled the loose wood aside and reached out to grab the lumber that was barring their escape. He lifted it, a searing pain shouting up through his right deltoid, and tossed it aside. He turned to his wife, still seated in a frozen ball, and reached out to take her by the hand. *No time for argument. They might not have heard outside. They might still be discussing something, arguing even. No plan. Just flight. Burst through that outer door. Run like hell. Into the night. Into the desert. Run!*

Cynthia was still petrified and conflicted. She was staggering as he dragged her through the inner doorway. A few more feet and he was at the outer door, and with her hand in his left he used his right to reach for the handle. Unlocked. He threw it open and as the night winds buffeted him he took a first frantic step outside. And that's when he was pistol-whipped.

He didn't lose consciousness exactly. But his thoughts were muddled as he felt himself being tackled, roughly manhandled, bound tightly, blindfolded once again, and dragged back into the dark shack, all to the shriek of Cynthia's hysterics.

*   *   *

The blindfold was ripped from his head, and a splash of water hit him in the face. He was dizzy from the blow to the head, and couldn't see clearly enough to focus. He felt Cynthia's hands move gingerly over his brow, and he winced with pain as her fingers stroked the swollen area over his right eye. She immediately pulled her hands away, and when he saw no blood on her fingers, he knew that the gun had not broken skin. Lightheaded and with a throbbing pain coursing across his forehead, he leaned back on the couch, and his whole body slumped in defeat.

"Very stupid," said Cobo, Federale 1, as he hovered over them. "Did you even have a plan?" Kyle looked at Cobo's left hand, saw the ski mask dangling from it, and realized that it, put on backwards, had been used to block his vision the second time.

Kyle said nothing, but the feeling of hopelessness returned ten-fold, and he was worried that he would start to unravel in front of his wife. It was Cynthia who erupted. "Why are you doing this?" she screamed at the men. "We're good . . . . " A sob escaped her. "We're good people."

Cobo ignored her, but turned to his partner, whose face was now exposed. Kyle took the smaller man in. His vision was still blurry, but the man he saw before him was no more than a boy, maybe late teens or early twenties. He must have felt the exposure now that the mask was gone, for he averted his eyes from Cobo and the Conways both, and he no longer looked menacing. He looked like a youth who was just now realizing that he was in over his head. His hair was closely cropped to his skull, and he had a thin mustache that just failed to meet the goatee on his chin. Judging from the expression Kyle read on his face, he might as well have been kidnapped along with Kyle and Cynthia. He looked forlorn.

Cobo pointed at Kyle, "You come with me now," he ordered as he reached for the handcuffs on his belt.

Cynthia's eyes widened. "No," she murmured. "No!"

"Shut up!" Cobo yelled. "He comes with me, we take care of our business, and then you go home." To Kyle he said, "Now give me your hands." Defeated, Kyle stretched out his open palms and Cobo slapped the cuffs on both of Kyle's wrists. Kyle was trembling. Ever since this had all started, he and Cynthia had been able to stay together. He didn't know if he could stay strong if they were separated.

Once the handcuffs were in place, Cobo reached between them and yanked on the chain that bound them, dragging Kyle to his feet. The blood rushed from Kyle's head, and he almost fell over. He felt like vomiting. Cobo gestured to Cynthia and commanded his now timid accomplice, "Mírala. Si intenta algo la bofetas." Kyle snarled at Cobo when he suggested that his partner should raise a hand to his wife, but Cobo wasn't intimidated. He pulled Kyle forward and dragged him through the inner doorway and toward the exit.

"Kyle," Cynthia called in her desolation.

"It's alright, baby," Kyle called over his shoulder, fighting down the bile in his throat. "I'll be back soon. Just do whatever he says, okay? Do whatever he says." And with that he was dragged through the outer door, out into the first rays of morning sunlight. Cobo got behind him and prodded him back toward the van. Cobo ushered him into the passenger's seat, went around the front and got into the driver's seat, revved up the engine, and they were off.

*   *   *

Terror kept springing up from the pit of Cynthia's stomach. But after an hour alone with the boy sitting across from her, her body began to shut it down as if to say *no more*. She was utterly exhausted as she pulled her body into an even tighter ball and let fatigue overtake her. After a time, she raised her eyes to meet those of her assailant.

As Kyle had, she observed how torn the youth appeared. He hadn't spoken at all since their capture, and he continued in silence now. She didn't understand, as Kyle had, that the meeting with *El Jefe* had shaken the boy to his core. She didn't know that he may have just now been realizing that his life was as forfeit as hers was if there was any deviation from the plot that had been set in motion, whatever that was. Ever so gradually, another truth began to dawn on her. As was the case with Cobo back at the border, she'd seen this young man before. She'd seen him back at AnimalE. He was the one who'd been watching them back at the bar when Kyle had refused to pay for the shots. He had been keeping tabs on them. *My God, they've* both *been watching our every move. WHAT IS GOING ON?*

"I know you," she declared defiantly, as if this statement might somehow push him off balance. "I know who you are."

She didn't expect him to respond, and true to form he remained silent. But he did meet her gaze. And as she studied him much in the same way two children might have a staring contest, something troubling began to dawn on her. He'd kept a safe distance back at AnimalE to avoid suspicion, and although she now recognized that this man in front of her was the same one from the bar, she realized that there was

Imaginary Lines

more to it than that. She'd seen this man even earlier. Before AnimalE. Before Tijuana. She'd seen this man once a long time ago. "Oh, my God," she whispered more to herself than to him. He turned away from her again, as if this is what he'd been fearing when *El Jefe* had first pulled his mask off.

"Oh, my God," she stated coolly. "I know who you are."

* * *

The van sped along the desert highway, the only indications of civilization the occasional road sign. Kyle was exhausted, and he would occasionally rest his head against the side window until the pain in his forehead reregistered. He thought about Cobo's earlier question about what plan he might have had. He'd had none other than to run as fast as his and Cynthia's legs would carry them, and to keep running until they'd outdistanced the two Mexicans and found a suitable place to hide. Save their lives. How very foolish that all seemed now. *I'm going to die out here.*

The van made a sharp and abrupt ninety degree turn onto a dirt road much like the one they'd all taken when they'd switched vehicles. And they continued along that road, heading east, for mile after tedious mile. On and on they rode, away from civilization, away from other men, deeper into the desert. Then the van swerved left, off the road, and they continued another few miles north, until it came to a stop in a wide clearing away from the brush and cacti.

Cobo cut the engine and came around the van to Kyle's door, throwing it open. "Out," he ordered. Kyle did as he was told. There was little defiance left in him. It had been suppressed the moment he'd been separated from his wife. "That way," said Cobo, pointing generally toward the northeast. Head pounding, hands shackled, and legs wobbly, Kyle shuffled his feet and moved in the direction Cobo had indicated. He walked only a few hundred feet before he found himself at the foot of a wide ditch, about four feet deep. Nearby a shovel lay on the ground and another stuck out of the earth, its long handle reaching up toward the sky. Cobo was right behind him, and with his mouth close to Kyle's right ear he said, "I know what you are thinking." He then shoved Kyle forward, and Kyle pitched over into the ditch, his body rolling toward the bottom. He frantically tried to pull himself erect, to face Cobo, to ascertain his intentions. Cobo merely stood over Kyle at the foot of the ditch, towering over him, the glock held firmly in his right hand.

"We dug this yesterday," Cobo began. "Usually in these situations we'd have you and your wife dig your own graves, but we didn't want to deal with all of the wasted time and carrying on while you begged for your lives." Kyle backed away from Cobo, until he was standing squarely in the center of the ditch. His breathing became deep and rapid. "I never really wanted to show you this place," Cobo continued, and Kyle noticed that the man's English had much improved since their capture. "But after your escape attempt, you've left me little choice."

This can't be happening. Kyle took another step away from Cobo, and waited.

"What tends to happen is that we would get you both on your knees, facing away from us, and then we'd put a bullet through the back of each of your heads. But I can see now that we haven't quite gotten through to you." Cobo straightened up to his full height and held the gun loosely at his side. "You and your wife will do exactly what you're told from now on. There will be no second chances. If you try anything else like you did earlier this morning, first we'll bring you both back here. Then I will shoot you in the stomach. You'll still be breathing when we shovel the dirt back on top of you. But not her. Your pretty wife, she'll be fucked a thousand times. She's a little old, but not too old. Maybe we'll send her down to Guadalajara where she'll learn to spread her legs for money. By that time she'll have been so pumped full of drugs that she won't even remember her own name, much less that she once had a husband and two sons. Perhaps now you'll see that we mean business."

Two sons? He knew we have kids. Cynthia told him so. But he never knew we have boys. Kyle could only stare back, petrified. "What do you want from us?" he pleaded. Then his voice rose to a shout, "You haven't even told us what you want from us."

"That will all be explained soon," Cobo responded calmly. "For now, I needed you to see how serious we are. I think you're beginning to understand."

Kyle broke down. He raised his left hand to his face to cover his shame. He carried on for a minute or so until he was spent. When he looked back up at Cobo, a giant in the sunlight, he saw a cruel smile begin to play at the corner of his mouth, twisting his mustachios. "Welcome to the Wild West, amigo."

*   *   *

"Look, we can work something out. Just you and me. Your partner doesn't have to know anything. You can just . . . just find a reason for him to slip away. And then take us back to Tijuana. Is it money? Is it? Is that what this is all about? We have money. We can get you money. Just please . . . please take us back so we can see my children again. Ple-e-ease."

The youth wouldn't meet her eyes. His expression had turned stony. He sat there, inanimate, on the folding chair across from her on the couch. He hadn't bothered to replace the one-time coffee table that Kyle had kicked off the cinder blocks. He wouldn't look in her direction; his gaze was fixed on nothing in particular. She had no confidence whatsoever that she was getting through to him. She wasn't even sure if he understood English.

He was certainly no decision-maker. Even without having followed the conversation outside only a few hours earlier, she knew she was looking at the lowest rank on the chain of command. Her only hope, in her mind, was to appeal to whatever sense of humanity he might possess, and then exploit it.

But he gave her nothing. Why would he let them go and then face being murdered himself? He might have felt remorse for the part he had played in this whole plot, but he certainly wasn't about to throw his life away for that mistake.

And how in the world would he even conceive of a scenario where Cobo would leave him alone with her and Kyle long enough for the three of them to abscond back to the border? The wispy young man sitting across from her was just as likely to try and overpower Cobo.

But what *could* she do? There was nothing to do but beg, try to reason with him, dangle some money in front of him, and then beg some more. She had absolutely zero leverage, and the torturous thoughts of the immediate future brought unthinkable courses of action to her mind. There was one card—*Don't even think it!*—she could still play.

I could . . . no, I could never do that. Never. I would die before I would . . . but what if that's what it would take? Kyle would never have to know. I would go to my grave with that shame. But what's a little shame if it meant I could see Cameron and Cal again. What sacrifice is a mother was willing to make for her children?

His head jerked and he looked at her for the first time in a long while, as if probing her desperate thoughts, as if alert now to her intentions from the strange energy in the air.

You caught him staring at you once, back when you first met him. Looking at you with longing in his eyes. It was off-putting for only a moment, but then—admit it to yourself—you were flattered. The way you caught him casting glances at your bare legs stemming from those little jean shorts. His failed attempt at stealth when he eyed your cleavage. He wanted to do nasty things to you then. You loved that men liked to look at you. And look at you now. Look at the situation you're in. This is justice for your terrible vanity. Look at the sinful act you're thinking about committing.

He was still looking at her. Right at her. She swallowed hard, and then slowly and sensuously pursed her lips, the tip of her tongue just staring to peak out. He stared. She leaned slightly forward. "We can . . ." she began. "We can . . ." Her fingers came up to the low collar of her blue tank-top, resting there, but tugging at it ever so gently, just enough to lower it mere millimeters. "No one ever has to—"

He shot up out of his chair and came at her, closing the distance between them in less time than it took for her to process what was happening. She shrieked and jumped back on the couch, and then he was on top of her, weighing her down, a tremendous display of strength for a man so slight of build. She reached up with her left hand, going for his face, to claw, to gouge, to defend herself to her last breath from being raped. But he easily swatted the hand away, grabbing her arm at the wrist, and he bent it back down over her shoulder while at the same time his right hand wrapped itself around her throat. Her eyes went wide, and she suppressed another scream for fear that he would apply enough pressure to smash her windpipe.

But he didn't squeeze. He remained on top of her, staring down at her with the kind of fire in his eyes that told her she was mistaken—young or not, he was not a man to be trifled with. Her womanhood would not be clouding his judgment on this day. He was breathing heavily through his nose, his face flushed with anger, and his grip remained fixed on her delicate neck.

She too was breathing heavily, and just when she'd thought that she'd been cried out, the salty tears sprang up yet again. Fear of death, fear of being raped, and the humiliation of what she may or may not have been willing to do a moment ago made the intensity of her predicament feel raw all over again, and she cried and cried and cried.

But as his fingers loosened and he removed his hand from her throat, standing up off of her, she felt something strange, an emotion out of place. It remained elusive until she recognized it for what it was. Gratitude. As he backed away and took his seat opposite her, she wondered if she might be succumbing to symptoms of the first stages of Stockholm's Syndrome. For all outward appearances, he'd been about to squeeze the life out of her, or enter her, or both. But he hadn't. And the gratitude she felt was multi-layered. She was grateful to him for having spared her life. She was grateful for having not been violated. But most importantly—and she truly was abashed—she was grateful he had toppled her when he had, and spared her from having to make the hardest—and perhaps the most foolish—decision of her life.

* * *

It was a small backwater town, little more than a village, that Cobo drove Kyle to. Cobo made sure to park on the outskirts in order to avoid being observed by any locals. He'd locked Kyle in the car back in the desert in order to change out of his Federale uniform into civilian looking fatigues: a blue-and-black flannel, button-down shirt over jeans with a large brass belt buckle, and cowboy boots.

Parked at the edge of town, with no one coming and going from the local businesses, Cobo decided that the coast was clear. But before they exited the van, he said to Kyle without looking at him, "You follow my lead. We'll only be here for a few minutes. There will be people about. I don't think that I need to remind you what will happen if you try to pull anything. Remember that my partner has your wife just a phone call away."

Kyle said nothing, only waited for Cobo to open the driver's side door and plunge them both into whatever the next phase of their scheme might be. "Let's go," Cobo said. Both men got out of the van, and then Cobo nodded northwards toward the center of town. Kyle began walking, with Cobo only a few steps behind. He hadn't needed Cobo to remind him of the seriousness of the situation. He had no illusions about what would happen if he were to do anything untoward. There would be no more escape attempts, or any deviation from Cobo's commands. All he could think about was Cynthia's safety, and how any move he made would affect that safety.

As they closed in on the small town, he noted that Cobo had indeed waited for the daily commerce to die down. There were very few people about, and those that were paid very little mind to the two approaching strangers. They passed one liquor store when Cobo took Kyle's arm and steered him left into an alleyway. They kept moving until they were about halfway down, and then Cobo told him to stop. He reached into his pocket and retrieved the cell phone he'd stolen from Kyle, a standard LG cell phone from Sprint. Cobo flipped it open and began scrolling through Kyle's contact list. Kyle looked back, out of the alley, and saw no one. He then looked past Cobo to where the alley ended on the west side, opening up onto a dirt lot, and still saw no one. Cobo found what he was looking for. Looking up from the phone in his hand, he said, "Now you call your brother."

Part of Kyle was surprised, and then yet again part of him wasn't. "My brother?" was all he could respond.

"You tell him that he has one day to get $1,100,000 out of the bank. You tell him that we will contact him later this evening with a time and place to meet tomorrow morning. Let him know that if he tries to contact the police, or does anything other than what we tell him, you and your wife will die."

There was some solace in the momentary relief that hit Kyle right then and there. He had been right all along. From the very beginning this had been nothing more than an old fashioned kidnapping and ransom demand. There was no intrigue or intricate plot here. Just greed.

But this relief was heavily outweighed by his shock. *$1,100,000? Two sons? Call my brother?* He had expected there to be some sort of session of information gathering, where Cobo figured out who to contact and shake down in order to broker the deal for his and Cynthia's release. But there hadn't been. Cobo already had all of the information he needed. And somehow he knew the exact monetary figure of the payday he and Kyp had just received.

He stalled, partly to get his bearings and partly to confirm another suspicion. "My brother doesn't have that kind of money. I don't know who it is that you think we are."

"Between the two of you," Cobo replied, not buying any of it, "in your joint business account, you have *exactly* that much."

The surprises just kept piling up. There was no way, no way whatsoever, that Cobo could have gained that kind of information after the abduction. That meant that he and Cynthia hadn't simply been picked out of a crowd. Cobo and his partner had known exactly who they were when they'd crossed the border, and had been waiting for them. Furthermore, and equally as disturbing, they'd known where and when to wait for them.

Paranoid thoughts went bouncing around inside of Kyle's head, and Cobo grew impatient. He pressed *send* on the phone, and then handed it to Kyle. Kyle held it to his ear, staring at Cobo all the while. The phone rang once. He hadn't been given much specific information to convey, just the wider picture of the situation and what needed to happen in the next twenty-four hours. The phone rang a second time. This could not have been the standard procedure for a ransom. It was too sloppy, with too many variables. Whatever science there was to the planning and execution of such an undertaking must have been tossed aside. Why head into a town where they could be seen? What purpose did that serve? *Maybe he needed a stronger cell phone signal.* The phone rang a third time.

"Kyle?" Kyp said on the other end, not a warm welcome, but a question.

Kyle was breathing heavily again, and he tried to collect himself. Here was a defining moment in his and Cynthia's terror. While under duress, with Cobo seemingly knowing everything about him and his life, he had to play this straight. "Yeah, Kyp. It's me."

There was no apparent alarm in Kyp's voice, merely concern. "Where've you guys been? We haven't heard from you. We called a few times and didn't get any answer. We're all packed and ready to leave."

"Kyp, listen to me. Listen very carefully." He took a deep breath. He needed to remain calm. "Something happened when we arrived in

Tijuana. Cynthia and I were taken by two men." At this Cobo reached behind him and retrieved his pistol, wedged between his belt and his back, and held it at his side. Obviously, even this last statement had given away too much information in Cobo's view. Kyle's heartbeat quickened. *Goddamn you, Cobo. It's not like this was rehearsed.* "We're being held captive."

There was momentarily silence on the other end, as if Kyp didn't know how to process this. "What? What are you talking about?"

"They have us, Kyp. They want money. They want you to get $1,100,000 together and wait for us to call you." The anxiety was making him dizzy, the act of saying it aloud making their danger all the more real. "If we don't pay them," he said, fumbling, while the phone shook in his hand, "then they're going to kill us."

"Who has you, Kyle? Where are you two?" As Kyp spoke Cobo leaned in closer to the phone, so that he too might hear what was being said on the other end. His eyes narrowed, and Kyle deduced that Cobo wanted him to keep the conversation moving along.

"Are you hearing what I'm saying, Kyp?" His voice raised a little, not from frustration, but for clarity. "They're going to murder both of us if we don't do exactly as they say."

Kyp chewed on this for a moment, and then proceeded carefully, the reality of the situation starting to sink in. "They want money. Where are they? How do I get it to them?"

Perhaps Cobo had heard this. He was growing visibly impatient. Kyle's instructions were to update Kyp on the situation, relay the demands, and then await further instructions. "Just get it together," Kyle continued. "And then wait for our call. There will be a time and a place to meet sometime tomorrow morning. I'm assuming down here somewhere."

"Kyle—Kyle, listen. Everything's going to be alright. I'm going to get you out of this. But I need some more information. Tell me what—"

"There's no time. They haven't told me anything yet. They say they'll be in touch tonight." He was conveying everything as he'd been instructed, and his eyes never left Cobo's. "Right now the important thing is that you get the money. Can you do that?"

"In cash? Do they think that I can just walk into the bank and withdraw that kind of money?"

"You have to," Kyle pleaded desperately. "You have to do whatever it takes." Cobo didn't seem pleased with the way the dialogue was flowing, and he reached out to take the phone from Kyle's hand. But Kyle had one last spark of defiance in him. He took a step back, just out of Cobo's reach. "No police, Kyp," he said quickly, knowing that the line was about to be cut. "Don't tell Sara. Don't tell Dad. Don't tell anyone!" And then Cobo got the phone away from Kyle. Kyle still heard his name being called through the receiver as Cobo studied the screen. He returned the gun to the small of his back and then, instead of closing the phone, he took it in both hands and then broke it in half. He turned and threw the two pieces down the alley. He turned back to Kyle and stared at him long and hard. Maybe he was displeased with Kyle's act of defiance, but hadn't he wanted Kyle to relay to Kyp that no police were to be involved. *Do these guys even know what the fuck they're doing?* Then he remembered *El Jefe*, and the threat on Cobo's life, and the time constraints. He realized that Cobo and his mute friend were probably now winging it, unable to take the time to truly think things through step-by-step. He stood his ground in response to Cobo's staring. "You said no police," he shouted, his emotions getting the best of him. "I was just doing what you said."

Too fast for Kyle to defend himself, Cobo swung his arm and gave Kyle a backhanded slap to the swollen area just above his eye. He staggered back a few feet, letting out a grunt of pain as he brought his palm back up to his already bruised forehead. "Lower your voice," Cobo said quietly as he took a quick look at both entrances to the alley to make sure there were no spectators.

Kyle leaned against the cement wall for support. He'd forgotten how instantaneously this situation could erupt into violence. Panting from the renewed pain in his head, he said, "So what happens now?"

"Now we wait for your brother to show us how smart he is. Come on. We're leaving."

* * *

The prolonged silence, the staring, continued between Cynthia and her guard. She could sense some kind of internal struggle going on just underneath his surface, regardless of how much he tried to project an air of soldierly passivity. He hadn't said a single word since she'd first come into contact with him, and yet . . . . Her conclusion was drawn from her instincts and from the energy that hung in the air between them.

He and Cobo were not the same. She was sure of it. He had either been dragged into this whole mess, or volunteered reluctantly. And now he knew that he had been thrust into a situation that he had absolutely no control over. And this frightened him.

It occurred to her that she might play on his fears, and let him know—even if she was bluffing—what dire consequences awaited him if American authorities were ever to catch up with him and his partner. But just as quickly as she thought it, she dismissed it. Why would he cower at the prospect of American officials, who had very little power in the way of hostage negotiations, extraction, or extradition out of their jurisdiction, when he had what appeared to be Mexican gangsters—a cartel perhaps—looming over them with the threat of death?

Perhaps she could threaten his soul. "We're good people," she blurted out. It was risky, considering the way he'd pounced on her earlier, but when she got no reaction out of him she continued. "I've never hurt anyone in my life. I work with small children. I get them ready to face this scary world we live in. My husband is one of the most decent men you'll ever meet, and compassionate." She found as she plunged ahead that she was becoming bold enough to insert forcefulness into her voice. "He employs dozens of underprivileged, poor, and down-on-their-luck Mexicans like you. He gives them a fresh start." Again, she had no idea whether he was able to understand her words, but she pressed on, hoping the meaning might be conveyed in her tone. "But you already know that, don't you? You know we're good people. You've seen it yourself. We've led good Christian lives, and we reach out to the people who need our help. And we don't ask for anything in return. We're happy to help, not because of where it might get us, but because it's the right thing to do."

Was any of this registering with him? Did her allusion to Kyle's employment of illegal immigrants resonate with him? She had no way to tell, but she kept her sights on his eyes, hoping that there might be a way to look into his thoughts. "My boys are nine and seven, and they'll be devastated if anything happens to us. I don't know, maybe you grew up without a mother and father. Was it hard? Did it make life difficult?

Can you imagine the pain it would cause you to know they were taken away from you by men who were driven purely by greed?"

He actually met eyes with her now, but there was no change in his blank expression. The silence, the unwillingness to be moved in the face of what she was saying, infuriated her, even if she knew deep down that she had very little chance of swaying him. "There's a special place in hell for men like you," she said with as much conviction as she could pour into her voice. "If Kyle and I die in this place, my family will grieve for us. People will miss us. And even if I know the pain of that will be unbearable for them, at least I'll know that after I'm gone I'll be at peace. Can you say that for yourself? Will anyone miss you when you're gone?"

She saw something in his eyes. She wasn't sure what it was at first. But she could offer herself a guess. What she saw was congruity. He agreed with her. He knew that he was damned, and her words changed nothing. She leaned back into the couch, defeated again. She wasn't telling him anything that he didn't already know himself. And this realization didn't encourage her; it disheartened her even more.

*   *   *

As they drove back they way they'd come, Kyle made up his mind about something. He needed to *help* Cobo. Playing it by ear as they had would surely get both himself and Cynthia killed. There was so much stacked against their chances for survival already: the fact that he now knew Cobo's name, the fact that he and Cynthia had both seen their kidnappers' faces, the bosses allowing their presence to be known. Statistically, he knew that these cartel types often reneged at the last possible moment, still collecting their money, but murdering their victims in the end, thereby tying up any loose ends.

It awed him that after so many years of coming down here to party with his friends that he hadn't really considered just how dangerous it could be. He'd had his share of scrapes with real policeman and Federales who were corrupt to their cores, but he'd always wormed his way out of each problem with a quick payoff. Hence the cockiness he'd displayed back in Tijuana when he'd been sure that Cobo was an actual Federale. What a fool he'd been.

And the rate at which these types of kidnappings and ransoms had exploded down here in the last year should have given him pause. But it hadn't. Professional criminals didn't ordinarily finger people of modest means like Cynthia and him, and decide they would make for a nice bounty. But now he knew the truth. These men had done their homework. They knew about Kyle's newfound wealth, even if it was modest when compared to that of many of the citizens of Southern California. And how in the hell had they known about that? How had they known the time and place to lie in wait? Certain suspicions were starting to nag at him, but he cast them aside for now. He had to stick to the situation at hand.

"Look, you have to give him more time," he said, hoping to at the very least appeal to Cobo's practicality. "He said it himself. You can't just walk into a bank and cash out that kind of money. You have to declare it, and they'll want to know why." He dreaded suggesting that he and Cynthia remain down here in this hellhole one more second than they absolutely had to, but if that's what self-preservation took then he would endure for a while longer.

Cobo took his eyes off the road and looked at Kyle. There remained the malevolent expression of a man who meant to do you harm, but there was something else there too. Doubt. *Holy shit, I'm getting through to him. These guys really don't have any idea what they're doing. They have no concept of how these things really work. Ignorant savages!* "If there could be some kind of legitimate transfer of funds, then maybe this could be taken care of in a day or two. But you're asking for the impossible."

He waited for Cobo to ask him what needed to be done. He waited to be asked how situations like this were actually handled up in America. But Cobo simply said, "You'd better hope that he finds a way. For *your* sake."

* * *

Cynthia actually did find some time to fall asleep for a bit. The tremendous mental strain had caused her mind to shut down, and with it came sleep filled with nightmares. She had never intended to shut her eyes, to let sleep take her. She couldn't afford to. Not here. Not now. But in the end she'd had no choice. She was exhausted.

When she awoke, it was with a start. Federale 2 was no longer seated across from her, but when she looked to her right she saw him standing at the boarded window, peaking through the cracks. She had no idea what time it was. Perhaps late morning or early afternoon, judging by the sunlight that managed to penetrate through the cracks.

She thought she heard the sound of tires on unpaved road, and she knew that Federale 2 wasn't merely on watch. He was making sure that the approaching vehicle held Cobo and Kyle. She heard the van approach to within a few feet of the building and come to a stop.

She prayed that when Cobo walked in, Kyle would be with him. And he was, his hands still cuffed in front of him. When her husband passed through the inner door he quickened his pace toward her, and neither Cobo nor his partner objected when they embraced. Kyle lifted his cuffed hands over her head and held her for a long time. They were together again. He closed his eyes and squeezed her more tightly, so grateful that she still lived and breathed. As he nestled his face into her hair, he heard Cobo say to the mute, "Tenemos que hablar." *We need to talk.*

Perhaps not any more relaxed, but definitely sensing no threat from Kyle or Cynthia, the two men stepped outside to have a one-sided discussion. When they were gone Kyle moved his head back and looked at her. "I don't know what to say."

"Your eye looks worse."

"Cobo popped me again. How about you? Did anything happen when I was away?"

"Nothing happened," she muttered. "I'm fine."

He wasn't convinced, but with the men outside, he knew that time was of the essence. "Listen," he began, glancing at the outer door. "I found some things out while we were gone. And it's not good." He knew he had to do this quickly, and yet he had trouble forming the words. "Back when we were in TJ, we weren't just another couple of marks. These guys know exactly who we are. They know about Kyp, and the boys. They know how much money is in our bank account." He waited for this to register. He waited for her to act surprised. She didn't.

"I know," she said.

He didn't understand at first. "You know? How? He spoke?"

"No, he hasn't uttered a word, but next time he comes in, take a good look at him. We've met him before, Kyle, years ago."

Every time Kyle absorbed a new piece of information, the amount of danger they were in seemed to increase. And now, at a loss for words, Kyle was being told that the mute partner was someone he should know. Not even a hint of familiarity had hit Kyle when he'd first seen the little man with his mask off. And now Kyle came to the conclusion that he'd been wearing a mask from the beginning not simply because he hadn't wanted his face to be *seen*. He'd been startled when *El Jefe* had pulled the mask off his head because he'd been afraid of being *recognized*. "Who is he? How do we know him?"

And Cynthia told him how.

* * *

"*So this your new A-Team?*" *Kyle asked Mauricio as he joined him on the front lawn of the latest site.*

Mauricio nodded. "*They work well together. Like carpenter ants.*"

Kyle smiled despite himself. Ever since he'd taken on Mauricio, the man had not only proved how able-bodied he was, but had also strived to better his English for the sake of both his family and his career. And the rate at which he had progressed had exceeded everyone's expectations, including Lorena's. In the here and now Kyle was impressed not only by Mauricio's cadence, but by his expanded vocabulary as well. This was good. Good for him. Good for Kyle.

He knew he'd done the right thing when he'd taken a chance on the kid. A little risky at first, sure, but whatever magic spell Eddie had cast after Lorena had announced her pregnancy had worked wonders. Mauricio was legit now. Immigration couldn't touch him.

Kyle looked at the skeletal beginnings of his next project, at how much progress the guys had already made, and he was very pleased indeed. "*This is excellent, buddy. Nice work.*"

Mauricio crossed his arms and allowed himself a grin of satisfaction. "*Thanks, boss.*"

"*Just one thing,*" *Kyle said delicately, not trying to spoil the positive mood, but still needing to protect his business. There's a city inspector coming by in a couple of days and I need them out of sight. We'll put 'em to work someplace else."*

Mauricio understood certain realities, and by now he and Kyle had developed a shorthand to avoid anyone's taking offense. *"No problem, boss."*

"Let's go meet them," Kyle said, and they both walked across the lawn and around to the backyard. There were men coming and going with nail-guns, electric power saws, bags of plaster, ladders, wooden planks, and levels. Everyone had a job to do. Everyone knew his place. And Mauricio had everything under control.

He felt as though he were looking at some well-oiled machine, a machine he himself had built and needed only to switch on. He was proud of himself.

Cynthia, who had been exploring the interior, came out through the frame of the back patio door, a large cylindrical thermos held by one hand and a sleeve of plastic cocktail cups in the other. *"Who wants lemonade?"* she called out to the crew. Most of the men glanced Mauricio's way, waiting for some kind of cue. Mauricio nodded to them all, gesturing with a wave that said yes, it was okay to take a break and join Cynthia for some lemonade. But not everyone did. Only about half of them joined her.

Kyle watched as the men gathered around his wife, thanking her graciously for the refreshment. When she'd offered them all lemonade, he'd wanted to blurt out something tacky, like, *"Hey how 'bout some beer?"* to show the Mexicans that he was an everyman, a guy's guy who might have a work ethic bordering on the obsessive compulsive, but who still liked to kick back and yuck it up with the boys.

Just as it was about to come out of his mouth, he stopped himself. He watched the men approach her, at first like dogs who didn't trust the hand that was offering them food. Then came a visible change, the softening of the postures, as Cynthia won them over with her cheery smile and magnetic personality. She had that effect on people, and Kyle loved her for it.

He stared at her as she handed out the lemonade. She was so beautiful, but not in a classical way. She was so dainty, and yet she had a gymnast's physique that was well toned and curvy in all the right places. Her face was cute rather than sexy, with the freckles that ran just around the bridge of her nose and under her eyes. Her golden hair was pulled back in a tight ponytail, and her summer garb was simple: a white tube top with jean shorts and sandals, an outfit that accentuated her best physical attributes without being too provocative.

But her appearance wasn't the only thing that attracted men to Cynthia. She had one of those inviting personalities that served her like some great beacon of empathy, and every man, woman, and child who came into contact with her appreciated her because of it. She was lovely, a little naïve at times, yes, but that's why Kyle was there: to bring her back down to earth from time to time. God, he'd struck gold!

He walked around the house to the backyard, not so much inspecting, but simply observing. Mauricio's word now had enough force behind it that Kyle trusted that the job was being done the right way with men who labored in harmony. The team wasn't all that large, about half a dozen or so, but they cooperated with the kind of efficiency that suggested they'd all worked together for some time.

Then Kyle stumbled across a possible red flag. Good God, how old is that kid? Kyle saw a boy kneeling as he laid concrete in the back patio area, and walked over to introduce himself. "Hey there," he said. "What's your name?"

The boy looked up at Kyle, one eye squinting in the sunlight. He stopped what he was doing, but didn't rise to meet Kyle's eyes. From where Kyle was standing the boy looked like he was in early adolescence, not older than fifteen or sixteen. His hair was just a bit too long, bowl-like and shaggy. His face was beardless, and Kyle wondered if he'd even started shaving yet. He waited for the boy to respond, but the boy said nothing.

"¿Como te llamas?" Kyle repeated. Still nothing. The kid continued to just stare up at Kyle. What's going on here? Does this guy really not know who I am? Kyle didn't think he was in any way coming across as intimidating; he was trying his best to appear friendly. "Where are you from, friend? ¿De donde es usted?" Kyle was now starting to grow irritated. Whatever this little stalemate was about, he didn't like it one bit. It was another worker who came to the kid's aid.

"Hola," Kyle heard over his shoulder, and turned to see a pudgy man in a straw hat holding a wheelbarrow. "I'm Martin," the newcomer said, putting his hand out. Mar-teen. "Thank you much for this."

Kyle took the man's hand and shook it. "It's nice to meet you, Martin. And it should be me thanking you for the great job you're all doing."

"We like to work in the sun," was all Martin said.

"So what's with this one?" Kyle asked, jerking a thumb toward the kid crouched down on the ground. "He doesn't talk?"

"Oh, no," Martin assured him, "he talks. But his English is not so good."

"I was speaking to him in Spanish," Kyle clarified.

"Ohhhhhh," Martin said with a frown, but then he quickly reverted to smiling. "Well, Davitos, he very shy."

I don't need this, Kyle thought. "I only wanted to know his name and where he's from," he said.

"Oh," Martin said jovially with a why didn't you say so? look on his face. "Me and Davitos are Mauricio's cousins. We're all from Ciudad Juarez."

Kyle was about to accept all of this and move on, then stopped. "Ciudad Juarez?" he said to Martin quizzically. He looked across the yard, searching for Mauricio, and found him stacking tile near the kitchen door. "I thought Mauricio was from Oaxaca."

Martin was the one to look confused now. "Oaxaca?" he said, appearing to think it over. "No," he said finally. "I know Mauricio since he was this high," he held his hand out to waist height, "and we all grow up in Ciudad Juarez."

"Huh," Kyle said, more to himself than Martin. He looked back down at the boy, who had gone back to work at their feet. All Kyle could see was black hair. "How old is he?"

"Eighteen," replied Martin.

"Hey," Kyle said more sternly this time, looking down at the boy. "Hey, you." Davitos looked up from what he was doing. "Go on." He nodded toward Cynthia and the other laborers. "Get yourself some lemonade. Vamanos."

Davitos looked at Martin for a cue on how to proceed, and Martin nodded. Davitos stood up and walked over to Cynthia. Kyle watched the boy go with mild displeasure. He turned back to Martin. "You obviously do the talking for the both of you. Let him know who's really in charge, eh?"

Martin nodded quickly and said, "Yes, sir."

"Cool. Now go get yourself some lemonade."

Martin took his hands off of the wheelbarrow and followed Davitos. Kyle watched both men approach Cynthia and accept the plastic cups, Martin thanking her promptly for the both of them.

Kyle watched Davitos' face, observing the failed attempt at being inconspicuous as he lustfully gave Cynthia the up-and-down. That's right, you little shit. That's what a real woman looks like. My wife. The boss' wife.

He decided to try to alter his thinking. He could straighten the kid out later, show him who the boss was. Another lingering thought that had been troubling Kyle came back to the forefront. Why the devil did Mauricio tell me he was from Oaxaca if he was really from Ciudad Juarez?

He suspected that he already had his answer. Ciudad Juarez was sometimes referred to as a cesspool, a breeding ground for young aspiring criminals and killers. Perhaps Mauricio had been told to lie when he'd first arrived here in the states, and had never imagined that he would advance to a station in life where he might have to one day tell the truth about his roots.

Kyle didn't like it. He didn't like it one bit. But Mauricio was unknowingly about to get a huge pass. He'd simply accomplished so much in so short a time that Kyle didn't want to risk creating strife at such a critical juncture of their business relationship. No, he'd give Mauricio the benefit of the doubt. He'd let it alone. For now.

* * *

He couldn't wrap his head around it. It was unfathomable. How could Davitos have had the audacity to abduct two people who'd shown him kindness another lifetime ago? Kyle's rage was rekindled. He imagined shattering the lantern at his feet over the boy's head when he returned, and then beating him to death with his fists.

I employed him. Cynthia quenched his thirst on a hot summer's day. We've been held captive for almost twenty-four hours and not even a scrap of food or a drop of water. How can these two things possibly add up?

He wondered, since he'd suspected all along that he and Cynthia would never survive this, what the probability of success could be in getting the jump on Cobo and Davitos. His fear made him rational; there was no way he and Cynthia could ever hope to rush the two men. But if he used his head, and started thinking *right now*, he might just be able to formulate some kind of escape plan. Not like the attempt he'd made earlier this morning when he'd panicked, but a *real* plan. Calm. Calculated. He could outsmart Cobo and Davitos. Those two hadn't even been able to pull off something as common as a kidnapping and ransom.

Don't forget that the game's changed now. It's not just these two bump-kins and their cartel bosses. It's much bigger than that. He still had trouble acknowledging it to himself, but the evidence now was insurmountable. He balled up his hands into fists and lowered his head, closing his eyes. Cynthia grew concerned.

This had been an inside job from the very beginning.

"I'll kill him," he said in a low voice barely more than a whisper.

Cynthia's frown deepened. "Who?"

"Mauricio."

Her eyes widened. She was still sitting next to Kyle, facing him with her feet up on the couch, and she leaned into him now, her right hand on the nape of his neck, her left one clutching his bicep. "You can't really believe he had something to do with this."

He turned to face her with an expression of pure bewilderment. "Can there be any doubt?"

"This is all purely circumstantial," she argued. "We have no proof that Mauricio—"

"We have all the proof, Cynthia," he shot back, his voice rising, frustrated that she wasn't drawing the same conclusion he was. "We have all the proof we need."

"Let's not get ahead of ourselves," she suggested, urging calm. "We *know* Mauricio. He would never—"

"What?" he interrupted, lowering his voice now as to not be heard from outside. "What do we really know about him anyway? He could've been anyone before he turned up in San Diego." He took her shoulders in his hands; she needed to see things his way. "We don't know for sure who he is or where he came from."

"It's too much of a stretch," she insisted. "Someone like him never could have orchestrated—"

"Cynthia," he hissed in exasperation. "They knew *exactly* where and when to wait for us. They knew about the boys, and Kyp, and who knows what else. For God's sake, they knew the exact figure to ask for when they demanded the money." He shook his head, resolute in his conviction. "There's just no way. No way in hell."

She must have sensed that he was bordering on the obsessive about it, for she changed the subject. "True or not, it doesn't do anything to change our current situation."

Oh, but you're sooooo wrong, my naïve little CC. You have no idea how much more danger we're in now. If I'm right and you're wrong, they'll kill us even after they get their money.

Learning that Davitos was Mauricio's cousin was like a final piece of a puzzle falling into place. Kyle had wondered from the beginning how two men who'd been so sloppy in their execution had managed to always remain one step of him and Cynthia. And it had all been about reconnaissance, information. Like knowing to wait for them at AnimalE, and hoping that Kyle just might do something stupid and screw up on his own, thereby making posing as Federales all the more convincing.

The most damning piece of evidence against Mauricio in Kyle's mind was something that would never hold up in a court of law if Kyle were lucky enough to live through this and try to implicate Mauricio. And that was something Cobo had said back in the desert, back when Kyle had been standing in his own grave: *Welcome to the Wild West, amigo.*

Cynthia would never understand. She was too benevolent, and trusting. She would never know the kind of intricate web that had been woven. But Kyle knew. He knew the truth.

Cobo and Davitos came back inside, both looking troubled. Cobo stopped at the inner doorway, his gaze fixed on the floor. He appeared to be staring at nothing in particular; the gears of his mind must have been turning. To Kyle he looked like he was on the cusp of violent action, as if at any moment he might start reaching for objects to hurl at the wall. But instead, he looked at Kyle and in a very collected voice said, "You come with me again."

Kyle felt Cynthia tense up beside him, and knew she was about to object. They had only just been reunited. Before she could say anything, he took her in a fierce hug, and pressed his mouth against her right ear. "Whatever you do," he whispered at decibels that barely registered. "*Do not* let on that we know Davitos. They'll kill us for sure."

Cobo reached over and grabbed Kyle's collar. Kyle quickly complied, and was up and moving in step with Cobo before the brute had a chance to get nasty. Kyle stole another glance at Cynthia's pained expression as he was dragged out again. Back outside in the afternoon sun, he passed Davitos, who was on his way back in.

It was more apparent now, the resemblance between this man and that wide-eyed boy from all those years ago. Kyle kept his head down and lowered his eyes. The danger to their lives just kept increasing. He needed to start coming up with some kind of plan right now.

* * *

Davitos came back into the small room to monitor Cynthia once again. And once again he tried to shield his preoccupations from her with silence and an unreadable expression. But whatever Cobo had said to him was troubling him; that much was apparent to her.

She hadn't had the courage to tell Kyle that she'd already revealed to Davitos that she knew his identity. She hadn't been thinking when she'd made that declaration to her young captor. *I really screwed up.*

She saw things from Kyle's perspective. It was bad enough that they'd both seen Cobo's and Davitos' faces, but now she'd let it slip that they had more information about their mysterious captors than merely the ability to identify them. Kyle would be furious.

Davitos took his seat, set a water jug down at his feet, and kept his eyes on her. He looked visibly conflicted as he reached for the breast pocket of his Federale vest and thumbed open the snaps. She held her breath as he reached inside the pocket; she worried about what he might be retrieving. But when his hand came up, all he had in it was a Snickers bar, which he slowly unwrapped halfway and handed to Cynthia.

She didn't want to accept it. He could've done something to it. But she hadn't eaten in over a day, and her hunger got the better of her. She took the candy bar and broke it in two, wolfing down the large piece that she'd freed from the wrapper. She kept the other piece for Kyle, hoping that Davitos wouldn't object. He didn't. Instead, he handed her the water jug and allowed her to drink all that she wanted. As she drank, he kept staring at her, a despondent look in his eyes.

She was no expert on reading human expression, but what she saw now was a look that gave her gooseflesh. Davitos was looking at her like a prison guard might look at a death-row inmate as he was served his last meal.

* * *

Cobo led Kyle, not back to the van, but about a quarter of a mile west of the hut. They approached a gradual slope adjacent to the dirt road that led in to this place. It was near the rusted remains of an old pickup truck that no longer had wheels on its axels. "Sit," directed Cobo.

Kyle sat down on the edge of a smooth boulder, and Cobo sat on the bed of the truck opposite him. Cobo had with him a plastic bottle of water, and he tried to hand it to Kyle. Kyle, wary of the offer, refused. "Think about it," Cobo said. "If I really want to hurt you . . ." He used his thumb and index finger to mime a pistol with his right hand, and pointed right at Kyle's head.

Kyle took the bottle of water and unscrewed the cap. He drained the entire bottle before Cobo had an opportunity to object. He hadn't realized how dry his palate and throat had been, how dehydrated he was overall, until this moment. He tossed the empty bottle aside.

Cobo looked mildly amused. "Now we wait."

"What for?"

"To call your brother."

"You said we weren't going to call him until tonight," Kyle said with alarm. He looked up in the blue cloudless sky, to the sun. On this August afternoon it couldn't have been any later than four or five o'clock, but here they were waiting to contact Kyp before he'd barely had a chance to process what was going on, much less gather the money together. "I told you before. You need to listen to me. He needs more time."

"We give him time," Cobo insisted. "But I don't want you anywhere near her," he said as he nodded back at the shelter. "No funny ideas."

"I think you made your point back before we went into town," said Kyle, annoyed that Cobo thought he'd failed to grasp how seriously escape attempts would be taken.

Cobo shrugged. "This will give us time to talk." He ran his hand over his shiny bald head, which was damp in the desert heat. "Ay, muy calor."

"Talk about what?"

"Details, Señor Conway. We talk about the details."

* * *

Cynthia knew she'd spoken out of turn, and may have earned herself and Kyle a death sentence in the process. But it was too late to backpedal now, and she was determined to use any means at her disposal to guarantee their safety. Previous attempts to appeal to any morality Davitos possessed had failed miserably, but perhaps it wasn't a lost cause now that she knew about the history she shared with the man: part of her suspected that she'd been chipping away at the walls he put up every time she interacted with him in Cobo's absence.

"Why are you doing this, Davitos?" He flinched at the mention of his name, the first time it had been spoken aloud in his presence. "We took you in. Maybe not into our homes, but we gave you and your family members a better shot at life. How can you do this to us? We were so good to you. I'm sorry you and your cousins got deported, but we had nothing to do with that. Kyle and I have never been handed anything in our lives. We've worked hard for everything we have. My God, I even care for Mauricio's children, *your* cousins, when he and his wife aren't around. They're best friends with my sons. Doesn't that mean anything to you? How are we the bad guys?"

Davitos remained motionless, but she took note of the way in which his chest was rising and falling with more rapid breaths. Was she getting through to him?

The emotional outpouring that had characterized the beginning stages of her captivity had abated. Part of her was calm and at peace. She put her fate in God's hands. "I just want to see them again. I'm afraid that I'm going to die in this place without ever telling them that I love them one last time."

He glanced over his shoulder as if he hoped that Cobo would return soon and spare him from Cynthia's outpouring. But Cobo didn't return, and she pressed on. "Maybe you think that one day you'll have built a better life for yourself with the money you've stolen from us. Maybe that you'll have your own family, and everything you ever wanted. And that maybe I'll be dead." She paused, gazing into his eyes, which he tried to turn away, and drove it home. "But I think that deep down, you're really a good person, and you'd live out the rest of your days haunted by nightmares about the things you might do. And then none of this will have been worth it."

* * *

"Look, you're only real hope is that he's able to take out a cashier's check," said Kyle. He knew he was making sense to Cobo on some level. Cobo hadn't thought his master plan through, and now he had the threat of death looming over him in the form of a cartel lieutenant.

But Cobo questioned this rationale. "A check? You must think I'm really stupid, gringo."

Damnit! "No, that's not it at all. But the bank is open for only half a day tomorrow, and it'll be closed on Sunday. They'll never let Kyp walk out of there with that much cash on hand." He leaned toward Cobo. "This is the reality."

Sarcasm from Cobo now. "So I take his check and go cash it at the bank? Just like that. And then you're on your way. No one will ever be able to come track me down."

"That's not what I'm suggesting. He can make out the check to some dummy business. It won't easily be traceable, and even so my country doesn't have the time or resources to follow through on something like that." Part reality, part bluff. Kyle wasn't sure if there was truth to anything he was saying, but he was one-hundred percent certain that Kyp would never be able to come up with the kind of cash being asked for without raising the alarm somewhere.

"Dummy business?" Cobo asked, and Kyle suspected the question was sincere.

"Yeah, like a front. Y'know. Any business your organization uses to launder money from. I'm sure your boss, the *Jefe*, has plenty of—"

Cobo swung his arm and backhanded Kyle for the second time, this time on the mouth. Kyle sagged off his stone perch and hit the dirt, reaching up to his now split lip. "You don't say his name!" Cobo shouted with an equal mix of outrage and fear.

Kyle lay there, stunned, and reminding himself to choose his words carefully. "Okay," he panted through rapid breaths. The blood was trickling through his fingers. "But you've got to realize that you're asking for the impossible. There's no way Kyp will ever be able to produce the kind of cash you're asking for."

Cobo stood up and walked away from Kyle, deep in thought. He walked west, away from the shelter, and stopped about fifteen feet away. The late afternoon sun was bright behind him. He turned around to face Kyle. "No checks," he said with finality. "No money orders. No

ATM. He has until Sunday morning to bring me $1,100,000 cash, or you and your wife both die."

*   *   *

Cynthia had been hoping for some indication of compassion from Davitos. His escorting her outside to a wretched outhouse and then walking away to provide her with privacy was not a pleasant experience, but at least it showed understanding and humanity on his part. When they returned to the concrete shack, her continued entreaties to Davitos became more about reassuring herself than appealing to him. As she moved forward with her narrative on how closely her life was intertwined with Mexican immigrants and culture, she found herself reflecting on what circumstances had caused her to arrive at this critical juncture.

One day a man decides to uproot his life and risk everything by coming to a land with abundant opportunity, only to find himself rejected soon thereafter. And then later down the road he finds the strength within himself to snatch away the livelihoods of two people who at one time embodied that opportunity, but now only serve to represent the rejection.

Such a vast discrepancy between wealth and poverty. Between security and instability. Liberty through determined effort or hopeless corruption. Not to say that everyone living down here was crooked and destitute. And not to say that Americans weren't often corrupt and living with an overabundance of material wealth. But it was strange, that line that cut across North America, polarizing two different peoples. The reason why so many Mexicans turned their sights north for a more meaningful existence, and why Americans turned theirs south for an escape into celebration and sin.

And oh, the symbiosis of it. Americans getting high off of cocaine and marijuana, not ever once questioning where it all might have come from and who might have died for it. Complaining about the meager wages of their faltering careers, or about the high-paying jobs that were disappearing overseas.

Meanwhile Mexicans harvested Yankee crops and scrubbed their toilets for five dollars and hour, keeping America's true infrastructure intact. And they rarely complained. Mexicans took it all with smiles on their faces, sending their meager wages back home to their families, while Americans stressed over the prices of the nursing homes they were about to place their parents in, or what private schools to send their children to.

That indifference changed only after one stepped onto Mexican turf at a time when a crisis such as this one had become commonplace. It wasn't that much of a stretch for Cynthia to see, from Cobo and Davitos' point of view, the justification in what they were doing. She recognized a certain leveling of the playing field, a bringing of incongruity into balance. *Once the line is drawn, be careful which side you find yourself on.*

"I got pregnant right before Mauricio's wife did," she continued. She was speaking to herself as much as she was to him. "I remember how happy I was when I first found out. I was going to be a mommy. It's what I'd always wanted." She began to smile to herself for the first time since her capture. "Kyle and I went to work on the baby's room right away. We'd never been such a team like that before, with his passion for building and my love of kids. Those were the early days of our marriage when everything was still perfect."

Her face fell a little, and she took on a melancholy expression. "But I lost the baby late in the second trimester. It was devastating. But what was even worse was that the doctors were unsure if I'd ever be able to get pregnant again. The loss, followed by the uncertainty, broke my heart. I became very distant in those first few days. Kyle was there for me, as loving and supportive as can be, but we both grieved in different ways. And when he saw that he wasn't reaching me, he pulled back and poured himself back into his work. We stopped talking about the situation after a while. But I remember . . . I remember right after Lorena announced that she was pregnant, the pain it caused me to hear that, like an old wound being torn open again. And I was happy for her, I really was, but there was one night . . . there was one night when Kyle was busy on another job, and I was home feeling sorry for myself. I remember thinking to myself that I would never be able to start my own family, and I broke down crying and curled up into bed. And even if Kyle had been there, there was such rift between us at the time because of the different ways we dealt with it, I don't even think he could've made me feel better then. So I just cried and cried. And then . . . then our maid," she looked right at him, "your other cousin, Angelica, came into the bedroom to ask for permission to leave for the evening. I was a mess, and wasn't too responsive to what was going on around me. But when she saw me like that, saw how much pain I was in, she did something I never would have expected. She crawled into bed with me and wrapped her arms around me, rocking me gently and repeating, 'Todo va a salir bien.' Everything's going to be okay.

"I can't begin to tell you how much better that made me feel. That this person who I hardly knew would extend such kindness to me. And I was so grateful to that sweet woman. So grateful."

Her eyes misted up again, but no tears fell. "And then, soon after that, she was deported. Probably along with you. I never really truly thanked her for what she did. Never really treated her like an equal after that. I went on living, got pregnant again, and she went back to being my maid. Everything went back to normal. Until immigration caught up with her.

"I was good to her while she was here. But I didn't raise a finger when they threatened deportation. I didn't fight on her behalf. I just went and got myself another maid. And looking back, who knows whether I really could have made a difference in the outcome. I was just another privileged *guera* who had no say in such matters. But I could have tried. I could have fought for her."

As if taking the broader view by dropping some unwanted platitude on Davitos in order to bring her cathartic anecdote to a conclusion, she said, "I don't know why we do the things that we do to each other, Davitos." And she didn't look to him for any kind of reaction or response. She pulled her knees up to her chest once more, and hid her face in her arms.

After a minute she heard Davitos abruptly stand up from his chair. She looked up at him, and he looked back for only a second. He walked through the doorway and across the other room. She peeked around the corner as he opened the door on the far wall and stepped through it, looking out to the west. She could see by orange tint in the blue of the sky that it was late afternoon. He turned around and saw her watching him, and then he shut the door and locked it.

* * *

"Showtime," said Cobo. Kyle was still sitting on the ground, slumped up against the stone, and Cobo reached out to grab him by his arm. Maybe Cobo thought that Kyle had grown a little too comfortable in this conversational posture the two of them had taken. He wanted to remind Kyle that in the here and now, even with Kyle offering advice on how to make this work, they were not equals.

After pulling Kyle erect, Cobo reached into a backpack that was sitting on the ground alongside his assault rifle, and retrieved what looked like a two-way radio. It was boxy and black with a long plastic antenna. He flipped it open, and Kyle realized that it was some kind industrial grade cell phone, maybe military. Cobo went about punching in a phone number, and waited for ringing on the other end.

Was this it? The moment where Cobo dictated the time and the place of the drop? Kyle thought that Cobo must've memorized the number earlier before he'd broken his own phone in half. Why drag Kyle into town when they had a reception here then? So that Kyp might recognize Kyle's number and answer? So that Kyle's calling in might legitimize how very real the situation was?

Kyle couldn't hear if anyone on the other end answered, but then without preamble he heard Cobo say, "We have your family." Then silence as Cobo listened. He held out the phone to Kyle. "He wants to talk to you."

With a shaking hand Kyle reached out and took the phone from Cobo. "Kyp?"

"Kyle, are you alright? Is Cynthia?" Kyle had never remembered his kid brother sounding so frantic. If he had indeed kept the earlier phone call to himself for all these hours . . . Kyle couldn't imagine what a tremendous burden that must have been.

Then again, maybe the police, or the FBI, were listening in. Maybe they were triangulating his position as they spoke, and at any moment a helicopter would come racing in overhead. *Wishful thinking.* "We're fine, Kyp. Both of us. Now listen—"

Cobo reached over and grabbed the phone out of Kyle's hand. "So now you know they're okay. Now we talk about—what? No, you listen to me, *puto*! I do the talking. ¿Comprende? Here's how it will happen.

At eight o'clock on Sunday morning you drive into Tijuana with the cash in your trunk. La policia will pull you over and search your car. When this happens you look across the street, and we'll let your brother and his wife out of the car. If we see anything, or anyone, we don't like, then we kill them right then and there. No second chances. Now tell me, do you understand?"

More silence while Kyp talked on the other end. "No, we'll know who you are. And we'll know where to stop you. This is a simple plan; very hard for you to make mistakes." He waited. "No, we keep them safe for the weekend. Give you another day to think twice about doing something stupid. No, that's it. A million plus one hundred thousand cash. Tijuana. Sunday morning. Eight o'clock." And then he ended the call.

He should have looked at least a little triumphant, but he didn't. He looked preoccupied. Not paying the least bit of attention to Kyle, he picked up his backpack and put the phone away. He put his arms through the straps and then picked up the rifle. He cradled it in his arms for a moment, admiring the steel craftsmanship, and then walked toward the van. Kyle wondered if Cobo had forgotten about him completely. The man's back was turned as he walked at a relaxed pace toward the van.

"It's all bullshit, isn't it?" he called to Cobo, trying to keep the fear out of his voice.

Cobo turned to face him, looking perplexed. "What is?"

Kyle's swallowed. "You're not going to let us go, are you? You never were."

Cobo stared back at Kyle with that same confused look, a deep frown underneath his handlebar mustache. He stared long and hard, across the desert sand, but said nothing. He turned his back on Kyle once again and resumed his walk to the van.

Kyle hadn't expected an answer. That's not why he had even asked. In the twenty-four hours since Cobo had turned his life upside down, he'd learned a few things about their aspiring cartel border lord. And one thing he'd learned was that the man had no poker-face. And the expression on Cobo's face when Kyle had asked him the question had told Kyle everything he needed to know. He fought down the urge to vomit. No, they weren't going to let them go. They had never intended to.

He brought a fist up to his mouth and leaned against the stone chimney for support. When he looked back at the shelter, where Cynthia was, he saw Davitos standing just outside the door, watching him.

* * *

Cobo brought Kyle back inside and sat him down on the couch. Cynthia immediately noticed his split, fat lip. "He hit you again?" she whispered.

"He's wound up pretty tight," Kyle said quietly. "Just sit here and don't say anything. I have no idea what might set him off." Cynthia watched Cobo pacing around inside the building in a state of agitation. Kyle's assessment seemed accurate. The man was on edge, and she imagined this had everything to do with events having unfolded in unforeseen ways. Things weren't exactly going according to his plan.

She hated being left in the dark. Kyle was the one was being used as liaison. She could only sit here and wait, desperately waiting for some words of hope from Kyle. "Did you talk to Kyp?"

"Only for a second," he replied, the pain in his mouth evident. He looked into the next room to make sure Cobo and Davitos weren't listening. "Cobo did most of the talking." He glanced in Cobo's direction again. "This isn't playing out the way he thought it would. He wants Kyp to come down to TJ on Sunday morning and make a drop of $1,100,000. Then he said he would let us go."

She was afraid to ask, and it took her a moment to get the words out. "Do you believe him?"

When Kyle didn't answer, the fear resurfaced. She knew he didn't really want to tell her what was on his mind, but there was little he could do to hide his own misgivings. It was evident in his eyes. "It was supposed to happen tomorrow. But Cobo gave him another day to get the cash together."

"Can Kyp even get that kind of money together? Wasn't it all deposited into the business account?"

"Kyp will figure something out," he replied, but now he wasn't able to meet her eyes. He had no confidence that what was coming would be an even exchange.

Short of another escape attempt, they were both utterly powerless to change their situation. They could only come along, praying every second that something didn't go terribly wrong. And then they just might be killed outright anyway. Why would Cobo want to leave any loose ends? There was nothing to stop him from executing them both the minute he had the money in his hands. And she didn't kid herself into thinking that the cavalry would be shadowing Kyp, just out of sight and ready to ready to make its move. That was just as likely to get her and Kyle killed as well.

And yet, although she was unable to explain it, she was more at peace with the possibility of impending doom than when she'd first been thrown in the van. It had only been a little over twenty-four hours, but she was just too exhausted, both in her body and in her soul. The fear had diminished. Whatever was going happen would happen. She couldn't change that.

Lost in thought, contemplating that these might be her last hours on Earth, she almost failed to notice Kyle listening intently to Cobo. He was talking quietly in the other room, and perhaps he still assumed that Kyle's Spanish wasn't proficient enough for translation.

"Tengo que hablar con el jefe," Cobo told Davitos. "Es necesario que te quedes aquí y mantenga un ojo sobre ellos." She heard the jingling of metal pieces clanging together. "Esposalos."

Kyle looked at her, and she mouthed the words *What's going on?* Kyle pressed his swollen lip to her ear and said, "He's leaving to go talk to their boss. He was supposed to have been rid of us by tomorrow. I think he needs to vie for more time."

Before she could respond, Cobo appeared in the doorway, Davitos lurking just behind him. Cobo stood there staring at them for a moment, the look on his face suggesting that he blamed them both for this unfortunate setback. He certainly wasn't optimistic about the coming meeting with his overlord. He looked apprehensive.

With his right hand he pulled his sidearm once more and pointed it right at Cynthia's head. Instinctively she closed her eyes and tensed up, letting out a whimper. Then she felt Kyle jump on top of her, folding her head in his arms, shielding her body with his own. "Stop it!" he shouted. "Stop pointing that fucking gun at my wife!"

They were wrapped together tightly, but she peeked out under his arm against her will. The gun was still there, but Cobo made no move. He just stood there, arm extended, the glock an extension of it. She could see how stressed out he was. His face was flushed and the veins in his thick neck were bulging. She closed her eyes again and prayed that this wasn't really the end.

No shot was fired. She looked again and saw him holster the pistol. He turned to Davitos, handed him two sets of cuffs, and repeated, "Esposalos junto." Davitos stepped forward and reached for Kyle's hands, which were still clasped together at the crown of Cynthia's head.

Kyle resisted as Davitos tried to pry his arms from Cynthia, and she said, "It's okay, Kyle. Just let go." Kyle didn't seem convinced, but his arms slackened as Davitos brought both of his hands behind him to slap the cuffs on. Cobo watched it all intently as Davitos did the same with Cynthia, first her left wrist, which he tugged on so that he could wrap the chain-link around the one that bound Kyle's hands, and then her left wrist. Still sitting on the worn-out couch, she and Kyle were now locked back-to-back.

"Me dan un par de horas," Cobo told Davitos. Then he turned around and walked out the outer door, slamming it shut behind him. She could turn her head just enough to see Davitos return to the window, and peek out through the cracks. She then heard the revving of an engine, presumably the van's, and then rocks and sand being kicked up as tires peeled. The sound of the engine grew faint, and then was gone entirely.

Davitos remained fixed at the window for another minute, watching the desert beyond. Then he turned and hurried out of the room, leaving the shack and locking the door behind him.

"What's happening?" she said over her shoulder to Kyle.

"I don't know," he responded with more curiosity than apprehension. "Listen," he said abruptly. "It's just Davitos now. I say if we have a chance, then we take it."

"How? We're totally restricted like this."

"I don't know, but if these cuffs come off for even a second, then I say we move on him. He's just a runt anyway. Together we can take him."

She hoped his mind wasn't made up. "We can't risk it," she said doubtfully.

"Cynthia, they're going to kill us. I saw it in his eyes out there. We need to fight back."

He was making sense, but she still stalled for time. "Just don't do anything until we have a plan. We need a plan."

"If I see an opening, I'm going for it," he said defiantly. He'd had enough.

They sat there in silence, and she wondered where Davitos had wandered off to. After a while they heard an approaching vehicle, and she grew anxious. If Cobo came back and found them left alone, then who knew what he would do. She didn't want to be alone with Cobo. The man's growing state of agitation was unnerving. Not that Davitos had been protecting them; he'd been silently following Cobo's lead from the very beginning. But there was something about the smaller man's presence that made her feel just slightly safer when Cobo was around. *Good cop, bad cop,* she thought.

The vehicle came to a stop just outside the window and was left with the engine still running. The sound of a lock being unlatched followed, and then the outer door flew open as Davitos came back in at a hurried pace. He came toward them both, and she saw that he'd shed his Federale's bullet proof vest and uniform in favor of a simple white T-shirt and jeans.

Davitos looked at them both, then just at Kyle, and she could sense Kyle looking back the man with defiance. Davitos must have sensed Kyle's intentions, for he drew the shiny Colt revolver from his waist and held it up to his chest for Kyle to see.

She had a strange feeling in her gut, and she wanted Kyle to abandon his plan to revolt. She also sensed that Davitos was now on to Kyle, and that he had no intention of slipping up even for a second.

Davitos tucked the Colt into his jeans, and then approached the Conways carefully. He took one of their arms in each hand and gently eased them up off of the couch. He slowly nudged them toward the inner door and led them into the outer room, and then through the door to the outside. Walking was a challenge in their precarious position, but they took small steps, unsure of Davitos' intentions. He kept a safe distance; he wasn't taking any chances. He must have read Kyle's violent intent from the moment he'd returned.

But he was also trying to make haste, and he pointed to an old gray Volkswagon station wagon that was waiting for them just around the corner. Kyle froze as if he imagined the end if he got into that car. But Cynthia wanted to believe, *needed* to believe, that this was the right move. "C'mon, let's get in," she said.

He didn't respond, and his feet remained planted. She turned her body as much as she could before it became too painful so that she could look at him. "Baby, we have to get in. You have to trust me."

A look of confusion washed over his features, as if trusting her had never factored in to the equation. He must have wondered what she was thinking that she would suggest that they willingly take another ride. "This is our chance," she said with conviction. "We need to take it."

It might have been dawning on him just what she was suggesting. He looked at her, and then at Davitos a few feet away, and then must have decided that he would take a chance on her intuition. He took a step toward the waiting car.

Davitos followed them both to the station wagon and then put a hand up to Kyle's chest before he could get in. He had the keys to the cuffs in his hand, and he freed one of Cynthia's wrists so that he could undo the criss-cross fashion of their entanglement. When she and Kyle were unhooked, he sat her down on in the back passenger seat, cuffing her to the handle just above the window of the interior. He then led Kyle around the car and did the same for him, watching Kyle intently the whole time. When Kyle and Cynthia were both settled in, he got behind the wheel and peeled out onto the dirt road that had led them in here when they'd first arrived. Cynthia sat behind him and Kyle's movements were restricted by the passenger side handle so that he was just out of the reach of Davitos.

They drove north on the open road for many miles. The only scenery to behold was the vast desert painted in vivid earth tones in the late afternoon sun. No one said anything as Kyle and Cynthia both wondered what their destination might be.

Eventually they came upon another turnoff, another dirt path, and Davitos took a wide right turn as he exited the paved highway and sent the car bulleting down the path. This time they drove up on what appeared to be mechanic's junkyard, with two buildings facing each other: a simple one-story auto shop and a wide, open garage that may or may not have once been used as an airplane hangar. Davitos drove into the garage and threw the car in park, climbing out of it and disappearing just out of sight around the corner.

Cynthia turned to Kyle. "He didn't blindfold us this time. Is that bad?"

Not if his intention is to take us back to those pre-dug graves and put a bullet in each of our heads. "I don't know. It could mean anything."

They continued to sit alone with their individual thoughts on what might happen. She wanted so desperately to believe that this was all just a turning point that Cobo never could have foreseen, that she'd broken through Davitos' shell. Kyle continued to play the odds of their survival in his head, and those odds continued to remain unfavorable.

Davitos startled them both when he returned a few minutes later and threw open the hatchback on the station wagon. Kyle craned his neck to see what he was up to. First their backpacks, which had been absent since the car-switch after their arrest, were carelessly tossed into the back. Then six plastic gallon jugs were placed alongside the backpacks, still dripping from a recent refill. Davitos covered it all with a black plastic tarp, and then slammed the hatchback closed. He returned to the driver's seat, threw the car in reverse, and backed the wagon back out into the fading sunlight.

As they peeled out once again, Kyle stole a glance over his shoulder. The whole yard was completely devoid of any human activity, not necessarily abandoned, but definitely unmanned for the moment. The only movement whatsoever that was discernible was the last few drops of water escaping a well's spigot, probably the same one Davitos had used to refill the water jugs. Kyle wondered what it all meant.

Northbound again. Then slightly northeast as the highway took on a slight curve. When they came upon a four-way intersection Davitos turned right and took the car east for another half-hour. As the wagon barreled along the highway, Kyle tried to deduce where they might be geographically. When they'd first been taken they'd headed south for quite some time before they'd both been blindfolded. There was no telling where they'd been transported after that, but his gut told him they'd traveled significantly southeast into the heart of the desert, away from the Baja peninsula. Now they'd made some ground heading back north, back toward the border, but he hadn't a clue what might lie to the east.

Eventually they entered another unmarked, unpaved dirt road much like the previous ones he and Cynthia were reluctantly becoming accustomed to. As Davitos banked the car left and plunged further into the unknown, Kyle noticed that the topography was getting hillier, more mountainous. The road became bumpier yet again, and from time to time he reached out for Cynthia's hand to see how she was holding up. She seemed more relaxed to his touch, more at peace with the immediate future, for better or for worse.

The road began to wind and incline as it sloped upwards toward a distant mountain range. After a while the road narrowed so much that travel by car was highly problematic. This old wagon they were riding in had never been meant to handle such rugged terrain; the tremendous strain of the journey was taking its toll on the wheels and the engine both, and Kyle feared that they might have a blowout before they reached wherever it was they were going. It never came to that: after proceeding with great care, when the road opened up into a wide clearing, Davitos hit the brakes.

Getting out of the wagon, he went around to the back and unpacked their gear before attending to the both of them. He unchained them from the back seat, keeping his revolver handy when it was Kyle's turn.

They stepped out of the car into the rays of the setting sun. Twilight was upon them, and Kyle looked northward to the twin mountains that were staring back at him, and then to the open canyon that cut between them. If this really was what he thought it was, what he hadn't dared to dream it was, then this was a very foolish time to set out on such a journey. But what else could be done? If indeed Davitos had decided to help them, they were now racing against a ticking clock, and weren't afforded the luxury of traveling in the daylight hours.

With his gun still in hand, Davitos took a few steps and backed away from Kyle and Cynthia, his eyes on them all the while. They both stared back at him, doubt tormenting them yet again. Perhaps they weren't out of this just yet. Perhaps Cynthia's faith in the man's greater good had been misplaced.

He stared at them both for a minute, not moving. His gaze seemed to hold a challenge, as if to say to the both of them: *So here we are. Now let's see how much we'll allow ourselves to trust one another.* He then tossed the keys to the handcuffs at Cynthia's feet. She had still been rubbing her sore free wrist where the steel had been biting into it, and her eyes went wide with disbelief when she looked down and saw the keys sitting there in the dirt. She looked over at Kyle for some kind of reassurance.

He didn't waste even a moment. "Pick them up," he commanded her. She slowly bent down on one knee and reached out for the tiny key ring. She fumbled with them for only a minute, and then was finally able to unclasp the second cuff, a feeling of previously unknown liberation washing over her as the pair of cuffs clinked to the ground at her feet. She took a quick stride over to Kyle to assist him with his cuffs.

Davitos, apparently convinced that they were starting to see the larger picture, went to work on their backpacks. He started to strip the packs of things they wouldn't need: semi-formal dinner wear, bathing suits, extra pairs of shoes, Cynthia's cosmetics, unnecessary toiletries, books, anything that didn't serve them on their coming journey. He piled it all in the back of the station wagon. Kyle and Cynthia simply watched, letting him work. He had his own simple black backpack, not a hiker's pack like theirs, and he stuffed one of the gallons of water into it. He did likewise with theirs, taking up the space that had only a moment ago been freed. He also folded and packed the black tarp into one of his backpack's side compartments.

Cynthia noticed that Davitos seemed more sure of himself in acting on his own, more efficient at completing the immediate task at hand without his burly partner looking over his shoulder and waiting for him to make a mistake. She couldn't imagine Cobo doing anything but killing Davitos outright if he ever caught up with them. For now, though, Davitos seemed at ease with doing what needed to be done.

Even without having spoken, he must have assumed that by now she and Kyle understood what he intended, and would think twice about trying to get the upper hand on him. He was now no longer their abductor, but their guide out of here, and he was probably gambling on the fact that they recognized how instrumental a part he would play in their regaining freedom. After all, if they hurt or killed him, then they were on their own, and good luck to them finding safe passage back into the states. It was growing darker by the minute.

When the old Volkswagon was loaded up with their excesses, he closed the hatchback once again and turned to face them. He picked up his backpack off the ground and ran both arms through the straps. He picked up his extra gallon of water and held it firmly in his left hand, nodding to the packs at their feet and the extra gallon of water each. He wanted them to follow suit, and they obliged him.

They stood there for a moment, facing each other and unmoving. Davitos' eyes scanned the ground for any refuse, any evidence of their passage. There was none. He'd retrieved both sets of handcuffs, and the only remaining testament to their presence here was tire tracks and the run-down station wagon. He eyed the gray car with a look of uncertainty, perhaps uncomfortable with the prospect of leaving such an obvious trail to follow. To Cynthia his furrowed brow made him look like he was in the midst of deciding something crucial, when something in the distance to the right caught her eye. The familiar tremor crept back into her voice when she announced, "There's a car coming."

Kyle and Davitos looked where she was pointing. To the south they could both see an approaching car's high beams bouncing as it ascended the slope that had taken them here. They were distant still, but growing larger by the moment. The car, and whoever was in it, would be upon them soon. Cynthia didn't take her eyes of this impending danger, but instinctively reached out and grabbed for Kyle's arm.

Davitos, who either didn't believe in coincidences or knew exactly who was coming, began to gesticulate wildly, waving his hand toward a hill just a few hundred yards away. His intent was clear enough. He wanted them to run and hide. Kyle didn't waste a single breath debating him. He clutched Cynthia's free hand and practically pulled her off of her feet, leading her toward the hill.

They started toward the hill at a dead run, and then something dawned on Kyle. He turned around and took off his backpack. Cynthia, in panic mode, said, "What are you doing?"

"Here, hold this," he commanded her as he handed over his gallon of water. "Got to cover our tracks." He looked to Davitos to see if he objected, but Davitos hadn't started to follow them. Instead he headed back to the station wagon, his backpack still on. He threw his gallon of water on the floorboards and then turned the engine over. Kyle had no idea what Davitos intended, but he had absolutely no time to think it over. Returning to their point of origin, he dropped his pack on the ground and used it to rake the earth in order to wipe away their footprints. He continued to do this as he backed away hunched over, not nearly fast enough to feel confident in what he was doing.

Back and forth he moved the pack, and his actions had the desired effect. He was covering their tracks, but it was slow going, and over his shoulder he heard Cynthia say, "C'mon, c'mon. They'll be here soon. We have to run for it."

"We'll never make it on foot. We have to hide."

Cynthia remained a few paces behind his back, moving toward the hill in a straight line so that Kyle could do his job more efficiently. But she kept looking toward the approaching headlights as they scanned the incline. She knew what Kyle was doing might save them both, but still she wanted to grab him by his collar and flee for the hill at a sprint. She looked over her shoulder at the hill. They were almost there. Almost.

Neither of them knew exactly what Davitos was doing, but they both grew confused as he hit the gas and picked up speed, pushing the wagon toward the edge of the clearing. He started cutting the wheel and spinning the car in erratic three-sixties. Cynthia bit her lower lip as she watched.

She and Kyle reached the hill and climbed over the crest. He was practically on all fours as he covered the last of their tracks. They both got down on their bellies, nestled in between two thick, bushy ocotillo plants. Kyle urged his wife to keep her head down as he carefully studied the area. There was nowhere left to run to, and no time. If they were discovered here, they were dead.

When he looked over the top of the hill, he watched, dumbfounded, as Davitos continued wildly to cut donuts into the dusty ground. Kyle wondered if perhaps Davitos had finally lost it in his panic, but then it dawned on him what the man was doing. The station wagon fish-tailed here and there as the tires lost purchase on the ground and Davitos struggled for control. However, his intentions were clear to Kyle now. He was using *the car* to cover their tracks, kicking up the desert sand that had their footprints all over it.

Just as this was dawning on Kyle, Davitos did something else very odd. He stopped cutting the wheel left and right and hit the brakes. He backed the car up toward their hiding place, and then threw it in drive and pressed down on the gas. Kyle watched, wide eyed, as Davitos gunned the car away from them, to the northeast, toward a hilly slope similar to the one they were hiding on now. The station wagon continued to pick up speed as it advanced on the rocky slope. Kyle was still wondering what Davitos could possibly be thinking as the wagon jumped up onto the hill, bounced fiercely, and then disappeared over the rise. He both felt and heard the terrible shriek of steel grinding against stone as yet another dust cloud shot up into the air at the top of the hill opposite them. There was the unmistakable rumbling of the station wagon as gravity tossed it end over end, until the sound gradually faded, and then ceased altogether. It must have been a long, steep drop on the other side.

"What just happened?" Cynthia asked with her head still down, looking up at Kyle.

It took a moment for Kyle to find his voice. "I have no idea."

The dust cloud actually had a chance to settle before the incoming car reached them. For as quickly as the three of them had sprung into action since Cynthia had first noticed the high beams, they'd gotten settled into their hiding spot with plenty of time to spare. They waited for close to five minutes before Kyle, relying on the car's own lights, was finally able to discern its make and model. It was a navy-blue Crown Victoria, sleek and streamlined, with a shiny exterior that seemed to repel the dust from the blustery desert air. It was a newer model, at least from the last ten years. It came to a stop at the end of the road within a few feet of where the Volkswagon had been parked only a few minutes before. The driver didn't kill the engine, but all four doors opened simultaneously, and out came four men.

Kyle lowered his head to Cynthia's level, out of sight. When she looked at him he put his index finger to his lips. He was worried their voices might carry in the open desert. He risked peeking from the hill once more. He didn't want to be any more exposed than they absolutely had to be, but they were in an extremely vulnerable position and couldn't afford to be caught unaware. At least if he saw them coming they could make a run for it.

He took a look. One of the men was Cobo for sure, and he appeared every bit as agitated as he had before, but this time it was more in a subservient sort of way. Sure enough, one of the other men was *El Jefe*. He had the same shadowy outline as he had earlier this morning, and he made the most minimal of movements as the three other men spread out and surveyed their surroundings. The high beams of the Crown Vic lit up the clearing, but Kyle noticed that only one of the other men had a flashlight. And only *El Jefe* wasn't visibly armed. He was content to let his henchmen search the immediate area with lethal force.

"[You seemed certain that this was where he'd run to, Cobo]," *El Jefe* said venomously. "[The trail ahead seems impassable by car. He would've had to have left it here.]"

"[Maybe we beat them here]," said Cobo, sounding unconvinced with his own words. Kyle wondered if Cobo had bet everything on the fact this had been Davitos' way out. Now he was arriving with his boss, believing that he had fouled up greatly, when in fact his intuition had been right all along. Kyle prayed that there was nothing left out in the open to mark their recent passage.

El Jefe said nothing, and Kyle watched as the man stared Cobo down for a long time. Just when Kyle suspected that it might all be too much for Cobo, and that he just might drop at *El Jefe's* feet to beg him for forgiveness, one of the other men called to them, "Por aqui."

Kyle looked to where the voice had come from. One of the anonymous cartel men, a medium sized man in a black leather jacket, was standing with a high-powered searchlight atop the hill over which Davitos had taken the station wagon, and was directing a strong beam of light down the other side into whatever lay beyond. His three companions rushed over to join him, and Kyle risked raising his head just little bit higher so that he might hear what was being said.

"[That's it!]" Cobo said excitedly. "[I'm sure of it.] He turned and faced *El Jefe,* hoping that this good fortune might be enough to redeem him in his boss' eyes.

El Jefe wasn't convinced. "[That's it? From way up here, you're sure that upside down wreck is his car?]" It sounded as if he had very little faith in Cobo's testimony. "[Would you bet your life on it?]"

Cobo was persistent. "[Look, see, it's the right color.]"

"[And how, if you're right, can we be sure that they're inside of it?]" *El Jefe* asked as if talking to a child. "[How are you going to confirm that?]"

"[It won't be easy, but I can hike down there]," Cobo pressed, trying to sound as if this was the most logical course of action. "[I can hike down, look inside, and then climb back up.]"

"[That would take a day at least]," *El Jefe* said with diminished patience. "[And you certainly won't be doing it in the dark.]"

"[Then I'll wait until sun up, and then go]."

"[You haven't thought this through, have you? What happens when you get all the way down there, and then their bodies aren't there? Now they've got a full day's head start on you. What then?]"

"[Then we split up. Two of us can stay here, and two of us will follow the trails.]"

El Jefe's voice rose to a shout. "[Will you listen to yourself? Hit the trails with only the stars to guide us? There's about a thousand different ways they can disappear into those foothills, especially under the cover of night. I've already paid off too many people to cover up your mistakes, and now you want me to go slogging through the mountains just to clean up the mess you've made? Tell me something, Cobo. What good are you to me anyway?]" He turned away from Cobo and left the three of them standing there as he headed back for the still running car.

Cobo chased after him, starting to plead as he caught up with him. "[Please, Boss. Please let me make this right. I'll do whatever it takes. Just let me make it right.]"

El Jefe turned and looked long and hard at Cobo, as if noticing something about him he'd never noticed before. When the two other underlings rejoined them, he said, "[I have a better idea.]" He gestured to the thug in the leather jacket, who drew his pistol on Cobo. "[Why don't you get in the trunk.]" As if he'd been awaiting this command, the other man, the driver, casually went over to the car, reached inside and popped open the trunk. Cobo stiffened as the man behind him pressed the barrel of a gun to his head. "[Let's go]," *El Jefe* said to Cobo with finality, nodding toward the waiting trunk.

Cobo, defeated, and out of options, did as he was told. Perhaps he realized that for the moment, at least, he was still alive. With deliberate, mechanical movements, the big bald man who'd brought so much terror into Kyle's and Cynthia's lives climbed into the trunk of the Crown Vic in silence. Just before the driver closed the trunk, *El Jefe* said, "[You brought this on yourself, Cobo]." And then the trunk was slammed shut.

The three men stood there, and then the driver got back into the car. *El Jefe,* who had never been anything more than a shadowy silhouette in headlights to Kyle, took a few steps forward and put his hands on his hips. He stood there for a minute, running his eyes over the mountains to the north. Trying to break the tension in the air, the man who'd put the gun to Cobo's head came up behind *El Jefe* and said, "[I don't really believe that they're down there. If we go after them right now we might still catch up with them. We can—]"

"[No]," *El Jefe* briskly cut him off. "[The mute will turn up. We'll deal with him then. Other than that I'm washing my hands of this whole thing.]" He went to the car and got back inside. The other man went around to the other side and got into the front seat. The Crown Vic backed into a wide turn, reversed direction, and then drove back the way it had come in, back down the winding dirt road.

Kyle watched it go. He slowly exhaled a long held breath. The night had grown quiet, and he lowered his head back down to look at Cynthia. She hadn't dared to speak throughout what had just transpired, and she still wouldn't, as if she was waiting for Kyle to confirm that they were truly gone. He reached a hand up and brushed away a lock of her golden-blonde hair, tucking it behind her ear. He then tenderly cupped her cheek with his hand. "It's okay," he said.

She still wouldn't lift her head to see for herself, as if she was expecting some kind of ruse. "What did they say?"

Kyle wasn't sure he really believed that *El Jefe* was simply going to forget about this whole thing. However, he needed to reassure her, and they needed to get moving if they had any hope of ending this nightmare. "I don't think we're going to be seeing any more of Cobo," he told her. That would have to suffice for now.

He stood up, the action meant to show her that the danger truly had passed, and gave her his hand to take. She looked up at him, and then slowly reached out her hand to let him help her up. He took it and gently raised her to her feet.

They grabbed their plastic jugs of water and then carefully climbed back down the hill and walked into the clearing. "Stay here for a second," he said.

She squeezed his hand tighter. "No," she said with alarm.

"Okay, okay," he said apologetically. "No one's leaving you. We just need to go see what happened. Come with me."

They put their waters down, and he led her by the hand to the hill where Davitos had gone. Together they climbed up to the top and looked down the other side. Kyle hadn't realized what a long drop it was over the craggy hill. The whole landscape dropped off into a heavily vegetated, boulder-strewn canyon that was as wide as it was deep. Neither of them could see the overturned car, not without a flashlight, but having launched over the precipice at the velocity Kyle had noted, it would have plummeted for quite some time before grinding to a halt. There was no way Davitos could have survived.

Just as he processed the thought, the two of them heard a rustling in the bushes to their right. They turned their heads, and Cynthia pressed her body into Kyle's when, amazingly, Davitos rose up into view.

He staggered a few steps forward, obviously dizzy, and then fell to his knees. Cynthia rushed over to him before Kyle could protest. She crouched down so that she and Davitos were face-to-face, and inspected him. Kyle joined them.

Davitos had a gash on the left side of his forehead, and a trickle of blood was running down the side of his face. It was immediately clear to Kyle that Davitos had not remained in the car on the way down. The wounds that he had suffered came from his jumping clear, and that even must have occurred soon after the car had began its plunge.

Cynthia took off her pack and unzipped it. She removed a gallon of water, and then took out one of her tank-tops. She used the water to wet the top, and then she reached out with the cloth to gently dab at the wound and wipe away the blood. Davitos winced, but he didn't object. She went to wet the shirt again, but this time Davitos waved her away. He still had his own pack on, and he unhooked it from his arms and went into it. First he took out a first-aid kid, from which he retrieved some hydrogen peroxide and a clean bandage. He went about cleaning and dressing the wound without Cynthia's assistance.

While he was doing this, Kyle was keeping watch on the road to the south, worried about the possibility, however unlikely, that *El Jefe* and his men might have overlooked something and decided to return. However, there was no more sight of headlights, no more rumbling of an engine.

When Davitos had bandaged his wound, he took the other object in his hand. It was a heavy, black steel Mag lite, and he switched it on as he stood up shakily. Cynthia rose up with him, eyeing him with concern. He shook his head as if to ward off the dizziness.

Kyle looked at him in disbelief. He was awed by the fact that Davitos was still standing here in front of them after pulling such a daft stunt. Davitos looked back at Kyle, and then shined the light over to where he and Cynthia had abandoned their water jugs. He wanted them to go get them.

As Kyle went over to pick up the plastic jugs, he considered the implications of this recent turn of events. They were right back where they had started only a short while ago, ready to hike through the mountainous terrain of northern Mexico in the dead of night. It would be cold, it would be exhausting, and it would be dangerous. But one factor had been removed from the equation. They were no longer being chased.

At least that was how it seemed. Kyle was reluctant to accept it, though. He couldn't afford to let his guard down simply because there was hope now. That might lead to a fatal mistake. He needed to remain on guard for Cynthia's sake.

He watched Cynthia as she held her arms out to support Davitos in case he stumbled. Saintly to a fault. He cursed under his breath. Davitos was not their savior. He was the one who'd brought them into this hellish contrivance, and Kyle would be damned if he was going simply going to dismiss that because Davitos had apparently had a change of heart.

The truth was that Davitos had still not uttered a word, and there was simply no guarantee that he was going to deliver the two of them to safety. Cynthia needed to stop searching for the good in people, Kyle thought, because people generally weren't all that good. Anything could still happen.

He walked back over them with the jugs of water. "He might have a concussion," Cynthia said. Part of Kyle hoped that this was true. Did they really need Davitos? If he were to lie down and go to sleep, never to wake up again, would he and Cynthia be in any more danger than they were already in?

But we might still need him, Kyle reminded himself. If these foothills were, in fact, too treacherous to navigate, then they might still need him to guide them through. He was torn, but he told himself not to make any rash decisions, even if he thought his chances were favorable. Davitos was still the man holding the gun, and he had to put his wife's safety first.

"What now?" he asked Davitos, not expecting an answer. Davitos picked up his pack and put his arms through the straps, tightening them as he pulled it closer to his back. He'd lost his spare water, and had only the flashlight in his hands. He moved past Cynthia and walked over to the foot of the path, lighting his way as he went. He stopped there, and then turned and looked at them both expectantly. Kyle and Cynthia exchanged looks. They said nothing to each other, and then she picked up her pack and put it back on. "C'mon, baby. Let's go."

There was nothing else to do. It would have been foolish to argue. This was their way out, their *only* way out, and they needed to take it. He followed Cynthia as she went to join Davitos at the trailhead. The three of them began their trek into the dark night.

Part Three

"The amateurs are more dangerous than the more sophisticated groups because they're unpredictable, less disciplined, and they're scared."

—Kerry McCown
2011

et three coffins ready.
    Welcome to the Wild West, Amigo.

Kyle awakened from his nightmare without a start, without calling out. He opened his eyes and acknowledged the cold sweat that soaked right through his clothes. Cynthia was already awake. It took him a moment to remember where he was and why he wasn't home with his wife, warm in his bed. He shuddered with a chill, and she pulled him closer to her inside of the nylon sleeping bag they shared, touching her forehead to his. "It's okay," she whispered just loud enough that only he could hear her a few centimeters away, "Just a nightmare."

"As opposed to reality?" he said skeptically.

"Things could be worse," she reminded him in the softest voice possible. "It wasn't too long ago things *were* worse."

My poor little CC. Always seeing the bright side of things. The world doesn't work that way. "You're right," he said, placating her. Usually lingering memories of his dreams evaporated within the first minute of waking up, but not now. His dreams wouldn't leave him, and they became intertwined with his current reality.

"You're shivering," she said sadly, and she tried to pull him even closer, bringing his face down to her chest. "Hold on to me."

Davitos sat only a few feet away on the other side of the dying fire. He was keeping watch throughout the night, ever-silent and eyes alert. He kept his long Colt revolver close, but Kyle and Cynthia hadn't thought of him as threatening in quite some time. Still, though, they kept their voices low as they talked, so that only they could hear each other.

"How long have you been awake?" he asked.

"Not long. I woke up shortly before you did. You were talking in your sleep."

"I'm sorry. I know we both need our sleep."

"Don't apologize."

"What time do you think it is?"

"Hard to say. Maybe three or four?"

They'd hiked through the greater part of the night. Kyle hadn't needed Davitos to talk for them to be in total agreement about covering some ground. Davitos had led the way over the rocky terrain with his flashlight, with Kyle and Cynthia following closely at his heels. They'd kept up a rigorous pace, even in darkness, for hours. The journey was not without danger. There were steep drop-offs from narrow ledges that hugged cliff faces. Rattlesnakes were more active at night. The mountain air was frigid, and even in this late August evening the chill caused them to expend more energy than was wise.

Kyle had stumbled and fallen twice, twisting his left ankle the second time. As the night grew darker and the terrain grew more vertical, Cynthia told Davitos that she and Kyle were too exhausted to go on. He marched them on for another half mile or so when they came upon an open fire pit area that from the looks of things had been frequented by many a traveler.

Perhaps it wasn't advisable to start a fire and increase their visibility, but the three of them actually believed that *El Jefe* and his men had simply given up their pursuit. Perhaps the cartel men truly believed that they'd perished in the station wagon, and it wasn't worth their time to follow through and confirm it. After all, *El Jefe* had Cobo contained now, and he'd seemed confident that either Davitos had perished in the crash or, if that was not the case, that one day he would slip up and make his presence known, in which case *El Jefe* could move in and disappear the mute at his leisure.

Kyle spent a lot of time trying to understand *El Jefe's* thought processes, but he only had the two times he'd very briefly observed the man to go on. How much of a threat did a loose end pose down here? Could *El Jefe* really afford to leave it alone if the Conways never turned up again on this side of the border? Was this kind of kidnapping and ransom such big business down here that an occasional slip up could simply be dismissed as overhead?

Both times *El Jefe* had taken care of business under the assumption that he was going unobserved by Kyle. The only ones he'd wanted to put a scare into had been Cobo and Davitos. He'd made it abundantly clear that he approved of their designs only if their captives had been taken care of quickly and quietly with a substantial enough bounty to make it all worth it. Well, Cobo certainly hadn't delivered in any of those regards, and now Kyle wondered how much energy—if any at all—*El Jefe* might expend on damage control before he just disregarded the issue all together.

These men had gathered enough information on his family to cause him to continue to fear for Cynthia's life and his own. The kind of intel gathering that had been done on the Conways provided evidence to suggest that the cartel had been doing reconnaissance stateside long before he and Cynthia had embarked on their weekend getaway. And not a moment had gone by since learning who Davitos really was that the implications had stopped weighing heavily upon him.

"How could he betray us like this?" he said so low that she almost didn't hear.

She was about to ask him who he was talking about, then realized that he was revisiting his suspicions about Mauricio. "You're not back on this again, are you?"

He tried to remain patient with her. She didn't view human nature through the same lens that he did. "CC, he lied about where he was from. He's first cousins with this kid. You'll have to come up with a pretty solid argument to convince me that his hands aren't dirty."

"It's not in him," she urged. "It just isn't. He never could have done something like this. It's not who he is."

"I'm sorry, but that's just not good enough for me. We can't just believe things simply because we *want* to."

"Kyle, you know his heart. Ask yourself if he could really knowingly put us through this."

"That's nonsense," he said, exasperation starting to creep into his whisper. "I don't know what's in his heart. I only know what's right in front of me. And he's *guilty*, that's all there is to it."

"You can't just condemn him without proof," she persisted. "There's more to—"

"No, Cynthia!" he hissed. "I won't stake my family's life on it. Do you understand? This thing is obviously more complex than we both originally thought." He glanced over his shoulder, and then lowered his voice once more. "And we cannot slip up and let Davitos know that we know who he is, or he might change his mind."

Cynthia said nothing to this, and Kyle failed to notice the flash of guilt that washed over her face and then vanished in a second. She held him in silence for another minute, and then kissed his forehead gently before saying, "We should try and get some sleep."

"Tomorrow's going to be dangerous," he declared grimly.

"What do you mean?"

"The desert. The afternoon sun. Do you have any idea how many skeletons they find along trails like this? Illegal immigrants die here every day. I doubt two gallons of water will even be enough."

She smiled. "At least we have a coyote."

He squeezed her more tightly, and she winced. "*Do not* trust Davitos," he said quietly but forcefully into her ear. "He is *not* our friend."

"I just meant that our chances will be better with him along," she said dejectedly.

There was something else that she wasn't considering, something he needed to understand if they were going to push themselves to their limits after sunup. "I have to get to a phone as soon as we get free. A cell phone, a pay phone, any kind. I've got to warn Kyp not to come down here."

"How much time did you say he has?"

"He's supposed to drive into Tijuana Sunday morning. That gives us one day and one night to get a hold of him."

"How far from the border do you think we are?"

"I don't know, but if we see any signs of man between now and then we have to do something." He closed his eyes, trying to think clearly. "Maybe Davitos has one of those heavy duty phones like Cobo had."

"But he doesn't talk."

"No," he said, conceding her point. "He certainly doesn't."

"Let's try to get some sleep."

* * *

They woke up at sunrise. All three of them took a swig of water, conscious of the need for conserving that precious commodity, and broke down their camp. Davitos shared some beef jerky with the both of them, and then extended his hand holding some kind of capsules. Kyle tried to turn him down, but Davitos was persistent with the hand-off. When Davitos wasn't looking, Kyle put them in his pocket and signaled Cynthia to do the same.

"What were those?" Cynthia asked him when Davitos was out of earshot.

"I don't know," Kyle replied, watching Davitos warily, "but if I had to guess, I'd say that it's some kind of Mexican speed. That's typically what they take on journeys like this."

"Do you think we'll need them?"

He turned to her. "No, and we're not going to take them. Another thing, though. We're both more wiped out than we realize. Our minds are on high alert, but we haven't had a real decent night's sleep. Now we're about to hike under a scorching summer sun. I need you to promise me—no matter what—that if at any time you get lightheaded or dizzy, you'll tell me. We've come too far to endanger ourselves with heat stroke."

"Okay," she said.

"Promise me," he urged.

"I promise."

As improbable as it seemed, the sky remained overcast throughout the morning as they were graced with a blanket of nimbus clouds that blocked the rays of the August sun. In spite of Kyle's worries regarding their plight, he was grateful for this remarkable condition. His main concern now was whether their path would cut its way through the rocky highlands, or if they were doomed to repeat the process of strenuous ascent followed by hazardous descent, a cyclical reality that would be so physically taxing on the both of them that it would matter little whether or not the sun was beating down on them.

For the most part they remained at lower elevations, skirting the edges of the mountains and following very gradual inclines that were just enough for them to handle. Kyle's twisted ankle irritated him, but he was able to keep up with the rigorous pace Davitos was setting for them.

Hours passed in silence. The only words exchanged were the occasional, "Watch out for that rock," or, "Be careful near here; it's a steep drop at the edge." As they hiked along, there was ample evidence that this trail was frequented by border crossers: fire pits like the one they'd camped at, trash strewn about, footprints in the sand. Each time they came across the physical remains of human contact, Cynthia allowed herself to grow a little more hopeful, a little more optimistic about seeing Cameron and Cal again. Kyle, on the other hand, grew inwardly agitated. Every time they passed another abandoned campsite, he grew more antsy. There was nothing to suggest that they were any closer to civilization, and Davitos certainly wasn't offering any ball-park estimates on when they might be. He needed to warn Kyp, and he needed to warn him soon. He would never forgive himself if he and Cynthia were to miraculously find their way back home, only to have his own brother deliver himself into the hands of *El Jefe* and his cartel thugs.

Around noon, after six hours of hiking, they stopped by a boulder to rest and hydrate. They had been disciplined in their water intake. Kyle and Cynthia had only drunk half a gallon of their two gallons of water, and Davitos, who'd left behind his spare jug in the wrecked car, forced himself to conserve the remaining one he had. He shared some more jerky and some dried apricots with Kyle and Cynthia.

It didn't matter to Kyle that they still had an entire afternoon and an entire evening to get word to Kyp. For all he knew they'd be on this monotonous trail for days, and his concern for Kyp was making him edgy. "Look, I don't know if you can talk, can't talk, or just choose not to talk, but you need to give me some idea of when we'll be near a phone. Gesture with your fingers, draw a goddamned picture in the sand, I don't care. Just give me *something* to go on."

Davitos simply stared back at him, and Kyle's anger started to come to a head. "I don't care that you've had second thoughts. My brother is in very real danger, and it's all because of *you*. You need to get us to a phone immediately. ¿Comprende? I've got to warn him."

Cynthia didn't like the steady rising of his voice, the combative tone. "Kyle, don't. Just try to calm down."

"No!" he bellowed, losing patience with her. "Do you have any idea what those men will do to Kyp? We're running out of time." For a split second Kyle revisited the idea of just tackling the smaller man, beating him unconscious and going through his backpack, looking for a phone just like the one Cobo had used. He looked Davitos dead in the eye. "Teléfono. Ahora." He took a step toward Davitos, who went for his gun.

Cynthia threw herself in front of Kyle, placing herself between the two men. "No, don't!" she pleaded. She put her palms on Kyle's chest. "Please. We've got to keep a level head."

Kyle ignored her, looking over her head at Davitos. "How much longer, damn you? How long are we going to be out here? You'd better start talking, or I'll make you talk." So obsessed was he with protecting his kid brother, that he didn't realize the potential danger into which he was putting himself and Cynthia. His body moved forward, pressing into Cynthia's, so that he was about to knock her over and launch himself at Davitos, gun or no gun.

"Kyle, stop! Just please stop!" She knew that he was relentless now, and she needed to find a more practical way to mitigate. She turned toward Davitos. "Please, you have to understand the danger Kyp's in. If there's anything you can do to help, even if it's just getting word to Mauricio—"

Kyle's eyes went wide. "Cynthia!"

Too late she'd realized her mistake. Shame washed over her, but she met Kyle's accusatory tone head on. "It's alright. He already knows. He knows we know who he is."

Apparently this was enough to deflate him. She felt the tension in his upper body relax, but she suspected that it was out of a feeling of betrayal. "You told him?" he said in disbelief.

"Back at the shack, I thought I could reason with him. It wasn't until after you warned me that it occurred to me—"

"Do you have any idea the danger you've put us in?" As if it was just now occurring to him that this changed everything, he studied Davitos' movements, looking for any adjustment in his body language that would indicate that he now had no choice but to kill them both. However, Davitos stood his ground, hand resting near the pistol at his hip, unmoving.

Cynthia felt the need to make things right. Looking at Davitos, she said, "Please, you don't have to say anything. Just nod your head if the answer is yes. Will we be out of this by nightfall?"

It was a moment before they got a reaction from Davitos. It was almost imperceptible, but his chin dipped just ever so slightly, indicating a nod. She looked back up at Kyle. "See? It's not too late. We can still get word to Kyp."

Whether or not Kyle was convinced remained to be seen. He must have recognized, however, that they were wasting time with this one-sided confrontation, and needed to make tracks. He blew out a breath he hadn't realized he'd been holding, and said to Davitos, "Well, what are you waiting for? Lead the way."

* * *

Two hours later, in a low valley heavily populated by boulders and lush ironwood trees, the blister on the sole of Cynthia's left foot became too much for her to bear. She'd tried as best she could to endure it and keep pushing onward, but now she realized that if she didn't take immediate action she might slow them down even more in the long run. Her yellow tennis shoes were no substitute for legitimate hiking boots on this terrain. When tears began to well up in her eyes from the pain, she called the group to a halt. "Stop, please," she pleaded. "I need to stop for a minute," she said as she plopped down on the ground, going for her laces.

Kyle hadn't realized how much the blister had been bothering her. He took his backpack off and went down on one knee to assist her. He gently tugged at her shoelaces until they came untied, and then slowly eased the shoe off of her foot. She winced in pain when he carefully rolled her sock off, exposing the inflamed flesh on the arch of her foot.

"Oh, CC," he said with her outstretched leg resting on his thigh.

"You should have spoken up earlier. We need to dress this and change your socks." He looked behind him, up at Davitos. "We need that first aid kit now."

Davitos was already retrieving it. He placed it on the ground next to Kyle, who began to poke through it. First he cleaned the infected area with peroxide and cotton balls, then he dried it, applied some ointment, and covered it with clean gauze. He wound medical tape around her foot several times until the gauze was held firmly in place, and then went into her backpack for a clean pair of socks.

Cynthia watched her husband as he worked, attentive and focused as he bandaged her, just like in every task he put his mind to. His eyes were narrowed in concentration, and she knew that this was the time when all other parts of who he was went somewhere else entirely, leaving only this diligent problem-solver behind to take care of business. He was so methodical in his processes. It was a large part of what had first attracted her to him. Now it was more endearing than ever, but somehow it made her wish she'd been stronger. "I'm sorry," she mumbled weakly.

He stopped what he was doing and looked up at her. She was so naked in all of her vulnerability, and never before in nine years of marriage had he loved her more than he did at this exact moment. He reached out his hand and cupped her face, then brushed his fingers over her cheek and ran his hand back to the nape of her neck. "Oh, no, no, baby. Don't be sorry. You have absolutely nothing in the world to be sorry about. You've been so brave. It's me who should be sorry."

One tear ran down her cheek, a sight that pained him. It hurt him so badly that he had to turn away. After two days in captivity, her discomfort now from this very trivial blood-blister was every bit as painful to behold as the anxiety and dread she'd endured while being held prisoner on that filthy couch. He wanted to take her pain away and carry it for the both of them.

"Goddamn you, Mauricio," he muttered under his breath as he dug his arm into her pack in search of a clean pair of socks. "Goddamn you for dragging us into this nightmare."

She heard him, wondering if he'd meant for her to hear or was just obliviously thinking aloud. As he tenderly worked the fresh sock over her toes and then her heel, she said to him in a pleading way that gave her voice a husky quality, "Kyle, you have to promise me that if we get back—"

"*When* we get back," he corrected her.

"Right, *when* we get back," she said with a forced smile. "When we get back, you have to promise me that you're not going to rush into action with your conspiracy theory."

He sucked in a deep breath and held onto it, choosing not to exhale until he'd come up with the right combination of words that would make her see their reality through his eyes. Finally, he let the breath go. "I *cannot* afford to give him the benefit of the doubt the way you do, CC."

She was so obstinate, so set in her ways. "Ask yourself how he could do such a thing. Ask yourself how he could knowingly put us through this."

"CC," he said with strained patience, the process of trying to get her to switch gears proving to be mentally exhausting, "It's all about greed. It's all about money. It's really just *that* simple." He tried his best to avoid talking to her as though she were a child, but her need to believe in the good in people just wouldn't wash when faced with their perilous situation.

"I'm not talking about *why*," she said calmly, undaunted by his patronizing tone. "I'm talking about *how*. How could Mauricio possibly bring himself to do this to us?"

Somewhat dumbfounded, he said, "I'm not sure I follow you."

She clarified her point for him. "He's a hard-working family man. He's achieved more than he ever could have dreamed of thanks to you. And he's a gentle soul. You said before that you can't know what's in his heart, that you can only see what's right in front of you. Well, think about what you've seen with your own two eyes in the last ten years, and then ask yourself, 'Could he really have had a hand in this?'"

"Yes," he said without missing a beat.

"But how?" she said, getting a grip on his forearm. "How can you be so sure? What are you seeing that I'm not?"

He'd actually thought about it a lot since learning that Davitos was Mauricio's cousin. And he hadn't needed to dwell on it for very long before he came to a plausible conclusion. "Everyone who knows us has been talking," he began slowly, "and I mean *everyone*, about how poorly I've treated him. How I've kept him down."

"What?"

"That's right. In the last year, whether it's been a snide comment right to my face or talk behind my back, everyone who knows the business has been saying the same thing—that I've mistreated him—and they've started putting ideas in his head."

She couldn't believe what she was hearing. "*That's* what's got you convinced? Petty gossip?"

"It's real," he persisted, "and it's been building up for a long time, this resentment. It came to its boiling point that cursed night when he asked for a cash advance and Franco's First Communion came up." *I don't think it's nice, you laughing. See, my mule don't like people laughing. He gets the crazy idea you're laughing at him.* "That was the night when everything changed."

Welcome to the Wild West, amigo.

She waited him out, but he said nothing more. And although the love that bonded them together was completely intact, she had never felt so far removed from his thought processes as she did now. It boggled her mind that he could have solidified his convictions with such hearsay. Yet he truly believed what he was saying, and he wasn't going to budge.

Conversely, she was completely on the other end of the spectrum. When she faced facts, she recognized that there were certain pieces of information that had come to light in the last two days that most people would agree were pretty damning for Mauricio, and yet she just couldn't see it. He just wasn't that kind of person, she was sure of it. However, she knew that Kyle simply couldn't accept this line of thought. To him, her reasoning was flawed, tainted by her hopeful optimism.

This left them at a psychological impasse that each of them secretly acknowledged but said nothing about. He helped her with her shoe, and tied up the laces after he slowly lowered her foot to the ground. She squeezed his forearm. He was looking down at her sneaker as he laced it, and she leaned forward and dipped her head to lock eyes with him. "Thanks," she said sincerely. "You take good care of me. I feel much better already."

"Of course."

"We should get going," she suggested, knowing that was exactly what he wanted. Still seated, she looked over his shoulder, and then frowned. "Where's Davitos?"

Kyle, still crouched, turned around and scanned the immediate area. There was Davitos' backpack, and his jug of water, but he was nowhere to be seen. Kyle slowly raised himself up to his full height. Apparently Davitos had slipped away, but where the hell had he gone, and why? Kyle stood still, listening.

Cynthia remained seated on the damp ground. This grove they had stumbled upon had seemed miraculous in this arid climate. There was moisture in the earth here at this oasis, which hydrated the tall green grass that grew throughout and around the outcropping of boulders and dense clusters of ironwoods. A warm summer breeze came billowing down the trail and whipped at the grass and wispy foliage. She sat there, motionless and alert, hoping the wind would carry a sound that marked Davitos' presence nearby. She heard nothing, however, and judging by Kyle's perplexed expression, neither had he.

He looked down at her and put his hand out, palm facing down. The look of confusion on his face turned into one of extreme caution. "Stay right here," he said, and he started walking up the trail in the direction they'd been headed before stopping. About twenty feet from where Cynthia sat, the trail began to taper and then disappeared beyond a clump of brush. Kyle made it exactly that far, peering ahead apprehensively. Then his whole body stiffened. From her viewpoint it was like watching a dog's hackles stand up. He turned quickly and jogged back toward her, scooping up both of their backpacks in his left hand as he came, but leaving Davitos' behind.

When he reached her, he hooked his whole arm around her elbow and pulled her to her feet. "We have to go," he said with a failed attempt to project an air of calm. "Right now."

"What is it?" she asked with rising alarm.

"Turn around. Let's go!" He held on to her elbow and—despite her blistered feet—began urging her along at a pace usually set by power-walkers, heading back the way they'd originally come in. She stumbled for a second, and then limped along in his grip as he tugged at her tricep, leading her along in a panicky manner that frightened her and made her forget about her blister. She stole a glance over her shoulder.

There were only two facts she could be sure of from that quick look.

One was that the two figures approaching were men, and the other was that they were both armed. However, just as quickly as this was registering with her, Kyle sensed that she'd snuck a look, and he herded her along with continued urgency. She didn't need much convincing at this point.

In a moment they saw another figure approaching on the trail from the opposite direction, brandishing a long hunting rifle with a large, cylindrical scope. Kyle's feet skidded in the dirt as he came to a halt, and Cynthia stood still behind him.

The man coming at them walked along at a leisurely pace, as if he were just on a stroll, but Kyle knew right off that this man was not out for exercise nor for hunting. He was a short man, only a little taller than Davitos, but more powerfully built. His facial features where obscured by his black Stetson cowboy hat, but he looked sinister enough with the rifle cradled in his thickly muscled, tattooed arms. He wore jeans and boots and a zipped-up, green military style vest, with a hunting knife's handle protruding from a sheath covering one of its breast pockets.

Kyle dropped the backpacks, using his right hand to keep Cynthia behind him. They slowly backed away from the newcomer, who came toward them with a swagger that might have suggested he was the owner of this land. His face came into focus when he was within a few feet of them. He was approaching middle age, with a long, black goatee coming to a sharp point underneath his chin. When his mouth opened into a wide smile, a gold tooth glimmered at the both of them. It was a smile that had no warmth to it. Kyle saw only enmity there. "Hola, amigo," the man said, his index finger lightly tapping the trigger on his rifle. "No parece que seas de aqui." *You don't look like you're from around here.*

Kyle turned to his right, facing northward, and saw the two other men approaching. One of them was a sinister looking brute, with a short-sleeved, collared flannel shirt worn open, with a heavily tattooed chest disappearing into a filthy wife-beater underneath. Below his waist he wore black cargo pants and heavy boots. He was beardless, and he wore a black bandana, rolled up like a headband and tied tightly at his forehead. Black flame tattoos crept up his neck, reaching for his jaw line. This one, too, had an authoritative gait, and he strutted along the trail with his shotgun in a loose grip, resting on his shoulder. He was grinning malignantly.

The third man certainly didn't look like the brains of the operation. He was young, in his early twenties. Perhaps his bushy mustache was meant to cover up his youth. He walked along somewhat uncertainly, looking to the man next to him for cues. He wore a dirty red trucker's mesh hat with the star emblem for Texaco gasoline, and a gray-and-white soccer jersey that was starting to fray at the bottom. This one had jeans with holes in the knees, and construction boots. A shiny .357 magnum was holstered at his side. This might make him every bit as dangerous as the other two, even if he didn't project their self-assured aura of malicious intent.

As the three men closed in nonchalantly, Kyle kept backing Cynthia up, until she was pressed firmly between him and the boulder behind her. He spread his arms out at his sides a little wider, as if to create an invisible barrier between him and Cynthia. "No queremos ningún problema," he said. *We don't want any trouble.* These men weren't passing themselves off for anything other than exactly what they appeared to be. Kyle knew who they were, although he was angry with himself for not having assessed this threat earlier.

Banditos. Roaming these hills, looking for illegal immigrants, and possibly their coyote guides, to prey on. Today probably started off business as usual, scouting the trails with the most frequent traffic when—*lo and behold, what have we here?*—two gringos should materialize out of nowhere. *What good fortune,* Kyle imagined them thinking. *Today's take will be far more fruitful than usual. Who knows what kind of treasures we might uncover from those backpacks.*

"Nadie quiere tener problemas," the lone man in the cowboy hat, the assumed leader, assured Kyle. *No one wants trouble.* "Pero estos cerros son muy peligrosas." *But these hills are very dangerous.* "Mis amigos y yo ofrecemos protección por una pequeña cuota." *My friends and I offer protection for a small fee.*

Kyle knew Cynthia probably wasn't catching all of this, but she was probably deciphering the menace in the man's tone. He felt her tense up behind him, her muscles going taut. That's when Kyle wanted to cry out in rage. That's when he feared that there was some great cosmic joke being played on him. He hadn't dared to believe that the worst was behind them, and now, just as he was starting to allow himself to believe that maybe everything was going to be okay, he realized that they had traded one Cobo for another.

Kyle gestured to the backpacks on the ground. "Toma lo que quieras." *Take whatever you want.* The leader grinned at him, once again flashing the gold tooth, perhaps amused by Kyle's impertinence considering the powerless position he was in. The man in the cowboy hat nodded to his cohort in the trucker's hat, who went and knelt down by both backpacks.

The thug in the black bandana headband, the scary looking one with the shotgun resting on his shoulder, watched Kyle with a nefarious grin on his face as his bandit accomplice unzipped the backpacks and flipped them upside-down, dumping their contents onto the ground. One of the water jugs cracked open and leaked water into the earth.

Kyle's heart was hammering in his chest. *This can't be happening. It was all good. We were going to make it.* He had had enough adrenaline coursing through him in the last two days to last him two lifetimes. He was reaching his limit.

While the young one sifted through Kyle and Cynthia's meager possessions, searching for anything of value, Cowboy Hat pointed up the trail to Davitos' bag, and said, "¿Dónde está tu amigo?" *Where's your friend?*

Kyle swallowed and thought about how he was going to answer. He didn't want to lie if he could help it, but he didn't know what else to say. "Es sólo a nosotros." *It's just us.*

Cowboy Hat's smile faded, and the barrel of his hunting rifle lazily started angling toward Kyle and Cynthia. Kyle pressed back into her with even more pressure. "No creo en usted," said the leader. *I don't believe you.*

Kyle's mind started racing wildly in an attempt to come up with something believable to say. Bandana took a step a step toward him and Cynthia, the shotgun slowly starting to slide off of his deltoid and fall into his one-handed grip. He didn't believe Kyle either. However, before Kyle could conjure up something credible, Trucker Hat saved him the trouble. He used the toe of his boot to kick at the pile of dirty clothing, the shared sleeping bag, and jugs of water. "No hay nada aquí." he said ruefully. *There's nothing here.*

The leader hadn't been expecting this, and his disappointed facial expression morphed into one of irritation. "¿Nada?" he said with disbelief. He, too, took another step toward Kyle and Cynthia. Trucker Hat stood to his full height.

Kyle tried to get his breathing under control. "No tenemos nada de valor," he said, addressing them all. *We have nothing of value.* He assumed a wider stance, trying to broaden his shoulders, trying to blot out Cynthia from their vision.

Cowboy Hat stroked his goatee with his free hand, studying Kyle, as if in searching Kyle's eyes he might be able to ascertain the whole truth. Then, after a moment, his eyes moved slightly to the left, altering his line of sight so that he was now looking over Kyle's shoulder, to Cynthia. "Siempre hay algo de valor." *There's always something of value.*

The man's intentions were clear enough. The three bandits would get *something* worthwhile out of this encounter. Bandana and Trucker Hat were now following the alpha's lead; they, too, were now staring hungrily at Cynthia, realizing that this encounter wouldn't be completely fruitless. All three men took another step toward Kyle and Cynthia.

Kyle had reached his breaking point. These men assumed that they had just happened upon two lost travelers finding themselves in the wrong place at the wrong time. They didn't know what the Conways had been through in the last forty-eight hours, how much their spirits had been brought to the brink. If Kyle and Cynthia had never been taken captive by Cobo and Davitos, if they'd never endured the outrages of the previous two days, then he wasn't sure how he would have reacted to this latest development. As it was, he was *done* with feelings of impotence.

He would give Cynthia a chance to flee. He would lunge at Cowboy Hat. He would punch, kick, head-butt, gouge, and even bite. He would have only a precious few seconds before he was overpowered, but he just might buy Cynthia enough time to get away from them. He would go down fighting, using his last breaths to urge Cynthia to run, to get as far away as she could. Even then, they might still catch up with her, but what else could he do? He had no illusions about what was about to happen to her. Cowboy Hat's lustful gaze had told Kyle everything he needed to know.

Shaking uncontrollably, and ready to pounce, his only hope was that Cynthia somehow sensed what he intended to do, and wouldn't let his sacrifice be in vain. The three men continued to leer.

Cowboy Hat rested his rifle against a nearby rock, and was going for the hunting knife sheathed at his breast, when something blunt and hard pressed into the back of his skull just underneath the brim of his hat. He froze as he heard the unmistakable sound of a revolver's hammer being cocked back.

Davitos stepped out from behind the boulder that Kyle and Cynthia were pressed up against. Bandana and Trucker Hat stopped dead in their tracks, taken totally unaware. Cowboy Hat remained completely still except for his pupils, which moved to the corners of his eyes. He knew that someone unseen had gotten the drop on him, and he instinctively raised his hands up in a gesture of surrender. Davitos pivoted around him so that he was in plain sight, and so that the other two bandits would realize that they'd now lost control of the situation.

No one moved, and Davitos said nothing. He used his head to nod at Kyle and Cynthia, indicating that they should step out from between the bandits on each side of them. Kyle didn't need convincing. He took Cynthia by the hand and, ducking down, slowly led her away from the boulder, careful not to make any sudden movements that might spook anyone into rash action. They went to stand behind Davitos.

Trucker Hat's hand gun was still in its holster, and Bandana's shotgun was still pointed at the ground. Davitos was able to look past Cowboy Hat and keep the other two within his sights. He kept the gun pressed firmly against the back of Cowboy Hat's head, and then looked at the other bandits' faces. They were looking to Cowboy Hat for some kind of signal, some unspoken instruction as to what action they should take. Davitos couldn't see Cowboy Hat's face, but judging by the searching looks of his two accomplices, he was either mouthing a silent command or using his eyes suggestively. Kyle saw what was going on and kept pushing Cynthia away from the group. The bandits were about to make a move.

Davitos must have sensed it too. He moved his gun hand slightly to the right and fired off a round, the thunderous shot echoing in the rocky surroundings. The report, just a few inches away from Cowboy Hat's ear, debilitated him as if from a hammer's blow, and he dropped down to his knees, crying out in pain. Bandana and Trucker Hat tensed up, their hands tightening around their respective firearms, but Davitos was quicker than they were. He had already cocked the hammer back again, this time lining up his shot at Bandana, who at the moment was the more serious threat.

Cowboy Hat remained on his knees, panting heavily and clutching at the right side of his skull, as if he could reach into his head and ease the pain in his eardrum. Davitos took a few steps back, keeping his Colt trained on the other two. He used his gun to gesture to the ground, a silent command for Bandana and Trucker Hat to drop their weapons. The pair of bandits had no choice but to obey, both of them slowly lowering their guns to the ground. With his outstretched arm he gestured for them to move closer to their fallen leader, bringing them closer to one another.

When they were bunched together he began to circle around them, moving toward their discarded weapons. He waved Kyle and Cynthia onward until they came within a few feet of the Magnum and the shotgun. Then Davitos nodded to the ground, beckoning for Kyle to pick up one of the guns. Kyle, unsure of how to properly handle a shotgun, smashed it and the hunting rifle against the rock, destroying both. He then went for the .357 and aimed it at the immobilized bandits.

Davitos brought his free hand to his belt, retrieving his sets of handcuffs. He held them up in the air for the bandits to see, dangling them by his fingers, and then tossed them at their feet. Kyle didn't know what Davitos intended. There wasn't a nearby object suitable enough for the three men to be handcuffed to. Moreover, there were three of them, and only two sets of handcuffs.

Davitos looked at Kyle and pounded his wrists together, hoping that Kyle took his meaning. Kyle did, and said to the three bandits, "Muñeca a muñeca. Enlacemonos ahora." *Wrist to wrist. Link up now.*

At the very least the men were smart enough to preserve their lives. The appearance of Davitos had shaken them and eroded their resolve. Bandana, staring cold death at Davitos and the Conways, reached down and picked up a set, slapping one of the cuffs on his left wrist, and then joined himself to Cowboy Hat, who was still dazed. When Trucker Hat gave Bandana a confused look, Kyle shouted at him, "Vamanos!" Trucker Hat hastily linked his right wrist to Cowboy Hat's free wrist.

The three bandits were now bound together.

Giving them a wide berth, Davitos began to circle slowly around the trio. Bandana warily kept his eyes fixed on the man who'd disarmed them as he moved around them. Kyle took a step toward them, leveling his gun at Bandana's head. "Los ojos en mí!" *Eyes on me.*

Cowboy Hat was coming to his senses, and the bandits began to back up toward the boulder, the same cornered position they'd had Kyle and Cynthia in only moments ago. Davitos got behind Trucker Hat and gave his back a shove, sending all three men staggering forward a few steps.

Kyle had no clue as to what Davitos intended, and just as he began to wonder, he heard Cynthia say from behind him, "Kyle, you don't think he's going to—"

Before she could finish the thought, Davitos raised his Colt into the air and brought it down hard on Cowboy Hat's skull, just behind the ear. The same ear that had just sustained damage from the gunshot Davitos had fired off at point blank range. Cowboy Hat's head jerked forward and his whole body convulsed before he collapsed in a heap, bringing Bandana and Trucker Hat each down on one knee.

Cynthia winced and let out a cry.

Bandana reacted instinctively, trying to whirl on Davitos, even in his precarious position, pulling on Cowboy Hat's limp arm in the process. Davitos reminded him who was in charge by aiming the barrel of his pistol between Bandana's eyes. Bandana thought better of his desperate act of defiance, body recoiling as he backed down. Davitos stepped away and moved around the men, returning to Kyle and Cynthia with his gun trained on the chained bandits the whole time.

Kyle understood Davitos' rationale. They couldn't very well kill the men in cold blood, but with nothing to securely cuff them to they had little in the way of options other than to ensure that at least one of them was dead weight. And who better than their leader, who probably already had a mild concussion even before Davitos had dropped him for a second time.

Davitos was about five feet away from Kyle when they locked eyes, and Davitos came to a halt. With the immediate danger behind them, it was just now occurring to both men that Kyle now had a gun. They stared at each other for a moment, Davitos' eyes searching Kyle's facial features, his body language.

Kyle looked down at the heavy Magnum in his hand, and then back on Davitos, whose expression betrayed nothing of his thoughts, his intentions as hidden in that blank stare as in his insufferable silence. Neither man raised his gun, but the standoff continued.

From behind Kyle, Cynthia said in both a plea and a warning, "Kyle, whatever you're thinking, don't."

Kyle continued to stare at Davitos, and Cynthia feared that he'd reopened that dialogue with himself as to whether or not they were better off without Davitos. Cynthia spoke again with an increasing sense of urgency. "Listen to me. We've come too far to risk it all now. He came back for us. He's proven himself." Kyle felt her voice getting closer as she came up behind him, speaking right into his ear. "We're not out of this yet. There's still *them*," she reminded him as she pointed to the bandits over his shoulder. "We need to stick together."

Kyle sighed heavily. *She comes right out of a movie.* Keeping his eyes fixed on Davitos, he slowly moved his gun hand behind him as he used his free hand to lift up the back of his shirt, tucking the Magnum between his belt and his sacrum. He turned to Cynthia and gave her a look that said that he was ceding all responsibility to her if there were any more life threatening hazards ahead. Then turning back to Davitos he said, "Let's get out of here."

They strapped on their backpacks and started rapidly back up the trail. Davitos took one last look behind him as they rounded a bend, then lost sight of the bandits. Even after they'd disappeared, all three of them heard Bandana calling after them, "Están todos muertos. ¿Me oyen? Muerto! Los encontrare y les purgare la sangre lentamente. Ellos nunca podran identificar sus cadáveres."

Cynthia was the only one who couldn't fully translate the threats, and yet the man's incendiary tone left no question as to what Bandana would do if he ever caught up with them. It made her relaxing pulse quicken again.

* * *

Kyle leaned back on his barstool and watched the young brunette stroll by them. Her display of sexuality beckoned to him as he watched her denim ass float up and down as she moved on. He groaned. "Oh, what I'd do to that." He shook his head and looked at Mauricio for a reaction. When he saw that Mauricio hadn't heard him, was still staring at the red label on the bottle of beer he held in both hands, he slapped his friend on the back. Mauricio's moping had to stop. He was bringing Kyle down. "C'mon, man. Cheer up. It's been over a week now."

Mauricio turned his head ever so slightly, just enough to meet his companion's eyes as Kyle leaned forward and rested his elbows on the bar. "It's not the end of the world, bro. You've still got them. You've still got us. We're just a little more spread out now."

Mauricio had always taken his social cues from Kyle. Kyle was his American mentor. Now, however, for the first time since Kyle had known him, Mauricio batted Kyle a defiant eye. Still though, he said nothing. Kyle saw that his positive spin on the situation wasn't going to improve his friend's sour mood. He changed tactics, opting for the compassion that never came easy to him when spoken aloud. "Hey, listen," he said in a softer tone as he placed his hand on Mauricio's shoulder, "I am truly sorry about what happened with your cousins. It's very unfortunate. We'll get through it, though. No one knows what will happen tomorrow."

Still Mauricio didn't speak, but Kyle could tell that he had his friend's attention. "You really do need to look at the bright side, though. I'm serious. If Eddie hadn't stepped in and intervened on your behalf, you would be right there with them. Think about that. At the very least you're in a position to help them."

Mauricio refused to respond to Kyle's platitudes. "We all work so hard for so little money, and this is how we're treated."

Kyle did his best to remain patient with Mauricio. What irked him first and foremost was the fact that Mauricio should have figured all of this out a long time ago. He'd been here long enough to have learned how the game was played. The deportation of his primos had always been a danger, if not an inevitability. It should not have come as this much of a shock, much less have been followed by some great revelation of social injustice.

The second reality that frustrated Kyle was that Mauricio had absolutely no right to piss and moan. The guy had struck the illegal alien's jackpot:

beautiful wife, delightful children, successful career, and an airtight citizenship. Sometimes Kyle wondered what kind of simple existence his friend had carved out for himself back in Oaxaca that could have left him so clueless as to how things really worked here in the states. "Hey, man, no one said you have to like it. Hell, I don't like it. It's a rigged game."

Mauricio swiveled on his barstool, turning to face Kyle. "My family was all I had. Before you. Before Lorena and the kids. We have history. It can be traced for many generations."

Mauricio's words reminded Kyle of a protestor he'd seen on the news once, out in front of City Hall just as the controversial immigration issue had become critical. Her sign had simply read: This is OUR continent.

Kyle was not without sympathy for his friend. In one fateful action, Mauricio had lost all of his extended family to deportation. This included the Conways' nanny, Angelica, and her twelve year old daughter, Carmen. Nineteen year old Enrique had been working as a dishwasher at a restaurant downtown. Allana was sixteen, and had been cleaning houses. Then there were his employees: Martin, Jaime, and the mop-haired mute whose name Kyle couldn't recall. Kyle thanked God that that affiliation had not been established when everything had gone down.

"My great-grandparents came over from Ireland on a boat with absolutely no money in their pockets," Kyle told Mauricio, hoping to force empathy. "They were treated like shit. They made shit wages. But in the end they proved to be the heart and soul of this country. Immigration is one of the things that made America great. I don't know how we lost sight of that along the way."

"My fathers were already here," Mauricio stated bluntly, holding his ground. "So what's changed? What's the difference between you and me?"

Kyle shrugged, willing to let this dialogue that was bordering on the absurd to run its course if only that would be the end of it. "I don't know, man. All of a sudden it just got too crowded, and then it was time to close the doors. And I'm not defending Europeans. It's the ultimate hypocrisy. Look at history. Act first, ask the moral questions later. That was the ugly side of Manifest Destiny." He wasn't sure if Mauricio even followed him at this point, if the historical references were lost on him. But on some level he wanted Mauricio to know that he really understood the helplessness that Mauricio felt, that he wasn't simply telling his friend what he wanted to hear.

"Now it's all backwards," Mauricio said with a toothy sneer, a display of disgust that Kyle had never seen from him before.

"Yeah," Kyle conceded. "It is. One great, big nationwide double-standard. It's not fair, and it's not right."

"You have to take what you can," Mauricio said with a faraway look in his eyes that seemed to suggest that he'd just solved some elusive riddle. "You have to look after your own."

This attitude of Mauricio's didn't sit well with Kyle. He'd always liked his friend the way he was—wide-eyed, and in awe of all the possibilities this great nation held. He didn't want to have a hand in turning Mauricio into a cynic.

"Yeah," Kyle responded carefully, "to a certain extent. But don't forget that you have your own family to worry about now. A family that needs you more than your cousins do."

Mauricio looked annoyed. "Of course I'd never forget that."

"Then do what you can for Angelica and everyone else, but do it from here. And try to remind yourself from time to time that you're one of the lucky ones."

* * *

The encounter with the bandits had spooked them into maintaining a more rigorous pace than was desirable considering Cynthia's blister and Kyle's twisted ankle. Rather than lead the way, Davitos brought up the rear, his oversized Colt revolver held at the ready. He frequently glanced behind them to make sure that they weren't being followed.

Twenty minutes after they had left the bandits, Cynthia stopped and looked at Davitos. "My God, Davitos, did you know that there were men like that out here?" At the very least she expected a nod of the head or a guilty look of admission. As expected, Davitos disappointed once again, moving forward on the trail as if he hadn't even heard her.

For the first time Kyle found himself defending Davitos, and it made him somewhat uncomfortable to say, "He probably knew, he just didn't have any other choice."

"He could've taken us back to the border at TJ," she suggested, wondering why Kyle hadn't seen this as the obvious course of action.

"Dropped us off and then driven away. We could have warned Kyp by now."

The last remark was meant to appeal to Kyle's fear for his brother. *Boy, does she have a knack for tapping into people's most vulnerable emotions and exploiting them. Yet here we are; nothing can change our current situation. What's the use in even pointing it out?* "He couldn't do that," he said with certainty. "His boss probably has his men crawling all over Tijuana on the lookout for us. Probably more Federale imposters, or police on the take, or both. It wasn't safe."

"Oh," she said, her thoughtful expression telling him that she hadn't considered that possibility. His CC wasn't as stubborn as he was. She was always the first to admit it when she was wrong. "Do you think there are any more dangerous men on this trail?"

Kyle felt reassured by the heavy steel at the small of his back. "No one's going to creep up on us like that again." The gun made him feel like he once again had some semblance of control over their fates. He could protect his wife from danger. He could offer her comforting words of reassurance that weren't merely empty promises with nothing of substance to back them up.

The trail rose once again, gradually and not too steeply, and when they reached another level, the terrain became more heavily vegetated, the lush green ironwood trees becoming more densely packed. Their path seemed to even off here, and it looked like they might remain at this elevation for quite some time without having to descend. Nevertheless, the trail eventually became so heavily wooded on both sides that it was difficult to see far beyond, or to detect threats that might lie in wait.

Davitos picked up the pace and strode ahead of Kyle and Cynthia, marching a good fifteen feet ahead of them. Kyle noticed his head turning left and right, as if he was scanning for something.

Cynthia hadn't noticed, her eyes fixed on the rocky path in front of her. She was still shaken, but she wanted to show Kyle that she was not only strong, but also practical. "Should we talk about the water situation? We did lose another gallon back there."

He felt another wave of concern for her when she said this. He wanted to take her in his arms and hold her tightly to him. He wanted to tell her that everything was going to be alright, and that they would soon be home with the boys and that no one was going to hurt her ever again.

He was still rattled himself. They'd averted a violent end back there, and he *hated* the fact that he owed their salvation to the very man who'd thrust them into this ordeal to begin with. He was about to answer her question, remind her that Davitos had confirmed earlier that they didn't have much farther to go, when Davitos came to a stop ahead of them and put his free hand up, indicating that they should do the same.

Considering what they'd just been through, Davitos' halt was not to be taken lightly. Cynthia tensed up, and said quickly, "What? What is it?" It was nerve racking to constantly be making inquiries of a man who wouldn't respond.

With his outstretched hand, palm down, Davitos gave them a subtle signal for them to stay put. They both watched him attentively. He seemed to be scanning the ground for something, particularly underneath trees and bushes. At one point he got down on his knees and bent over, running his fingers over the dusty ground.

"What—?" Cynthia began.

"I don't know," Kyle said, just as confused as she was.

Davitos stood back up, frowning, but with a look in his eyes that suggested that he was satisfied with what he'd found, as if he'd just confirmed a suspicion. He walked back over to them, and stopped just in front of them, putting his Colt away. He took off his backpack and unzipped one of the side compartments, then reached inside. Kyle and Cynthia waited patiently, wondering what he was up to now.

When his hand came out of the backpack, he was holding both of their wallets. He handed them to Cynthia, and she looked at them as if she was holding a lost family keepsake that she'd never expected to see again.

Davitos ran his arms back through the straps of his pack, pointed at the trail ahead of them, and then headed back they way they'd come. He walked away without looking back.

Kyle was elated. *This can mean only one thing.* "C'mon, CC. Let's go."

But Cynthia stayed fixed in place, watching Davitos' back as he retreated. She was still confused, but there was something else written on her face that Kyle didn't like. Maybe disappointment?"

He gently took her elbow in his hand. More softly, as if to demonstrate patience even when time was of the essence, he said, "C'mon. We have to go."

Still, she remained in place, watching Davitos with that confused look on her face that was really starting to fluster Kyle. "Davitos?" she called after him.

Davitos stopped and turned around. He looked back at Cynthia, and he held her gaze for a long time. His face was a blank slate, something he'd been able to maintain since he'd made peace with his decision to turn them loose. For just a second, however, right before he broke eye contact, Cynthia thought she saw a flash of contrition in his eyes.

Kyle didn't know what to think. Too many of his emotions were competing for dominance. However, as he watched this unspoken exchange between his wife and their kidnapper, he saw if for what it really was. This experience, from beginning to end, had created a bond between them, and that appalled him.

Davitos turned his back to them and retreated down the trail. Within seconds he had disappeared from sight.

Cynthia looked at Kyle with a *what does it mean?* look on her face. *I'll tell you later,* he thought to himself. "Let's go," he said.

Later he would worry about this very odd mental connection she'd established with that low-life. For now all that mattered was that they were no longer captives.

* * *

Lorena lathered sunscreen over her body until she'd covered everything but her back. She handed Mauricio the bottle and leaned forward on her beach chair. "¿Ayudame?" she prompted.

He squeezed a capful onto his palm and then rubbed his hands together. As he ran his hands over her, she watched Franco and Maria playing on the beach, building sandcastles down near the tide. To her, it was a vision of perfection. "We should go see them," she suggested, not taking her eyes off of the kids.

"¿Quién?" Mauricio asked.

"Tu familia," she said, closing her eyes as he rubbed the tension out of her muscles.

"No," he said flatly.

"Why not?" she asked, turning to face him.

"It's a bad idea," was all he offered.

"It'll be fine," she insisted. "I think the kids should know about their heritage. See the place their father grew up."

"It's a bad idea," he repeated with a lack of understanding that drove her crazy.

She squinted at him, even though he couldn't see it through her sunglasses. "Are you ashamed or something?"

He didn't rise to meet her in her erect seated position, but leaned back more heavily into his beach chair. "Don't be ridiculous."

"Then why not?"

He met her question with one of his own. "What good will it do?"

She didn't follow. "What do you mean? It's your family."

"I don't want the kids to see that side."

She leaned toward him and took his face in her hands. "Mauricio, you know everything about me and my world. I want to know a little more about yours."

With subtle equivocation that she knew was merely disguised finality, he said with a smile, "You and the kids are my world now."

* * *

"Let's drink some water," Cynthia suggested.

Kyle agreed, loosening the straps on his pack. His fear for Kyp and their race against time had returned, but he recognized that that they needed to stop and hydrate. "How's your blister?"

"It's better. Really, I'll manage."

"Okay," he said, pulling a swig, looking to the sky to pinpoint the location of the sun.

She wanted to reassure him. "Kyle, did you ever think that maybe he didn't listen, and that he did contact the police?"

"It crossed my mind," he admitted, "but if I know Kyp, he kept his mouth shut. He might've brought dad in on it, but that's it."

Cynthia knew what a renegade Jack Conway was, and imagined him and Kyp driving down to Mexico together, armed heavily, ready to take matters into their own hands. She hoped that wasn't the case. "Well it can't be too much longer—"

She fell silent, then jerked her head to the right, to the trail ahead. They had both heard approaching footsteps. Cynthia wasn't able to see around the brush, but Kyle could see who was coming from where he was standing. The tension in his facial muscles fell away as his mouth opened a little. She saw him reach behind his back, going under his shirt for the magnum revolver at his belt, and her heart started pounding again. *No! Not again. Not now.*

But Kyle didn't raise the gun into a firing position. Instead, he tossed it away from them both, over some cacti and out of sight. Then she heard something that didn't sound real at first. "U.S. Border Patrol. Let me see your hands."

Kyle raised his hands high, and Cynthia followed suit, stepping out from behind Kyle so that she could see the speaker for herself.

Two men in dark green police uniforms approached them slowly on foot, their gold badges gleaming in the sun. Cynthia clasped her hands together and closed her eyes. *Oh, thank God. ThankGodthank-God. Thank you so much!*

Kyle called to them, "We're U.S. citizens."

The one who'd spoken, a hefty man with a crew cut and a mustache, said, "Okay, well we'll figure all of that out in just a moment. Right now I need the both of you to take a seat on the ground."

Kyle and Cynthia did as they were told without argument, taking their backpacks off and sitting down on the dirt, back-to-back. Both of them kept their hands out in the open.

When the Border Patrol officers were within a few feet of them, the second one, a slender man with thinning blond hair asked them, "What are you two doing out here?"

Kyle dove right into it, speaking rapidly and with a sense of urgency. "We were kidnapped in Tijuana, and then brought here. One of the guys, he's not too far from here. He's just a ways down the trail. You can still catch him if one of you goes after him."

Cynthia's eyes widened. "Kyle, no!"

Kyle couldn't believe his ears. Was she out of her mind? He ignored her and continued, "He's about five-five, with a shaved head and a mustache. He's got a bandage on his forehead, and he's wearing a white T-shirt and jeans."

He glanced at Cynthia, and her features were turned down into a look of disappointment. At that moment he resented her for looking at him that way. "Please hurry," he said, and he half-expected one of them to take off at a trot. When neither of them made a move, he asked, "What are you waiting for?"

"First, let's just get a few things straight," the thick one with the mustache, whose nameplate read "Sanderson," said with his hands up in a calming gesture.

"You're not listening to me," Kyle fired back. "He's getting away. You can't let him get away."

"Stop it, Kyle! Please."

"No, Cynthia," he said, his voice rising. "What is wrong with you? They need to go after him right—"

"Sir!' Sanderson yelled over him. "I need you to calm down right now." He waited to see if Kyle had finished, and then continued. "Now, first thing's first. Do you two have identification? Proof of your citizenship?"

"Right here," Cynthia said, handing over their wallets. The other officer, whose nameplate read "Ziegler," took them and inspected the contents. He pulled out their California driver's licenses and examined them.

Kyle said, "I'm sorry, but we are who we say we are, and we're telling you the truth. The man who kidnapped us is less than a mile from here on this trail."

Sanderson and Ziegler exchanged glances. "Call it in," Sanderson said, and Ziegler went for the two-way radio on his belt.

Kyle looked up at the two men from the ground, glad that he was finally being taken seriously. "Thank you," he said, letting out a long breath, then added, "There's more. There are three men who tried to harm us. They're farther along the trail, but they're handcuffed together, and—"

"Whoa, whoa!" Sanderson said, putting a hand up. "Let's take this one step at a time. Now let's take a deep breath and then start from the beginning.

As Kyle told their hellish tale of the last forty-eight hours, Sanderson listened intently, taking notes on a notepad as Kyle spoke. Ziegler continued to communicate with whatever central office there was, and it wasn't too long before a helicopter came swooping in overhead. Kyle watched with grim satisfaction as it circled, and he leaned back into Cynthia. He realized as it continued to pass over the immediate area that it was already searching for Davitos.

"You need them to fly farther south," Kyle suggested.

Ziegler countered, "We can only patrol American airspace, sir."

Kyle and Cynthia were slowly stood up and patted down. Kyle told Sanderson about the gun he'd tossed, wanting to cooperate now that he knew these officers meant to help them.

"Sounds like you two have been through one hell of an ordeal," Sanderson offered compassionately. "But you're safe now."

As if only hearing it from Sanderson's mouth made it true, Cynthia wrapped her arms around Kyle's waist and buried her face in his chest. It was over.

Kyle held her tightly, his face pressed into her hair. He was so relieved. He had never really let himself believe that they were going to be completely okay. Still holding her tightly, he said to Sanderson, "And my brother?"

"Don't worry," Sanderson reassured. "We're taking care of it."

* * *

"It's not my intention to downplay the tremendous strain this ordeal has put on the both of you," Alec Cusamano, FBI agent, told Kyle and Cynthia, as they sat side by side in two arm-chairs in one of the stuffy offices of San Diego's downtown police headquarters, "but I cannot emphasize enough how lucky you two are."

Kyle and Cynthia had been told this repeatedly by various officials of American law enforcement. First the Border Patrol, then the police, and now the FBI. Kyle was getting weary of hearing it.

"First off, these cross-border extortion rackets don't typically have happy endings. A lot of times the kidnappers will execute the victims whether or not they receive ransom, either because they're scared, or just to make a point."

Tell me something I don't know, Kyle thought. It had been his greatest fear the entire time they'd been in captivity.

Cusamano was a well-built man in a perfectly tailored black Armani suit. He casually sat opposite them with his arms crossed. "Secondly, these negotiations can sometimes drag out for months while these violent gangs try to barter for more money. In some extreme cases, it can take over a year.

"Third, oftentimes these cartel types will send videos to the victims' families for proof of life, sometimes with mutilations happening on camera. Sometimes these videos will be accompanied by a severed finger, or an ear, and—"

"Agent Cusamano, please," Kyle said with a look of irritation, glancing at Cynthia.

Cusamano realized his mistake. "I apologize," he said sincerely. "I didn't mean to upset you. I just wanted to convey how fortunate you both are to be sitting with me here now. Moreover, it's almost unheard of that one of your captors should have a change of heart. That, in itself, is a small miracle."

Kyle didn't want Davitos' name being associated with small miracles. He wanted the man brought in to answer for his crimes, tried, sentenced, and then sent off to prison for the rest of his life. It only pained him to know that that would probably never happen.

Davitos had disappeared. The Border Patrol had failed to locate him. Kyle and Cynthia had been found wandering the foothills north of the Mexican desert just east of the city of Tecate. The agents had been alerted to the Conways' presence when the couple had set off ground sensors placed along the path they'd been traveling on. This is probably what Davitos had been looking for when he'd given Kyle and Cynthia back their wallets and then retreated. The Border Patrol had initially brought them to their headquarters at the Tecate Port of Entry. They had both given their statements there to a deputy-chief, and then been picked up by two San Diego police officers who had brought them here.

Cynthia was anxious to get back home to Cameron and Cal, but this follow-up statement was, to her, an unfortunate necessity. It was Kyle who understood how important all this information sharing was, because Kyle knew that everything was *not* back to normal.

They'd been unable to successfully identify *El Jefe* or Cobo from photos they were shown. They'd never actually clearly seen *El Jefe's* face, and none of the dozens of photos they'd been shown looked anything remotely like Cobo, a name that was most likely an alias. So that was a dead-end.

Although Kyle was frustrated with his inability to provide the FBI with any information of substance, he had learned a few things about the workings of the cartel networks. After relaying the details of the first meeting between Cobo, Davitos, and *El Jefe,* Kyle learned from Cusamano that the "H" *El Jefe* had referenced when referring to Davitos' aspirations, stood for Hawk, a low level cartel scout. The "Central" that *El Jefe* had referred to when entertaining the possibility of Cobo's rise, was the next step up on the cartel's chain of command, a position that usually handled the many payoffs that kept Mexican officials looking the other way when *indiscretions* occurred. This hadn't been a mere kidnapping and ransom. Cobo had wanted to prove himself to the cartel, and had most likely presented *El Jefe* with information on some wealthy traveling Americans, followed by his scheme to make a quick profit, a scheme *El Jefe* had never embraced whole-heartedly. But who'd provided the information?

That left Davitos, or more specifically: David Esteban Solares Ramirez. First cousin of Mauricio Solares. Twenty-two years old. Born in Ciudad Juarez. Later found living in San Diego by U.S. immigration agents and swiftly deported. No documented history of either a physical or psychological trauma that would explain an inability to speak. No prior criminal record in Mexico. Current whereabouts: unknown.

"So you have nothing to go on?" Kyle asked disgustedly.

"We're not even sure which cartel we're dealing with," Cusamano replied neutrally. "All signs point to the Zetas, but we have no proof. Also, as you may know, inter-agency cooperation with the Mexican government is often tumultuous. We can't just cross our fingers and hope for them to provide results." He sighed. "It's unfortunate that Kyp didn't come to us with this first."

Kyle knew what Cusamano was referring to, and the agent's comment angered him. Kyp had been scared in those first few hours, unsure of what action to take and whether he should keep the ransom situation to himself. He had paced his apartment frantically for a long time, wracking his brain for the solution that was most likely to ensure Kyle and Cynthia's safe return, but nothing had come to him. He hadn't even trusted himself enough to go into the bank and attempt to withdraw the demanded $1,100,000 without calling too much attention to himself. Finally, he'd panicked and called their father, Jack.

Kyle had wondered the whole time whether Kyp would have contacted the police outright, or kept the burden to himself. When the pressure had proven to be too much for Kyp, he'd reached out to their dad. The answer to Kyle's question was one he would not have expected. Kyp hadn't called the police, but neither did he feel like he could handle the situation himself. Jack, a hard-nosed individual who preferred action just outside of official channels, had immediately taken control of the situation and called some of his "people."

Within the hour Kyp had gone to his father's house to broker a deal with Altegrity Risk International, an expensive private firm that specialized in resolving international kidnappings, and boasted a near-perfect recovery rate. Their consultants had been listening in when Kyle and Cobo had called Kyp for the second time. It was too late in the game for them to have inserted one of their own hostage negotiators. Cobo had been very clear during that first phone call. They had planned on sending one of their own men in, posing as Kyp, to make the drop on Sunday morning, while a team lying in wait closed in on the location to make a move if the kidnappers reneged at the last minute. Then the police had called Kyp and told him that they'd recovered Kyle and Cynthia in the desert near Tecate, and that he should stay where he was. Kyp was now on his way to pick up Kyle and Cynthia.

Kyle knew that Kyp must have feared that if he'd played along on his own as he'd been instructed to, he might have gotten himself killed along with Kyle and Cynthia. However, neither had he wanted to risk alerting the FBI, who may or may not have been in a position to take sufficient action to rescue his brother and sister-in-law.

Enter Jack Conway and Altegrity Risk International. Kyle had to applaud his father's intuition. Private firms like that always kept a low profile and tended to cooperate with U.S. law enforcement, moving through Mexico discreetly. The most important distinction, however, was the firm's ultimate objective: victim recovery, whereas the FBI would most certainly prioritize Kyle and Cynthia's liberation alongside its need to gather intelligence on the greater networks of the cartel.

"Kyp did *exactly* the right thing," Kyle said in recrimination. "What do you have to tell me?"

Cusamano looked taken aback. "I beg your pardon?"

Kyle didn't know why this man was trapped in the recent past when he should've been focusing on the immediate present. "What's being done about Mauricio?"

Cynthia sat up straighter, rubbing Kyle's back gently. She wanted to monitor this line of inquiry closely.

Cusamano looked momentarily confused. He still failed to grasp the scope of Kyle's apprehension. "As I told you earlier, we brought him in for questioning."

Kyle raised his eyebrows. "And?"

"And he was cooperative, answering all of our questions thoroughly with no discrepancies. He confirms that Davitos is his cousin. He confirms that Davitos used to work for you, and that it was he who brought Davitos onto your team. He states that he lost touch with Davitos soon after his deportation. He claims not to have been privy to any of your financial affairs, and that he has no idea how much money you cleared on your last job. He's been with his family the entire time you've been in Mexico. This was confirmed by his wife, Lorena. We checked his phone logs. No incoming or outgoing calls out of the country, or any other suspicious phone activity for that matter."

Kyle broke eye contact with Cusamano and looked off to his left. This was not what he'd been hoping to hear.

Cusamano continued. "We contacted his relatives down in Ciudad Juarez. They haven't seen Davitos in over a year. They say he fell in with a bad crowd and then disappeared. No one's heard from him since. Yes, Mauricio told you he was from Oaxaca when he was, in fact, born in Ciudad Juarez; but his cousin Martin says that he spent a lot of time working odd jobs in Oaxaca, and that might explain why he claimed to be from there.

"Everything he told us checks out, Kyle. We had no reason to keep him."

Kyle was rubbing his hands together and shaking his head back and forth as if to say, *no, this isn't right.* Cynthia continued to rub his back, and when he looked at her, she gave him a look that pleaded for him to just let it go. Cusamano picked up on the general mood in the air and said delicately, "I know what you're thinking, Kyle, and I know this isn't what you want to hear, but it's more than likely that this stress has caused you to jump to the wrong conclusion. Our agents are *very* good at picking up on duplicity, and we got none of that from Mauricio. He seemed genuinely surprised and concerned."

"They knew things," Kyle said quietly, staring at the ground, refusing to meet Cusamano's eye. "Things they shouldn't have known."

"And that's what makes these criminal organizations so complex," Cusamano offered. "They do their research. They gather intel. They wait for these opportunities to pounce on unsuspecting targets. Sometimes for millions, and sometimes for only a few hundred dollars. It sounds more to me like these men used their knowledge of *Mauricio* to get to you. It's really not that far-fetched."

Kyle was dirty, and exhausted, and he wanted to go home to his sons. Why was it so hard to get reassurances from the FBI? "Will you at least keep an eye on him?"

"Of course," Cusamano said. "We'll be watching him very closely."

Just then one of the detectives handling their case opened the door a crack while softly knocking on it. "Excuse me," she said guiltily, "but would it be possible to borrow Cynthia for a moment?"

"We weren't exactly done here," Cusamano said, annoyed.

"It's alright," Kyle said, putting his hand up. He looked at Cynthia. "You should go with her."

Cynthia didn't know why she was being separated from Kyle. She didn't want Kyle and Cusamano to continue their talk without her, and anything the detective wanted to talk about could be said in front of Kyle. "What for, though?"

"It'll just take a moment," the detective said soothingly.

"Go," Kyle said, nodding. Cynthia thought that perhaps Kyle wanted her to leave so that he could pick up his and Cusamano's discussion regarding Mauricio's culpability without her input. "I'll be fine. Really."

She got up and walked toward the door. As she moved past Kyle, she bent over and kissed him on the cheek, and whispered into his ear, "I love you."

It was strange, but at that moment he was thinking about how angry he'd been with her after she'd tried to stop him from sending the Border Patrol agents after Davitos.

She walked out and the officer gently closed the door behind her. When they were alone, Kyle turned to Cusamano and said, "Tell it to me straight. Is my family safe?"

Cusamano mulled it over for a moment. "I understand your concern. You're worried about a cartel presence here in San Diego."

"Yes."

"Then I hope that what I have to say will put you at ease. First, though, let me be blunt. Yes, there is a cartel presence on this side of the border. Yes, it's a deeply entrenched network. But you've got to consider that we're watching over you now, and they wouldn't dare risk sticking their necks out. They don't move as freely up here as they do down there, and they don't want to draw attention to themselves for fear that we'll move in and smash their organization. You said it yourself: their boss, the *Jefe*, was reluctant to even give the go-ahead. It's safe to assume that he'll go even further underground now that the plan he signed off on has gone straight to hell."

Kyle stared back blankly. One thing he was sure of was that from here on out, very little would be done to bring the men who'd kidnapped them to justice. He just knew it, and there was nothing he could do about it.

Cusamano said, "You should brace yourself for the possibility that you may never learn the whole truth."

Kyle looked Cusamano in the eye. He stared at the agent stonily, but said nothing.

"I'll have some of my men posted outside your house tonight if that makes you feel better. A civilian car, nothing too conspicuous."

Kyle rubbed his hand along his jaw line, staring at the floor. *It's not enough. Not nearly enough. You're the all-powerful FBI. How can the danger not seem real to you when it's so very real to me?*

"What about a doctor for that eye?"

"I'm fine," Kyle said distantly.

Cusamano reached over and patted Kyle on the knee. "It's all over, Kyle. You're home now, and you're safe."

* * *

The female detective escorted Cynthia into another small office and closed the door for privacy. She motioned Cynthia toward a gray, vinyl-covered chair, then took a seat herself.

She was a pretty black woman with soft features and kind eyes. Cynthia had met her briefly when they'd first been brought in. Her nametag read *Harris*. "Are you comfortable?" she asked Cynthia in a motherly tone.

"Yes, thank you," Cynthia replied, wondering what this was all about. "How can I help you?"

"The reason I wanted to speak with you in private, Cynthia, is because I deal primarily with battered women, and I wanted to give you the opportunity to share with me anything you might want to discuss, strictly off the record."

Cynthia was confused. *Battered women?* "You don't think that Kyle—"

"No, no," Harris said serenely. "That's not it at all." She touched Cynthia lightly on the arm. "I need to know if anything happened to you while you were Mexico. Were you . . . violated in any way?"

Now it all came together for Cynthia. "Oh, no. No, no, no, nothing like that happened."

"Cynthia, you can tell me if something did happen. No one else has to know. I can refer you to a female gynecologist who handles these types of cases, and if you'd like her to examine you—"

"No," Cynthia insisted, her voice starting to crack. "I'm telling you nothing happened. Alright?" Her eyes teared up and her lips pressed together tightly. "Nothing happened. You need to believe me." Two unwelcome tears raced down her cheeks.

"I do," Harris assured her. "I believe you."

Cynthia sniffled. "I'd really like to see my boys now."

* * *

It was just after seven o'clock when Kyp picked them up at the police station, having left Grandpa Jack behind to watch over Cameron and Cal. He put his arms around Kyle and Cynthia in a prolonged hug when he met them in the main lobby. This loving embrace marked the end of the kidnapping ordeal. All formalities with the police and the FBI had concluded. It was early evening, and they were going home to get back on with their lives.

They rode back up to Rancho Bernardo in near silence. Kyp had questions, but he respectfully declined from asking them in view of the psychological trauma his brother and sister-in-law had endured. The questions could wait. Now was the time for healing, and Kyp would be there for them to lean on him when they needed it.

Kyle stared out the window and watched the various gas stations and strip-malls pass by. It would be interesting to decide how to break this to people, since very few knew what had happened. Kyp had canceled their trip to Mexico in a very vague text message to Sara after the first call had come in. The only person he'd told about the kidnapping was his dad, and they'd been negotiating in the shadows with Altegrity when Kyle and Cynthia had turned up in the custody of the Border Patrol.

According to Cusamano, the only people who knew anything about what had really gone down were Mauricio and Lorena, and they didn't know everything about the ordeal. Kyle closed his eyes. *But you do know, don't you, Mauricio? You know about everything that's transpired since Thursday afternoon.* Kyle closed his eyes and leaned his head against the glass, taking a deep breath. *Focus on the boys. Focus on seeing them again.*

Kyle and Cynthia had washed up as best they could back at Border Patrol headquarters, but they were still wearing the same filthy clothing, and both dreamed of a long, hot shower.

Cynthia's Saab had been picked up by San Diego PD down in San Ysidro, and towed to one of their lots. It would be awaiting the Conways for pickup, free of charge. She was glad for that. She didn't want to go anywhere near the border anytime soon.

When Kyp got off I-15 at their exit, he said to the both of them, "Guys, I would never presume to tell two parents how to behave toward their kids, but you both need to understand that they really have no clue what's been going on. They know something's up; that much is obvious to them, but they don't exactly what. They're both really confused right now. I just thought you should know."

"Thanks, Kyp," Cynthia whispered gratefully. "We'll act accordingly."

Kyle said nothing. *How do you act in a situation like this? How much should we tell them? Are they even old enough to know the truth?* He thought of a German shepherd he'd once owned that had always picked up on his mood, good or bad, adjusting her behavior toward her master accordingly. *Dogs are intuitive like that. They know how to act when their owner's in distress. But my sons aren't dogs.*

Cynthia experienced a wide range of emotions as they turned into the neighborhood, and she was nervous. She didn't want to be nervous anymore. Her nerves were shot. She reached over for Kyle's hand.

They turned onto their street, drove another hundred yards, and then pulled into the driveway. The front door was open, and Jack stood at the foyer with Cameron and Cal in front of him, a hand on each of their shoulders. Cynthia began to open her door before Kyp had come to a complete stop, and Kyle urged, "Easy, CC. Stay calm."

She realized that they had just talked about this, and that Kyle was right. She collected herself and stepped out of the car, hurrying to the front door with forced self-control.

"Mom!" the boys said in unison, delighted with her return a day early, and eager to hear about their parents' adventures down in Rosarito.

"Oh, boys," she said, barely able to contain the relief that washed over her as she knelt by the top step and wrapped her arms around both of them, pulling them to her. She recognized that she was holding them perhaps a little too tightly, but she couldn't bring herself to loosen her hold on them. She kissed their cheeks and made sure that her head was pressed between theirs so that they couldn't see her tears. "Oh," was all she was able to mutter. Already she could feel them squirming under the strength of her embrace, and she imagined them both thinking, *Why's mom acting this way?*

Kyle came up the walkway slowly and stopped just short of the steps, taking in this scene with the same sense of relief and joy that Cynthia felt. With his hands in his pockets he drank in the sight, savoring it. He was home with his family.

"Dad," Cal said, breaking Cynthia's grip and running to his father. Kyle scooped his youngest son up in his arms and held him tenderly to him. Cameron followed his brother and hugged Kyle around the waist, and Kyle ran his hands through his son's hair.

"What happened to your face? It's all blue and lumpy?"

Kyle didn't want to lie to Cal, but he had to tell his youngest son something. "That's a story for another day," he said, and he left it at that. For whatever reason, Cal seemed content with the dodged explanation.

Kyle looked up at his father, who looked back at his son with a pained, contorted expression on his lined and silver-stubbled face, an expression that gave way to one of gratitude. The message was clear: *I'm so very sorry for what you've been through, but you've come back to us, safe-and-sound. That's all that matters.* "C'mon, boys," Jack said. "Let's get inside. Your folks have had a long trip."

Kyp came up behind Kyle, and the six of them went into the house and closed the door. Kyle set Cal back down on the ground, and Jack, still well-built for a man of sixty-five, put his thick arm around Kyle's shoulders. "Welcome back, son." he said. Kyle patted his father's back twice in unspoken acknowledgement, then broke the contact.

"Tell us about Mexico," Cameron said enthusiastically.

"Boys," Jack said a little too sternly, "your mom and dad are a little exhausted from their journey. Right now they just need to relax."

"Did you bring us anything?" Cal asked excitedly.

"Cal," Kyp admonished, "what did Grandpa just say?"

Kyle noticed that Kyp and his dad were speaking for him and Cynthia, perhaps trying to buy them time to collect themselves and re-accli-mate to their surroundings. He was touched.

Cal walked over to Cynthia and tugged on her wrist, ignoring his cranky uncle. "Grandpa made us hotdogs for dinner, but he wouldn't let us have any ice cream for dessert. Will you give us a bowl?"

Kyp, not a parent himself, shrugged it off and let it go, not really knowing how to proceed in these types of situations. Jack tactfully said, "Boys, you need to listen to your Uncle Kyp when he tells you some-thing. Your mother needs some space right now. I'll get you some ice cream."

"No, it's okay," Cynthia interrupted. "I'll get it for them." She nod-ded to her father-in-law and gave him a look that said, *No, really. Thank you, but I've got this.*

Jack must have sensed that the most therapeutic course of action for Cynthia right now was for her to immerse herself in the family routine, busying herself with taking care of the boys. "Alright then." He turned to Cal. "Your mother's on the job. Let's go finish watching *Finding Nemo*."

"Okay," Cal replied emphatically, and he darted off to the comfort of the den.

Cameron remained where he was. Maybe his younger brother was content with a movie and the fact that his parents were home now to care for them. For Cal everything was as it should be in the Conway household, but Cameron seemed to have caught on to the fact that something was not right. He looked his father up and down, observing the grime that had collected on his shirt and shorts. "Do you need a bath?" he asked Kyle, frowning. "Those are the same clothes you had on when you left." Kyle didn't respond right away. He barely noticed his older son, staring at him but not really seeing him, and Cameron knew that his father's thoughts were elsewhere. "Dad?"

Kyle snapped out of it. "Yeah . . . a bath. A bath sounds great right now. Why don't you run along and finish your movie with Cal and Grandpa."

"Okay," said Cameron, deeply curious about his father's strange mood. He stayed fixed where he was as Kyle shuffled to the staircase and headed up to the master bedroom. From the kitchen doorway, Cynthia watched him go.

When Kyle had disappeared from sight, Cameron joined his brother in the den, and Cynthia turned and went into the kitchen. Kyp stood in the living room, alone. He thought about calling Sara, and wondered when the right time would be to tell her about everything that had happened. She was still in the dark, and she was probably furious with him.

Kyp walked to the kitchen and leaned against the doorjamb. Cynthia stood at the counter, her back to him. She had two porcelain bowls laid out in front of her alongside a half-gallon of Breyer's mint chocolate chip ice cream. She held an ice-cream scoop in one hand, but she made no move to fill the bowls. Kyp continued to watch her, and he wondered if she was aware of his presence. Still, she made no move to scoop the ice-cream out of the carton. He wondered what was going through her mind right then. "Are you okay?" he asked softly, and he realized, just as it came out of his mouth, how foolish it sounded. "I mean . . . are you okay all things considered?"

She slowly turned to face him, the impacts of joy and recent terror cancelling each other out, so that her face was a blank. "I have my boys back," she said.

Kyp smiled at her, the weak smile of a man who wanted to offer support, but didn't even know where to begin in voicing words of encouragement.

"Thank you, Kyp," she said, her voice low, barely above a whisper. "For everything . . . I know that this thing has shaken you too. I can't even begin to imagine what you—"

"Hey, hey," Kyp said, putting his hands up. "No need for that. It's all behind us now."

Was it? she thought to herself. *Someone needs to tell Kyle that.*

* * *

Jack stood behind the couch his grandsons lounged on as they watched their DVD and patiently awaited their dessert. When he was convinced that they were both settled in and their attention was fixed on the TV screen, he walked out of the den and headed upstairs.

When he knocked on the door to the master bedroom, he got no response. "Kyle?" he said gently into the door. "Can I come in?" Still no answer. He opened the door a few inches and peeked through the crack. Kyle was sitting on the foot of the bed, still fully clothed. He was hunched over with his elbows resting on his knees and his head in his hands, lost in thought. Jack walked into the carpeted room and approached his son carefully. "Kyle?"

Kyle didn't look up to meet Jack's eyes. In a voice devoid of the high emotion that had dominated him over the last few days, he said in a low tone, "I couldn't protect her, Dad. Not even for a second. They stood over me, threatening to kill her, threatening to . . ." he cleared his throat, and it sounded to Jack as if he were choking. Finally he raised his head and looked up at his father, and Jack saw the pain there. "You have no idea what that feels like. The *helplessness.*"

Jack combed back his silver hair with his fingers and took the last few steps to close the distance between him and Kyle. He clasped his hand on his son's shoulder, giving it a squeeze. "No, I don't," he agreed. "Not even when your mother passed." Jack kept his hand placed firmly on Kyle's shoulder. "We'll get through this, son. I promise you. We'll get through it together, one day at a time."

Kyle inhaled deeply, held it, and then let the breath out in an audible "whoosh." Jack stood next to him, waiting silently and patiently. He'd stay there with his son whether Kyle chose to speak again or remain silent. Kyle said nothing else.

Neither of them heard the car that pulled up to the house and parked beside the curb, but Jack had left the bedroom door ajar, and both of them heard Cal downstairs announce excitedly, "Franco and Maria are here!"

Kyle bolted upright and rushed over to a window. He stuck his fingers between the slats of the blinds, parting them and peeking through. There they were. The Solares family was getting out of Lorena's Buick.

Kyle's breathing grew more rapid. "No," he said through gritted teeth, and he practically dove into the walk-in closet. Jack watched his frantic movements, dumbfounded. He hastened over to the closet's doorway and watched Kyle, down on his knees, punching in the combination to his electronic floor safe. Jack heard Cynthia, downstairs, call after Cal, "Cal, no. Come back here right now." He turned back to Kyle, whose fingers were flying over the digits of the keypad with an alarming sense of urgency.

*   *   *

Cal ignored his mother's command, throwing open the front door and pushing his way past the outer screen door as the Solares started heading up the driveway. Kyp had gone after him at Cynthia's behest, but he was still a few steps behind when Cal reached the top of the front stoop. "Hi," he called out, happy to see his friends again.

Kyp came outside and put a hand on Cal, uncertain of how this was going to go. Cynthia joined them a moment later, and Cameron tried to wedge his way past his mother and his uncle. Cynthia took hold of Cameron's arm and then looked toward the Solares approaching in the twilight. Lorena was holding a foil-covered pan in both arms, and was smiling uncertainly, but when she saw the worried look on Cynthia's face, her pace slowed.

Cynthia looked torn, and she glanced over her shoulder, back into the house, just in time to see Kyle come barreling down the stairs, Jack trying to keep up behind him. Kyle burst through the outer screen door, which crashed against the house with enough force to startle his two sons, and all four of the Solares stopped dead in their tracks. Kyle stood in front of his family straddling the top two steps, his arms held out wide. Waving them back into the house, he shouted, "Get inside! All of you, right now!"

Mauricio and Lorena exchanged troubled glances, and Cynthia was about to protest when she heard Jack quickly urge, "C'mon, Kyp. Help me get them back inside." Kyp seemed indecisive, but he followed his father's lead and turned Cal around. Cynthia was about to put up further protest, but Jack shook his head and shot her a warning glance that said, *He's the man of the house. Let him do what he has to.*

Right now she had little choice. Her first priority was her sons, and she didn't want them to witness whatever calamity was about to unfold. She took Cameron by the hand and led him back inside. Kyle shut the screen door behind her, but she handed the boys over to Kyp and Jack and said, "Take them into the den and close the door."

When Jack and Kyp respected her wishes, she whirled around to make sure Kyle didn't do something very foolish, but Kyle had closed the screen door behind her and was standing with a wide stance on the stoop. He pointed right at the Solares and said loudly enough for the whole neighborhood to hear, "Turn around and get back in your car! Get back in your car and drive away!"

Lorena apparently didn't know what was going on, but her children were frightened now, and that was all the reason she needed to order them back to the car. With her hands full, all she could do was escort them back, glancing over her shoulder as she hurriedly walked away. The sight pained Cynthia, and she went to turn the handle on the screen door with hopes of intervening, but Kyle heard her and commanded her with exasperation, "Stay inside!"

Lorena was hustling toward her Buick with a confused Franco and Maria, but Mauricio stayed where he was halfway up the driveway. Lorena called after him, but he chose to ignore her. "Kyle, what is this?" he asked, dumbfounded.

"You shut up!" Kyle shouted, scanning the street for the surveillance car that Cusamano had promised, but apparently had never delivered. "Get out of here, now!"

"I don't understand what's happening," Mauricio said, looking hurt.

You're a fine actor, Kyle thought. "You know goddamned well what this is. You know that I know what you did." The doors to the neighbors' houses started opening one-by-one as Kyle's voice rose, but he didn't care. "Maybe no one else knows the truth, but I do."

"What truth?"

"Mauricio, get back here!" Lorena called from the street.

"Don't you fucking play dumb with me, you traitor!" Kyle said with fury. "You're not going to talk your way out of this."

Mauricio took another step forward. "Please, let's talk about this."

"Stop right there!" Kyle yelled, his face twisted by rage.

Mauricio's expression showed a combination of hurt and confusion. "We can't leave things like this, Kyle." He took another step forward.

Kyle took a step back and put one hand behind him, reaching up under his shirt. His chest heaved, and just as Cynthia decided that she'd heard enough, he bellowed, "MAURICIO, I HAVE A GUN, AND IF YOU TAKE EVEN ONE MORE STEP TOWARD THIS HOUSE, I WILL SHOOT YOU WHERE YOU STAND!"

Mauricio froze, and Lorena gasped from far away. Kyle stared Mauricio down, and Mauricio had sense enough to start backing away slowly. When he reached the street, he took three great strides to his wife's car and opened the door. He got in, and just before he shut the door, he heard Kyle say, "Don't ever come back!" Lorena started up the engine and threw the car into drive, giving the car enough gas to make a swift exit without going so far as to peel out and frighten her children even further.

Kyle watched them go, and even after they'd gone he stayed planted firmly in place on the top step. He offered no response to his neighbors' concerned looks of inquiry; he didn't even meet their eyes. After a time, he turned and opened the screen door, heading back into the house.

Cynthia was speechless, and she was looking at him as if he were a stranger. He walked right past her and headed back upstairs, saying nothing.

* * *

Cynthia's calls kept going straight to voicemail. "Lorena, it's me again. Please call me back when you can. I'm so very sorry. I can't even begin to tell you how sorry I am. I promise I can explain everything. I promise I'll make this right with us. Call me back." She pressed "end" on her cell-phone.

Jack came down the stairs and into the living room. "The boys are in bed," he said. He walked over to her. "I don't think they heard anything. They'll keep for tonight."

"Thank you, Jack," she said weakly. She stepped to him and rested her head on his shoulder. "Thank you for everything."

He put an arm around her and held her. "I'm going to go now. I'll be back first thing in the morning. Do you need anything?"

"No, thank you," she said into his chest. "You've been so great about everything. I'm sorry to have put you through this."

He took a step back and held her at arm's length with both hands on her shoulders. "Don't be ridiculous," he said, perturbed. "You have nothing to apologize for."

"We're going to need you, Jack. In the days to come."

"And I *will* be there for both of you, CC. Anything you need. Anything at all."

She leaned in and kissed him on the cheek, and he broke contact and headed into the hall. Before he went, he said, "He loves you all so much, it hurts. That's why he did what he thought he had to do."

She stared back at him.

"Just think about it," he said, and then he left, passing Kyp just outside the front door and exchanging a few words with him.

Kyp came back into the house and came to her. "I explained what happened to the cops. He has a license for the gun, and this is his property. He never drew it, and no one got shot, so no harm, no foul as far as they were concerned."

There's been plenty of harm done, she thought bitterly. *Irreparable damage.*

"I'll stay here tonight," he suggested. "On the pullout couch."

"I think . . ." she stammered. "I think I'd like that." She broke eye contact, trying to busy herself, once again, with the hospitable tasks that would help her take her mind off of her dark thoughts. "Let me get you some blankets."

"No," Kyp insisted. "I'll be fine. You go upstairs and get some rest. Go be with your family."

Too exhausted to argue, she concurred. "Alright. Thanks again for being such a help. I'll see you in the morning." She hugged him fiercely and headed upstairs.

She hesitated when she reached the master bedroom, hovering outside. When she'd gathered her courage—*Why should I be apprehensive?*—she turned the knob and opened the door. In the corner of their bedroom was a leather arm-chair, and Kyle had pulled the matching Ottoman up to the window so he could sit while he watched the front lawn and the street outside. The glow from the street lamps came through the blinds and painted him in bands of phosphorescent light that contrasted with the shadows cast in the darkened room. Still, he had not changed out of his dirty, sweat-stained clothes. She saw his black, .38 snub nose revolver in his hands, resting just between his knees. He didn't acknowledge her presence.

She was heartbroken that it had come to this. She knew that his erratic and frightening behavior had been born out of his need to protect his family, and she knew that she needed to give him the benefit of the doubt. Still though, his condemnation of Mauricio bordered on the obsessive, and she feared that he had started down a path that she wouldn't be able to bring him back from.

"Can we talk about it?" she asked hopefully.

He looked at her. "Do you really believe he's innocent, or do you just plain forgive him?"

"I haven't had time to think about it," she declared sadly. "All that mattered was getting back home to the boys."

"Well, that's all I *can* think about, CC. I have you and the boys to protect, and I don't really believe that the danger's passed."

"Let's go to bed," she pleaded.

"No, you go ahead. I'm going to stay up a little bit longer." He went back to staring out the window.

Perhaps he expected her to go to him and put her arms around him. Instead, she turned and walked down the hall to the boys' bedroom. The room was cast in the soft orange-and-green glow of an aquarium themed night-light, and she saw that her sons seemed to be sleeping soundly. She went over to the bunk beds and sat down on the mattress of the lower bunk, gently stroking the hair at Cal's forehead. She lay down on the mattress and draped her arm across him. "Cameron," she whispered. "Are you awake?"

"Hhhhnnnnn?" Cameron moaned groggily.

"Climb down her, sweetie."

"Why?"

"Because mommy's asking you to. Just please do it for me."

"Okay," he agreed reluctantly, and she saw his narrow legs descend the ladder.

Cameron's feet hit the ground, and she extended an arm to him. "Come here."

Cal began to stir.

"What?" Cameron protested. "There's no room for all three of us."

"Please, honey," she begged, failing in her attempt to mask vulnerability.

Perhaps he had remembered that something had been a little off when his parents had returned, an intrusive tension in the air that he might never understand, but he looked into his mother's eyes and seemed to comprehend how much she needed this. He crawled into Cal's bed and nestled up next to her as Cal mumbled softly.

"Mom?"

"Yes, Cam?"

"You smell bad."

She burst out laughing, tears welling up in her eyes, but it wasn't humor that moved her. It was a laugh of joy, and gratitude. Utter gratitude. The three of them fell asleep like that together.

* * *

It was early afternoon on a blue-skied Saturday when Kyle's pickup truck pulled into the Home Depot parking lot. He drove around to the side and slowed to a stop, then rolled down his window and stuck his arm out, waving to the unofficial leader of the pack, calling him over.

A lanky man in paint-stained khakis and a denim button-down shirt sauntered over to the car and stood by the driver's side door. This was a man Kyle knew. He'd put him to work before.

The man, too, must have recognized Kyle. When he saw who had arrived, he smiled widely, revealing a missing front tooth and a remainder that had turned to a dark shade of yellow-brown. "Hola," the man said with anticipation.

Kyle cut right through the pleasantries. "I need six of you. Just this one afternoon. I might have some more work for you later this week."

"Okay, okay," the man said, obviously happy to take on whatever work he could get. He turned and waved to the rest of the men huddled around the chain-link fence of the side entrance. "Cinco mas," he called. "Vamanos."

Five more men grabbed whatever gear they had and came trotting over to Kyle's Ford. They began climbing up over the tailgate and onto the truck's bed. They knew the drill, and they went about it quickly and efficiently, filing in one-by-one so that they faced each other in two groups.

When the five were all settled in, their spokesman was about to join them, but then Kyle looked over the man's shoulder and told him to wait. "What about that guy?" he said, pointing to a slender, unkempt youth in tattered clothes, sitting on the curb and looking distant and dejected.

"Who, him?" the man said, turning around and following Kyle's line of sight.

"Yeah, him. What's his deal?"

The spokesman scratched the back of his head, squinting into the rays of sunlight. "He new here. I work with him once. He okay. He a good worker, but you say you only need six."

Kyle stared at the young man. He looked so pathetically lost. He reminded Kyle of a rural villager who'd just stumbled into the big city for the first time. Kyle let his arm fall slack and rest on the door while he considered. "Bring him along," he finally decided. "We'll find something for him to do."

"Okay," the other man said. He turned and waved to the youth. "Vamanos. Rápido." The last day-worker scooped up his backpack in one hand and came to join the rest of the group.

"He can ride up front with me," Kyle said.

"Sí," the spokesman said, and headed towards the back.

The newcomer came around the front of the truck and opened the passenger side door, tossing his backpack on the floor and climbing into the cab. As he got settled in, Kyle reached behind him and slid open the small back window. "Alright, boys," he said through the opening, "we don't have far to go, but I don't want to get pulled over, so stay low. ¿Todos entienden?"

The six men in back all nodded their heads. "Sí."

"Alright then." Kyle slid the glass back in place.

He put the truck in drive and pulled out of the parking lot, turning left onto a side road and heading away from downtown traffic. He glanced over at the passenger seated next to him, and noticed the kid was avoiding eye contact, staring out through the windshield. "New in town?" Kyle asked casually, as if the kid had nothing to lose.

No response. "¿Habla usted inglés?"

The kid shook his head, his shaggy hair sweeping across his forehead. "No."

"No hay ningún problema. Hablo español." No problem. I speak Spanish.

The kid smiled timidly, nodding.

"¿Cuánto tiempo han estado aquí?" Kyle asked. How long have you been here?

"No hace mucho tiempo," the kid replied, warming to Kyle just a little. Not long.

Kyle smirked. We'll get this one to come out of his shell yet, he thought. "Usted debe tener hambre." You must be hungry.

"Sí, un poquito," the kid admitted.

"Pues bien," Kyle reported, happy to be helping someone who appeared down on his luck. "No te preocupes. Tengo un refrigerador lleno de sándwiches que mi novia preparó, y ella es buena cocinera." Well, don't worry. I've got a cooler full of sandwiches that my girlfriend made, and she's quite the cook.

"Muchas gracias," the kid responded graciously.

Kyle braked at a red light, and then extended his hand to his passenger. "Kyle," he said warmly, introducing himself. The kid, smiling politely, took a firm hold of Kyle's hand, and shook it. Kyle was glad for having gotten through to this one so quickly.

"Mauricio," said the kid.

Coda

A clear, sunny afternoon, typical for a Southern California summer, drew San Diego's residents outdoors, the absence of humidity making it a perfect day for Little League sports. Franco's team, the Camo Padres, was down five runs to three at the top of the sixth-inning against their rivals, the Gray and Blue Padres. Mauricio watched his son deep in right field. Franco's hands were on his knees as he stood, hunched over and awaiting a shot that might arrive at any moment. The batter's count was three and two, and he was one of the opposing team's most intimidating sluggers. Mauricio knew that Franco was not one of his team's more valuable fielders, and he hoped that his son would take the advice he'd given him earlier, taking a few steps back if the batter drove that ball his way and assessing its line of trajectory. Franco could always move in quickly if the ball were to lose momentum and fall short. Too many times Mauricio had watched in frustration as Franco took a few hasty steps forward when the batter connected, only to watch the ball sail right over his head, costing his team a run or two.

The pitcher nodded his head to his catcher, confirming a fast ball, a possible folly as he threw the ball right over the plate in what was only a little more than a lob. The batter got a piece of it, and sent a potentially disastrous line drive toward third base when the third baseman made an impressive dive into foul territory, the ball disappearing into his glove with an audible smack, and supporters of the Camo Padres let loose with hearty applause. Three outs. Franco and his teammates came jogging in toward the dugout.

Mauricio was clapping along with the other parents when he heard a voice behind him. "Hey there, Mauricio." Mauricio turned around on the bleachers and saw Kyle sitting there right behind him, a major-league Padres hat pulled down low over his brow. Kyle didn't smile, nor did he frown. He wore a neutral expression on his face, as if he didn't know how to proceed with formalities until he could gauge Mauricio's reaction. Mauricio continued to stare at Kyle in stony silence, so taken aback by his one-time friend's sudden reappearance that he himself was searching for the most diplomatic way to correspond with Kyle in this very public setting populated by other families.

Mauricio took a quick look around to see who might be observing, as if their history was a part of public record, and then slowly turned back around to face the playing field. "What are you doing here Kyle?" he asked with rising apprehension.

"I wanted to talk to you," said Kyle, and he, too, kept his eyes fixed on the ball players.

"Lorena will be along with Maria shortly," Mauricio said warningly. "You'd better not let her see you here."

Now it was Kyle's turn to take a quick look around. "What I have to say won't take long," he said after surveying the area.

Mauricio was silent for a moment, and he continued to watch the opposing team's players hustle as they took the field. Then, without turning around, he said, "I'm listening."

The way they were conversing reminded Kyle of a police drama where a cop clandestinely met with his confidential informant, only Kyle didn't know which role was which. "I wanted to set things straight between us," he said with chagrin.

The first pitch was thrown, and Franco's teammate hit a hard grounder that got past the short stop. Man on base.

Mauricio clapped, and then said, "I don't suppose Cynthia put you up to this?"

Kyle felt a tightening in his solar plexus. No, Cynthia certainly hadn't put him up to this. These days Kyle and Cynthia rarely spoke, though not for his lack of trying.

Kyle and Cynthia had been legally separated for close to four months now. It had been nearly a year since they'd been taken hostage in Tijuana. Since those two dark days, Kyle had slipped into a worsening state of enmity and paranoia that led to behaviors of irrational hostility. Consequently, his mental health, his career, and his family had all suffered. One day Cynthia had decided that she simply couldn't bear it anymore, and asked him to leave.

The FBI had opened up a dialogue with their Mexican government liaisons in the hope of uncovering the whereabouts of Davitos and the mysterious criminal organization he'd been working for. For the FBI, this dialogue had been frustratingly inconclusive, and after a few months, the bureau, its patience worn thin by the lack of information sharing, set the case aside.

Kyle and Cynthia's abduction had been part of the first wave of an unprecedented and disturbing rise in violence down in Tijuana. An all-out drug war had been declared by rival cartels, and firefights in both residential and commercial districts were a daily occurrence. Mutilated and dismembered bodies were piling up on the roadside in the sur-rounding areas, and the Mexican president sent in the army to quash the drug lords' war of attrition. The army's first move was to disarm the local police officers, most of whom the military suspected of working for the narco-traffickers. Ballistics reports were run on the seized guns with the hope of matching them up with some of the weapons used in many of Tijuana's unsolved murders. The reports were never released, but the public, on the whole despising the municipal police, welcomed the army's arrival. The military commanders swiftly appointed their own police-chief in Tijuana, a retired lieutenant-colonel, who went right at the cartels with a decisive show of force. The well-funded cartels fought back, however, and the body count rose. Sadly, the kidnapping and extortion of many wealthy and middle-class Mexican families then happened with such disquieting frequency that many families fled to the United States in search of asylum.

Kyle had continued to live in fear for his family's safety. He'd ar-dently made a case for his family's immediate departure from San Di-ego, possibly changing their names in the process. He'd been convinced that it was only a matter of time before the gang, or cartel, came for them, and in those first few weeks after they'd returned home he'd been scared witless by nearly every car he'd heard passing by their house. One night Cynthia had been shocked upon discovering that Kyle no longer kept his gun in the safe in the closet, but was hiding it under the mat-tress while they slept. This had been one of his first steps toward alienat-ing himself from his family.

When he'd come to the conclusion that no case was being built against Mauricio, and that no charges would be brought against him, he'd taken matters into his own hands, hiring private investigators to do some digging on his former employee. These investigations had yielded no results. The investigators' fees were hefty, and the Conways' accountant had uncovered this financial discrepancy at tax time. Cynthia had been beside herself with a sense of betrayal.

The nightmares couldn't be held against Kyle, but nevertheless they served to drive a wedge even deeper between him and his wife. The dreams were always the same: Kyle found himself back in the desert at the foot of the grave Cobo and Davitos had dug for them, side-by-side with Cynthia, both of them on their knees. Their executioners stood behind them, unseen, but their sun-eclipsing shadows loomed over the terrified couple, until Kyle heard an ear-shattering pop, and then blood would splatter the dirt in front of them as Cynthia slumped over and rolled into the ditch. He always woke up drenched in a cold sweat, a silent scream forcing its way out of him as his heart hammered against his rib-cage.

Mauricio had never returned to work, and Kyle had dismissed anyone who didn't have legal working papers, which meant practically everyone other than Kyp. Kyle promised his brother that they would endure, citing their construction company's now solidified reputation in the greater San Diego area, and they might have prospered had there not been an unfortunate, and arguably unforeseen, development. Toward the close of 2007, while Conway Brothers Construction was in its prime, the American real estate bubble burst, a near devastating blow to their livelihoods. This catastrophe almost ruined them, as foreclosures swept the entire country, a key contributing factor to the nation's sudden economic decline and eventual recession. Adventurous free spirits, the likes of Frankie Molinelli, became fewer, as countless well-to-do Americans wised up and judiciously protected their assets. Conversely, the low-income households that made up the other end of the socioeconomic spectrum, who had been hastily signing off on mortgage loans at the behest of persuasive real estate lenders, found themselves on the verge of homelessness and bankruptcy. It was an utter disaster, and the Conway brothers almost didn't recover.

Mauricio had persevered with his head held high. After Blain Lindeman had heard of his separation from Kyle's company, he moved in on Mauricio with the hopes of scooping him up, dangling a generous salary in front of the humble worker. However, Mauricio declined the offer, and joined other former employees of Conway Brothers Construction. These men had carved out a very comfortable existence for themselves, contracting down in the predominantly Hispanic towns of Lemon Grove and Spring Valley, southern municipalities of San Diego that boasted very modest one-story stucco homes. They were more than happy to bring Mauricio aboard: the man was practically a local celebrity in their profession. Mauricio's prestige continued to grow as he found himself comfortably working alongside his own people, immersed in a common cultural heritage.

Lorena had regrettably broken off her partnership with Cynthia immediately following Kyle's very public meltdown in front of the Conways' home. She had wanted to remain supportive of Cynthia and sympathetic to her plight, but she continued to maintain her husband's innocence in the alleged kidnapping conspiracy, serving as his alibi in the time leading up to and during the Conways' disappearance in Mexico. She would never forgive Kyle for having threatened Mauricio's life in front of her children, and the rapport between the two families dissolved literally overnight. Cynthia, with much heartache, had taken on another partner, while Lorena had sought work elsewhere. Although it was never spoken aloud, Kyle suspected that Cynthia, who usually had forgiveness in her heart for all, had secretly resented him for the falling out.

Despite his suspicions, Kyle had continued to lean on Cynthia, practically begging for them to pick up and leave. She fought him at every turn. It confounded him to no end. How could she not see how very real the danger was? Her faith and her ability to see the good in people be damned. It made him seethe when he thought about the likelihood that she'd probably forgiven Davitos for what he'd put them through. And Mauricio? She'd never truly believed that he'd played a part in their drama. This is primarily what had driven them apart: her naïve positivity coupled with his deeply rooted cynicism.

The night before she'd asked him to leave had involved an inciting moment leading to their separation. An old high school friend of Cynthia's and her husband had invited Kyle and Cynthia over for dinner. In the middle of their meal, the husband had unthinkingly let it slip that he and his wife were about to vacation in their annual spot down in Cabo San Lucas. The wife, mentally slapping her palm against her forehead for her husband's insensitivity, had tried to cover for him, but the damage had already been done. Kyle had immediately launched into a vicious tirade about what a lawless, corrupt, and dangerous hellhole Mexico was, and had made an awful scene. Out of respect for the hellish experience the Conways had both been through, the hosts had patiently waited Kyle out, but Cynthia had been mortified. She was done with her husband's outbursts. The next day she told Kyle that it would be better for her and the children if he moved out.

It *killed* him inside. What they'd been through should have solidified their bonds. Having survived what they had together should have strengthened their love, but in the end it had done just the opposite. It was not as though Kyle hadn't seen exactly what was happening. He'd felt Cynthia slipping away from him a little further, day-by-day, since they'd made it back home. Yet he'd been unable to alter his course of action in his conviction that none of them was safe. He'd thought it had been very foolish of Cynthia to want go on living their lives as if nothing had ever happened, even though he knew that she, too, bore the mental scars of the terror they'd endured. In the end, though, she had her faith, and that had given her the strength to move on with her life, while he still felt like he was drowning.

He'd awkwardly explained to Cameron and Cal why he and their mother needed some time apart, and then had gone on to rent a simple townhouse in the quaint town of Ramona. In the days that followed, while trying to keep his career from falling apart, he'd sought counseling, something Cynthia had been urging him to do for quite some time. He'd found a psychiatrist who specialized in post-traumatic stress disorder, and began making weekly visits. The man was a professional, and dealt primarily with veterans from the wars in Afghanistan and Iraq. Kyle hadn't witnessed any killing or bloodshed while in captivity, but that didn't make the taxation on his psyche any less real. His doctor listened to his woes with patience and compassion, and after a time Kyle felt that he was actually making progress. Following his wife's lead, he even gave church a try. It helped a little.

The next batter had a three-and-two count when he was walked. Man on first and second. Another kid took stepped up to the plate. Franco was on deck. Kyle watched him take a few practice swings. "No, Cynthia doesn't know I'm here."

"It's never going to be the way it was," Mauricio stated flatly, still facing the game. "You know that, don't you?"

"I do," Kyle said, and he was at peace with it. "But I figure I can repair some of the damage that's been done."

Strike one.

Mauricio once again turned around to face Kyle. "Why are you here, Kyle? Are you hoping that I'll beg for your forgiveness?"

Kyle shook his head, his expression saddened. "No, that's not it at all. I wanted to give you this." He reached into the breast pocket of his collared shirt and took out a folded piece of paper. He handed it to Mauricio.

Ball one.

Mauricio unfolded the slip of paper and studied it. He saw that it was a personal check, in the amount of $90,000, made out to him from the Conway Brothers Construction Company. He looked truly confused. "What's this?"

Ball two.

"Do you remember when I worked you all so hard last year? It was all for this. This was the bonus we earned for completing the Molinelli house two weeks early. We had always planned for you to have it. It was meant to give you a head start, but also a way of saying thank you. After everything that happened, I wasn't able to give it to you."

Strike two.

Mauricio looked at the check in his hands for a long time, and then back up at Kyle, his gaze boring into Kyle as if he might be able to discern some strange motivation. After a moment, his expression softened a little as he came to the conclusion that Kyle's intentions were genuine.

Then he tore the check in two. "I can't accept this."

Kyle's shoulders slumped in defeat. "Why would you do that?"

"Maybe because you need the money more than I do right now, or maybe just to make a statement."

"What statement?"

Mauricio held up the two pieces of the check, looking like he'd called Kyle on some bluff. "This is why you're here? What does this prove?"

Ball three.

Kyle was at a loss. "What else could I possibly have in mind?"

Mauricio opened his mouth to speak, and he looked like he was about to confirm a suspicion. "I can see it in your eyes. You still think I had something to do with it, don't you?"

Kyle had lived the last year of his life trying to let go of the hate that was weighing him down. He didn't want it anymore, and he'd successfully rid himself of it. He had a year's worth of soul searching and professional therapy to assist him with it. In a courtroom, a prosecutor had to present a case that proved a victim's guilt beyond a reasonable doubt. Kyle had believed in Mauricio's guilt from the moment he'd learned that his cousin was one of the men who'd taken him and Cynthia captive. He'd spent the last year gradually accepting the possibility of reasonable doubt, even though all signs seemed to point toward Mauricio's culpability.

He owed his old friend the truth. "I don't know," he said with feeling, as if he truly wanted to believe in Mauricio's innocence, "but that's not why I'm here."

"Then why are you here?" Mauricio asked, holding up the pieces of the torn check even higher. "For this?"

Pop fly to the other team's bleachers. Foul ball.

"No," Kyle said longingly, desperately wanting Mauricio to see that he'd changed. "You asked me if I came here so that you could beg for my forgiveness. It's just the opposite. I want you to forgive me, Mauricio."

Mauricio looked taken aback. "What?"

Kyle needed to let it all go. It's what his therapist would have wanted. It's what Cynthia would have wanted. "I want you to forgive me for the way I treated you. It wasn't right, and I have no excuse. Please forgive me. For everything." As he said it, there was satisfaction in his words. *He* needed this in order to move on.

Tip of the bat. Foul ball.

Mauricio didn't offer the forgiveness Kyle sought, but said instead, "I would never do anything to hurt you or Cynthia, Kyle."

Kyle offered Mauricio the slightest of grins. It *was* entirely possible. "Let's focus on moving forward, shall we?"

Mauricio nodded in assent.

Strike three. One out. Runner on first and second. Franco at bat.

"Yeah, Franco!"

"Go get 'em!"

"Eye on the ball, Franco."

The family members of the players of the Camo Padres erupted in cheers for Franco. Mauricio and Kyle both started calling his name and offering thunderous applause. Franco looked up at Mauricio before stepping to the plate, a wide smile on his youthful face. He didn't notice Kyle sitting right behind his father.

"C'mon, Franco!"

The first pitch was a fastball, and the fans on this side of the field jumped up in delight when they heard the sweet metallic crack of Franco's aluminum bat connecting with the ball, sending it over the second baseman's head and between the right and center fielders. Franco pumped his legs as he sprinted, and he rounded first as the base coach waved him on to second. The center fielder got the ball in, but not before Franco made it to second, and not before his two teammates rounded third base and crossed home plate. Franco looked up to the bleachers, beaming with pride over his two RBIs. The game was now tied at five-five.

Mauricio clapped emphatically, pumping his fist into the air to show his son how proud he was, and Kyle clapped with him.

Mauricio had been right. Things were never going to go back to the way they were, and Kyle still had a ways to go before he'd completely be at peace with himself. But here he had taken the first step toward making amends, and for now that was enough. And in time, who knows . . . ?

And maybe, just maybe, someday soon Cynthia would see just how far he'd come, how much he'd changed, and would consider taking him back. He knew that he couldn't allow his happiness to be completely contingent on her decision, because that would have defeated the whole purpose of his being here now. He needed to do this for himself. Standing here now, cheering for Mauricio's boy, he knew he was on the right path.

He'd taken a promising first step.

About the Author

Douglas Grant is the author of the 2010 novel *Preemptive*. He earned his BA in English at the College of Charleston and his MA in Education at Point Loma Nazarene University. He lives in San Diego.

Visit the author's Amazon web page at: amzn.to/YBLgYo

Also by Douglas Grant

Growing up in Manhattan, Zack McCrady did not have an easy life. First, his father died in a skiing accident. Then his mother was diagnosed with a brain tumor. Eventually Zack was left orphaned, and his big sister Jenny took over parenting and provided him with the unconditional love he craves. But after Jenny's death during the 9/11 terrorist attacks on New York, Zack begins spending his days pondering his rage toward Al-Qaeda, his dark feelings toward his own government, and his enduring pain and inner turmoil.

On the other side of the world, Afghanistan is rotting from within. The Soviets have withdrawn and, technically, the Mujaheddin have won. Hakeem Rashid, raised by a surrogate father since infancy, is bright and gifted and knows the lessons of the Koran in depth. Despite growing up in war torn Herat, Hakeem has managed to remain civilized and with a sense of purpose, but when Hakeem's real father returns, everything is subject to change.

Zack is involved in a violent crime.

Hakeem has become his father's minion.

As two men on opposite sides of the world battle intense psychological tumult, one of them is about to uncover a truth that will change him forever.

Buy this book on Amazon at: amzn.to/15A59Ev